A
LADY
IN
DANGER

A NOVEL BY

SUSAN PAYTAS

A Lady in Danger

ISBN:

To my parents, Nancy and Bob

Chapter 1

C ally Bank focused on the two cables in front of her. Arms wide and over her head, she tightened her grip around the soft foam handles. Resisting the impulse to yank the bar, she concentrated on isolating the lat muscles. *Set three. Twelve Reps. Deep breath.* Her tired muscles screamed as she pulled down. The metal plates rose surely, evenly upward. When they reached the top, Cally held them for a slow count of two, then eased the bar up and let the weights lower into place. Dropping her head, she felt the pulse run through her body.

"That's a serious grind you got going there."

The voice jolted her. It was deep and a bit ... sarcastic? She'd been the only one in the room, and she liked it that way. Cally raised her head to respond, but he continued.

"I should probably tell you that this section of the gym is reserved for Two Rivers cops between six and eight p.m. It's going to get crowded, and you may feel more comfortable over by the cable machines." He pointed to the room behind the glass wall, the side of the gym with lots of machines and lots of people.

"Thanks for telling me," Cally said, wondering who he was. Most of the staff at CrossTrain were serious bodybuilders. This guy was tall and on the leaner side. But he didn't look like a cop, either. His chestnut hair was a tad long, and he had a dusting of stubble on his chin, which gave him a somewhat scruffy look.

"Wouldn't want you to …"

"No problem." Cally could have gotten into it, but she was already behind schedule. She used her towel to wipe the leatherette seat. "It's all yours." She threw him a perfunctory smile and headed off toward the dumbbells.

Grabbing two twelves from the knee-high rack, she sat down on the edge of the flat bench. She looked at her reflection in the wall of mirrored glass and nodded slightly. The hard work was paying off. No one could say she wasn't in shape. Inch for inch, she was in better shape than any of her brothers. If only she was a little taller. Five-nine would have been nice, would have made things a little easier. But five-foot-six would have to do. It was what it was.

Cally looked over at the guy on the lat pull-down machine. He'd find out soon enough she was a cop. He'd find out soon enough that the legendary Bank family was about to add one more to their dynasty of cops, tomorrow night, at the annual TRPD banquet. She had a lot to live up to—four older brothers and a dad on the most prestigious police force on the Jersey Shore. She clenched her hands. Back to work.

Hoisting the dumbbells, she started curling. From the corner of her eye, she noticed Mr. Law and Order toss a white towel over his shoulder and head her way, claiming the upright bench right next to her. He sat down heavy, sighing as he did, and Cally detected a small smile on his lips. Gathering himself, making a rather big show of it, he lifted fifties directly up, and tapped them slightly above his head. He wasn't half bad—nice muscles, broad shoulders. He shifted his gaze her way, and she dropped her eyes.

"You lucked out tonight," he said. "I guess there's no harm since it's quiet."

And since I'm a cop. She started her second set, aware of him watching her for a few moments before he picked up his weights and began lifting again.

When he finished, he turned to her and asked, "Are you training for a contest?"

"Excuse me?" No one had ever asked her *that* before, and it took her off guard.

"A bodybuilding contest."

Cally rested the dumbbells on her thighs and considered how to reply to this guy who seemed so interested in striking up a conversation. Honestly, all she wanted to do was workout in peace and make it to her parent's house without being too late. When her mom said dinner at seven, she meant it. The places would be set, the food would be getting cold, and her mom would be watching the door. Cally sighed. "I don't mean to be rude, but I'm trying to finish my workout. Do you mind?"

"I don't mind at all," he said, grinning in apparent amusement.

"Thank you." Cally turned her shoulder. She raised the dumbbells and began her last set. Her arms were exhausted and quivered under the weight. She'd been lifting for an hour and every rep burned.

"You might want to try decreasing the weight and adding reps." He picked up his dumbbells and raised them easily over his head.

"You'll never add muscle mass if you don't push your limits," she eked out in a breathy reply, struggling to raise her own dumbbells.

"Is that so? Are you defending yourself or giving me pointers?"

"I'm stating a fact." She dropped the weights to the rubber mat and shot him a look.

"Well, I'll have to remember that."

Was he being serious or joshing her? She couldn't tell, but she was glad it was time to go. The guy was making her flustered. She cleaned the bench, bid him good night, then made her way to the exit. She pulled the door and made it past one, two, three cable machines before she couldn't resist and turned back to sneak a look through the glass.

He sat on the edge of the bench leaning forward, his forearms resting on his knees, his hands clasped, his cool green eyes pointed right at her. He smiled and winked. It was a very cocky, very cop-like wink, the kind she knew well.

Turning brusquely, she raised her chin, flicked her ponytail, and headed off to the ladies' locker room.

***

Luther Minx rubbed his hands then pulled the dark cap further over his ears. Exhaling anxiously, he watched the vapor curl toward the steering wheel and disappear into the frigid air. The dashboard clock read 6:55 p.m. For the fourth night in a row, he'd watched the parking lot from a secluded space next door. He'd noticed one gal who always parked toward the back. She'd walk to her red KIA and fumble with keys once she got there. She came out all three nights soon after seven o'clock, when the rest of the parking lot was quiet. She looked like she was in her mid-twenties—perfect—and she wore a ponytail, also perfect.

Luther glanced at his watch glowing silver under the moonlight that filtered through the windshield. Almost time. Two middle-aged women carrying bags, appeared on the sidewalk and walked to a silver Toyota Camry, just like his, and got in. A blonde approached her car, wisely parked by the door, and drove off. The minutes ticked away, ebbed and flowed, Luther's breathing becoming more erratic, shallower, with each person who entered their car and left. He became aware of his heart, beating against his breastbone. Sweat dampened the fleece lining of his black leather gloves. He licked his dry tongue against the sour taste of his teeth.

She would come now. She would walk out that door any minute. He placed his hand in the deep pocket of the wool-lined overcoat. He felt the club hammer in his gloved hand. He pulled it out and checked its weight, pulling it up and letting it back down. It was heavy enough. He knew it was. He'd checked it fifty times already.

The red SUV was waiting like a patient mule. And there she was, coming to the glass door, pushing it open, zipping her jacket. This was it. Here she came. He pulled the car's handle and placed a booted foot on the macadam.

She walked quickly to her car. He approached from behind. He looked at the narrow hips, the slender shoulders, yes indeed, she was a perfect size two. Every hair on his body shrieked in excitement as he saw her in the red organza, elegant and timeless. The dark hair? The olive skin? She would look beautiful. He stood erect in the cold night air, took a deep breath. It was time. She was perfect. They all would be.

Chapter 2

Murphy's law—she caught the drawbridge. Cursing her bad luck, Cally shifted into *Park* and tucked her hands under her thighs. She glanced at the dashboard's digital display which read sixteen degrees, and she shivered. Felt more like sixty below, with the dampness and wind that could wreak havoc at the shore. Now she was stuck as the warning bells clanged, and the bar lowered in front of the bumper. I am going to be so late, she thought. Glancing in the rearview mirror, she saw nothing but empty road. A gust of wind sent a swirl of white dust over the blacktop. It must have flurried while I was in the gym, she thought.

To the east, the rigs of a commercial fishing boat approached. Several heavily clothed fishermen pulled lines and scrubbed the deck. She watched them work as a crew, noticed one who seemed to be instructing, one mopping, others guiding the large nets into their brackets. She was reminded of her brothers—pulling duty together, watching each other's backs, the sad times and the festive they'd worked as police officers. Soon she would be there, too, working alongside them, upholding the family legacy.

Excitement flushed up her cheeks. She couldn't wait. It seemed such a long time coming, but at last her turn had arrived. The elegant old vessel appeared beyond the raised bridge, effortless in the still water. It blew its horn as if to offer congratulations. She leaned back and took it in—the shine of the moon, the boat cutting through the water, the eve of a very big day. The atmosphere seemed almost custom made, God's little way of telling her she would do great. She nestled deep into the down of her ski jacket.

Eventually, with a hearty creak, the bridge started to descend. Another car approached in the rearview mirror and came so close to her tail that the headlights got lost under her bumper. Watching in the rearview mirror, she saw the overhead light illuminate. A man in a dark ski cap sat all the way forward, both arms over the steering wheel. He glanced over his shoulder and turned, reached back and adjusted something in the backseat then turned forward again, and nosed the vehicle closer.

"Hold your horses," Cally mumbled. Did he want her to crash through the safety bar?

A moment later the gate's lights began to blink, and the warning bells clanged. The guy behind nosed up even tighter. When the arm rose, she stepped on the gas with more pressure than she'd intended. The tires skidded and the car fishtailed. She straightened the car as a feeling of annoyance and unease curled up her spine. Too bad she didn't have her badge yet. Too bad she wasn't on duty. She'd pull him over and slap him with a ticket for tailgating.

When Cally arrived at her parents' house, the driveway was crowded with six cars parked double and three deep. She entered the center hall Colonial in which she'd been born. The sound of clanking spoons greeted her, and immediately, she smelled the rich aroma of onions, Swiss cheese, and tomatoes. Excellent, Cally thought, suddenly very much in the mood for her mother's soufflé.

The family was already seated at the table, her mom at one end, brothers around. Her Dad's place was empty as expected. Cally apologized to her mom and blew kisses around the table. Suddenly ravenous, she sat beside her brother, Colin, and stuck her nose in the soufflé cup already set at her place.

Her mom cleared her throat. Judith Bank was a petite woman who tonight wore her auburn hair in a neat twist that spiraled up the back of her head. She was dressed in a well-fitted burgundy cashmere sweater with matching shell beneath. Setting her shoulders at their usual erect posture, she said, "Now that we're all here, I'd like everyone's attention, please." Her mellifluous, French-accented voice filled the suddenly quiet room.

"I wanted to get you together while your father is at the station, so we could talk about tomorrow night. It's going to be a very important night for him, and several other members of this family." She looked at Cally and smiled. "I want to make sure that no one does anything out of line. No hanging by the bar, *comprendez*?" She glanced at Charles. "I want you all in dark suits, preferably navy.

There are going to be pictures and I'm hoping to get a nice family shot."

"We'll look like a bunch of undertakers," Chris complained.

"You'll look like respectable, handsome men, Christian," Judith replied. "The way I understand it, they'll honor the retirees first, so go straight to the table. When your father gets up to receive his pin, I want him to look out at our table and see every one of his children looking back at him."

Charles snatched Chris's bread. Chris grabbed Charles's wrist and took it back.

Judith let the altercation play itself out. "Next, they'll introduce the graduates. That means Cally's turn." Cally thought she saw her mother's eyes moisten. "Cally has waited a long time for this. She's worked very hard. I want you boys at the table supporting her."

Cally looked around the table. Her brothers looked like a bunch of boys thrown in detention. "It's, okay, Mom. You don't have to be so serious. I'm sure they'll be great."

"I'm sure they will, too, but I'm not taking any chances."

"Any other instructions, *Maman?*" Charles teased.

"*Oui,*" she replied with a smile for her second son. "Don't forget that Clyde is being recognized, too. He's at the end of the evening with the special honorees, so be sure not to leave the table."

Cally gazed at her eldest brother. How could anyone possibly forget that night six months ago? She could hear the story a million times and never tire of it. She felt the familiar tug of gratitude for the man who had saved Clyde's life. Someday, she hoped to meet him, thank him in person.

When dinner was over, Cally helped her mom clear the plates. At the kitchen sink, she grabbed a towel as her mom donned an apron and rubber gloves. "So, what are you wearing tomorrow night?" Judith asked, pulling at the gloves as they suctioned against her skin.

"I bought a new black suit. It's nice. Simple pants and a cropped jacket."

"Pants?" Her mother grimaced. She took a flat baking tray and started to scrub. "How about that nice maroon wrap-around?"

"Please. I've worn that dress to every function for the past two years." Her mom handed the tray and Cally wiped it dry. "Plus, I don't want to show up in pantyhose and heels. That's not the impression I want to make."

"And what impression would that be?"

"That I'm the Bank boys' little sister, all dressed up in her party clothes. I'd rather wear pants and a suit, just like the guys."

"Oh, I see." Her mom flashed an amused smile.

Cally watched her mom pull a pan from the pile of dirty dishes. It was the pan upon which she'd placed the soufflé cups, and Swiss cheese had burnt a coating of black over the surface. Cally hated to see her mom scrubbing away after she'd prepared such a nice meal. "Let me switch with you," she offered.

"I'm fine," Judith replied. "But honestly, Cally, I think that's nonsense. This is not the 1970s. There are plenty of female police officers."

"Not in Two Rivers."

"Perhaps not but you'll do fine. You'll probably move up the ladder faster than your brothers just because you *are* a woman."

"Don't even say that. I don't want special treatment of any kind."

"I know you don't, dear." Judith smiled warmly. "What about Monday? You ready for your first official day on the job?"

Uneasiness niggled through Cally's veins. She thought of her brothers and the mixed responses she'd gotten about joining them on the force. "Have the boys said anything lately?"

Cally waited as her mom drained the sink and refilled it with clean water. Eventually, her mom turned to face her. "You're their baby sister. They have some concerns, sweetie, but only because they love you. They want to protect you."

Cally clenched the towel. If she heard that line one more time she might explode. "I don't want to be protected!"

Her mom laughed. "Don't worry, dear. I have a feeling your fellow officers are going to find that out soon enough.

Chapter 3

Jack Brant turned from the bar and watched the banquet hall. Tables were filling and noise in the room was starting to build. Katrina was deep in conversation with the wife of an officer with whom they socialized. Jack tapped his fingers and waited. Leave it to Katrina to order the most exotic drink and send the bartender scrambling to the main bar outside the banquet hall.

He took a swig of the Modelo Especial and gazed out the wall of windows at the Ocean Place Resort. The banquet room was located on the tenth floor with gorgeous views that spanned the shoreline of Long Branch and beyond in both directions. A luminescent beach stretched before him; a ship blinked on the horizon; waves crashed white against the night sand. He gazed at the myriad of high-rise luxury condos that had sprouted up along the coast in the last ten years. He saw the complex in which he'd just invested, currently just a steel frame. When he'd heard, a couple years back, that Netflix was buying up the old Fort Monmouth Army Base to move substantial operations to the Jersey Shore, he'd invested. This particular residence offered even more amenities than the other complexes, and on a huge beachfront lot to boot. He figured he'd hold on until the construction was completed and sell afterwards and make a nice profit.

Drumming his fingers on the bar top, he turned in the direction that the bartender had disappeared. What was taking so long? Coming through the broad double doors of the hall, he saw a band of men in dark suits. They wove their way through the maze of round tables, fanning out like politicians. As they approached, Jack noticed it was the Bank brothers, and in their midst, right in the middle of the pack—was the woman from the gym.

His pulse jumped. His gaze locked in on her. What was she doing here?

He adjusted his tie as he watched her chat with the Bank brothers. Man, did she look great. Even prettier than yesterday. Her skin seemed to glow under the ambient lighting. Her blonde hair was pulled back in a high ponytail, higher than the one she'd worn at the gym. The way it hung over her shoulder, the light blond against the black of the suit, looked sexy as all get-go. The jacket was short to her waist, and the slacks fit smoothly against slim hips. He was reminded of the tight, toned body that had so enthralled him at the gym—and the feisty spirit beneath.

Jack smiled, shook his head as he recalled the several occasions he'd tried to strike up a conversation. Each time he'd been met with a polite, but disinterested response. Now Jack watched with curiosity as Colin Bank, the rookie, led her to the bar across the way. The rest of the

Banks closed in. Charles Bank gestured to the bartender who placed several bottles of beer and a cocktail in front of him. As Charles Bank reached for the drink, an attractive older woman with auburn hair in a French twist, came up from behind and snatched it away. She wiggled her finger in front of his nose and proceeded to usher the group to its table. Mrs. Bank, Jack assumed.

He glanced back at his own table and saw Katrina glaring. She raised her hands and cast an impatient scowl. He turned away and surreptitiously watched the gym gal sit down beside Colin Bank at what looked like a family table. Who was she? What was she doing with a Bank? Jack felt a flicker of envy as Colin placed his arm over her shoulder and whispered something in her ear.

The bartender finally returned and presented a martini glass filled to the brim with blue liquid. Now how was he supposed to carry that back to the table without spilling it all over the place? Throwing a last glance the woman's way, Jack placed a ten in the tip cup and carefully walked to the table.

"Who's that?" Katrina asked when he gave her the drink.

"Who?"

"The woman you were watching."

"I wasn't watching a woman." He raised his glass and said, "Cheers."

Eying him skeptically, she toasted him back. Jack released a long breath. In the six months since they'd started going out, she'd become increasingly possessive. Non-stop text messages, impromptu drop-ins. She'd even managed to sneak into his apartment last week. He'd blown a gasket, and she'd responded by insisting the door was unlocked. He couldn't prove otherwise, but it had been the last straw. He'd broken things off then and there, telling her that their relationship was not working and that he needed space. But then she started to cry. She asked about the banquet, and he felt bad ... so here they were. He hoped he'd made it clear enough.

Glancing around the room, Katrina said, "So when do you get your award? You *are* the guest of honor, aren't you?" Her eyes gleamed.

"Toward the end, I think." Jack smiled, but it felt tight. He didn't really want the award. He'd done his job; any other cop in that position would have done the same. He'd already won awards; it felt selfish getting two more. There were other officers who'd done some amazing things this year, and plenty of grateful residents to prove it.

He took a swig of beer as Katrina dropped into a dissertation about a fashion show she was organizing. Jack zoned in and out, the beer hitting the spot. He started thinking about work, about last week's homicide—a prostitute found strangled in a motel room. He had to return to the motel, he decided, re-interview the manager. And Kurt. He needed to sit down with Kurt and review his report face to face. Surely there was some anomaly in the M.E.'s report he'd missed.

A tap sounded from the microphone. Chief Robert Grainer stood at the podium. Tall and thin, with a shiny balding head which shined under the lights, he blew into the mic and called for everyone's attention. After a short welcome and appreciation to the organizers, he announced that it was time to honor the retirees. He began summoning the retirees to the stage one at a time. Two officers were honored and given their pins. Next, the chief called for Deputy Chief, Clyde Bank, Senior. Applause exploded as table after table stood. Jack could see the gym woman's profile. She smiled and clapped then settled back into her seat as the racket died down. She listened attentively as Chief Grainer extolled the former Deputy Chief's virtues. Jack leaned back, happy for his former boss. Katrina sipped her drink and placed her hand on his thigh.

It burned a hole straight through his slacks. He reached down and removed it. Tomorrow, he would lay it out in terms she could not fail to understand. They were through. It was over.

***

Tommy Doone raised his eyes from the saltshaker. His father was speaking to him. "Pay attention, for Christ's sake."

"Did you even watch your father get his pin?" his mother hissed.

"I'm sitting right here, aren't I?"

"You seem more interested in that saltshaker than your father."

"This is a very interesting saltshaker."

He laughed. They didn't. What else was new?

Truth? It wasn't the saltshaker he was interested in. And it sure as hell wasn't the boring retiree speeches. He allowed his eyes to roam back to where they'd been. Front of the room. Center table. On Cally Bank.

He wished he could stop looking at her, but he couldn't. When she talked to her brother, Tommy could see her profile. She looked beautiful tonight. Pretty in an old traditional sense, with smooth skin, delicate features, like Sleeping Beauty. Hair like Rapunzel. It hung like a golden tassel, long and heavy, and it looked silky as anything. He liked watching it swish from side to side.

"You see that?" his father said. "You know why she's here tonight?"

Damn. His father had caught him looking.

"Because she made it through the academy, that's why. Even the daughter can make it through and you telling me you couldn't?"

"I could have made it through, Dad. I didn't want to finish."

"Bullshit. You were asked to leave."

"I failed the tests on purpose, Dad. I told you I didn't want to be a cop."

"What do you want to be, huh?" His father hunched over the table. His voice was low and cutting. Tommy looked around. Luckily, no one seemed to notice or care except the family of Hispanics sharing the table with them. They were starting to fidget.

"You don't want to be anything. You sit up in that room of yours and do nothing. You're a lazy bum."

"I wanted to be a doctor," Tommy retorted, using every ounce of restraint to keep his voice down. "But you wouldn't help me, would you, Dad?" He didn't want to talk about this. He was here supporting his father like they asked him to, why couldn't they leave it alone?

More applause broke out. Tommy looked up to see Mr. Bank leave the podium and a captain take his place. The captain banged a finger against the microphone. The crackling sent a shiver up Tommy's spine.

"May we have the graduates, please!" he announced.

***

Cally took a deep breath. Colin nudged her, pressing his elbow into her side, and wished her good luck. Around the table, everyone watched as she stood and placed the napkin on the seat. She walked toward the stage with her fellow rookies closing in. Her buddy, Juan, whispered a quiet, "Yo, babe," in her ear, making her smile like he always did. She'd made it!

She looked out over the audience and saw her brothers, smiles all around. Her parents' eyes sparkled. She felt her own sparkles coming out and she blinked to keep them at bay. Merino, a huge man with shoulders a football field wide, spoke about what a great class they were, how well they would do. Then he called the first name in a voice as big as his shoulders. Suddenly, it was like every good thing in life had come up on the stage to surround her, warm her, pay her back for all the hard work. The hours in class, the hours at Judo, the hours at the gym, the hours at video games, home plate, dodge ball, flag football, the basketball hoop. She'd struggled at every one, lost most of the time, but she was here now.

And she was next. She concentrated on Juan getting his badge. She put her two hands together and clapped. Then it was her name, OFFICER CALLANNE BANK, booming over the microphone, her hand, reaching out to receive the rolled diploma and the shiny brass badge for the second time that day. Her lips stretched into a big smile as a camera flashed in her eyes.

She returned to the table in a veritable haze, awash in a spray of congratulations. Chief Grainer had returned to the podium and clinked a fork against the microphone as she took her seat.

"Folks, if I could have your attention, please," Grainer announced. "We've got one more set of very important awards to give out, so if you could please stay seated for a few more minutes." His voice was stern, taking command of the room that had begun to rumble as drinks kicked in. "I'd like to take this time to honor the officers who have performed over and above the call of duty. Would the following three officers please take the stage: Lieutenant Clyde Bank, Junior; Patrolman Michael Gallagher; and Senior Detective John Brant."

Her brother, Clyde, took a deep breath and raised his brows expectantly. "Here we go," he said into Jennifer's ear. Cally watched as he kissed his wife then stood. He fidgeted with his tie as he approached the stage. Cally turned to the audience.

Finally, she was going to meet Jack Brant.

Scanning the room, she waited for him to stand, the elusive detective who had saved her brother's life. She'd read about him in the newspaper—detective in four years; senior detective in four more; six closed homicides under his belt. Impressive. But besides that one article, information about the man had been scarce. The article had been accompanied by an old academy photo, and Cally got the feeling he'd ducked the media the same way he'd been ducking her mother's invitations to dinner. At last, she would meet him tonight. Maybe he'd shed some words of wisdom. One by one, members of her family stood and started clapping. They turned toward a row of tables behind them.

"Where is he?" she asked Colin, dying to see what he looked like. Her eyes scanned back and forth. Behind them, people were stirring at a table, talking, moving chairs, and she noticed the guy from the gym stand up. The talky one. The guy who kept interrupting her workouts. She wanted to shout, *Sit down! Jack Brant is about to receive his award!* This guy was diverting attention from the one man who deserved it most. She leaned into Colin and said, "I wish that guy would sit down. Where is Jack Brant?"

"Right there. That's him." Colin replied.

She followed his long, lanky arm; his finger pointed at... *the gym guy?*

Her heart stopped dead. The guy who had tried, several times, to strike up a conversation? The one she had most definitely brushed off? Jack Brant? Uh oh. She wanted to disappear under the table.

Through a barrage of handshakes, he walked to the stage. At one point he caught eyes with her and smiled. She smiled back, of course, although she was sure that the word *guilt* must have been written in bold letters across her forehead. Whatever was she going to say?

The chief began telling the story Cally had heard a hundred times, but this time, the blank figure of thirty-three-year-old, Senior Detective, Jack Brant, the man whose praises her family had been singing for the past six months, was colored in. Yes indeed, boy oh boy, was it ever.

"Ladies and gentlemen," Grainer began. "As many of you know, Monday July fifteenth was a tragic day on our police force." The chief put his head down for a moment. "Tragically, one of our finest lost his life. We've honored our fallen colleague but tonight marks our first opportunity to honor the three surviving officers who acted so courageously that night." The chief's voice filled the quiet room. "Detective Brant," he reached his hand out toward him. "Would you step forward, please." Brant put his head down and took a step up. So here he finally was—the illustrious, the elusive, Detective Brant.

"As police officers we practice how to respond to situations," the chief began. "We practice down to the number of breaths we take, the number of steps we take, the exact words we say. But no amount of practice in the world can prepare us for the kind of trap these three men walked into that night. Detective Brant, you drove into the worst possible crime in progress—a deserted alley, two officers down, another officer out of sight. Two empty, bullet infested squad cars. We learn in training to wait for backup. But we never learn how to watch the blood drain from our fellow colleagues." The chief looked at Brant.

Cally felt the tears well in her eyes. Her nose started to tingle the same way it did every time she pictured her brother, down on the street, dying. Clyde had been perilously close to death. Had Brant not gotten him and Gallagher into safety within those few minutes, her brother would have died for sure.

"By maneuvering your car as you did, by using all of your resources and thinking on your feet, you accomplished what protocol tells us is impossible, what training tells us not to do. You displayed quick thinking and extreme bravery. You endangered your own life for the sake of fellow police officers and for that, you receive our highest honors, Two Rivers' Medal of Valor and Officer of the Year."

The hall erupted—whistles, hoots, and thunderous applause. Brant smiled, raised his hand in brief acknowledgment before shaking the chief's hand and accepting each of the two small velvet boxes. He walked back to his place on the stage, shaking the outstretched hands of Michael Gallagher, and her brother, Clyde.

Clyde and Michael were next. When the Chief announced the two men, everyone in the room stood. The clapping was loud and lasted for what felt like minutes.

Cally had never felt prouder of anyone. Watching her brother receive his medal, her eyes welled up again.

When the hoopla finished, people began gathering their belongings and heading for the exits. Clyde put his hand on Jack's shoulder, and they talked on the stage for a moment. At one point both men looked her way. Cally watched as they walked down the steps and headed toward her. A part of her wanted to turn and make a beeline for the ladies' room, while the other side wanted to have a normal, redeeming conversation. It was too late now; they were just feet away.

"Cally," Clyde said when they reached her. "Want you to meet someone. This is Jack Brant."

"Hi," she said with an awkward smile.

"Hello," Jack replied. "I was just telling your brother that we've run into each other at the gym. When you were introduced on stage, I assumed you were married to one of them. I had no idea they had a little sister."

"A *sister*," Cally corrected him.

"Cally hates when people refer to her as our *little* sister." Clyde clarified.

"I'll have to remember that." Jack suppressed a smile. "Well, it's nice to actually *speak* to you...Cally." He offered a handshake.

Sparks raced up her arm as she took the big, rough, hand. Close-up and in a suit, he looked even more handsome than at the gym. Now, as she uttered some reply, she couldn't help noticing his clear green eyes. How his hair turned up ever so slightly at the tip of the forehead—a very nice forehead, flat then curving slightly back into the perfectly placed hairline.

"About the gym—" she started to say.

"Jack!" her mom cried, squeezing in beside her. She took his hands and kissed him on both cheeks. "At last! We've been trying to reach out to you! We would absolutely love for you to come to our home for dinner. Could we set a date right now?"

"Dinner with the whole family?"

"Well, yes, but don't be intimidated; we don't bite."

"You sure?" He glanced at Cally.

Cally felt her cheeks flush. Her mom laughed and batted her eyelashes like a schoolgirl.

"I'd love to come," he said with a playful smile.

"Really! I thought we'd never get a yes out of you. How about next Sunday?" Her mother was still holding his hands, and she gave them a little bounce before she released them. "Cally, you're not working Sundays this month, are you?"

"I'll … uh, have to check," she stammered, growing more embarrassed as she replayed their gym meeting in her mind. She had not been exactly rude, but...

"I do hope not," Judith said. "I think the only person who's working is Colin, unfortunately. Oh well. Nice we don't have to worry about your father's schedule anymore, isn't it?" She laughed gaily.

Cally nodded along. Just then, she was bumped at the elbow. Lurching forward, she turned to see a tall, attractive brunette beside her, strong jaw, wide mouth.

Jack stopped smiling. He shifted his feet and jammed a hand in the pocket of his slacks.

"Well, Jack, aren't you going to introduce me?" the woman asked. Her dark eyes seared into him.

Jack cleared his throat. "Cally, Mrs. Bank, this is my ... friend, Katrina."

"Oh, and Jack, feel free to bring a guest, of course," her mom said, smiling at Katrina. "It's all set, then. Cally, give them the address, will you? It's so wonderful to finally meet you, Jack, dear."

Cally wondered if her mother had had a few too many. When she grabbed Jack's hands and squeezed them again, Cally was sure of it.

"*Au revoir*; see you Sunday!" Her mom waved to both Jack and Katrina and left to join the family already assembling at the bar. So much for family lectures.

Chapter 4

Jack drank the last of a tall coffee and chucked it in the waste can. A sliver of pink filtered through open blinds onto his desk, showing the first glimpse of sunrise. The weekend had passed quickly, most of it spent at the station on the Miskavitch case, the prostitute found strangled in a room in the Cozy Up Motel off Newman Springs two Fridays ago. He grabbed the murder book and opened it, hoping something new might pop out at him.

He turned the pages, reading snippets of the various reports, searching for answers. He stopped at the page analyzing time of death. Kurt Potovich, the medical examiner, had placed Miskavitch's time of death as the previous Thursday night. Now, what came somewhat unwillingly to Jack's mind, was the missing person report he'd initiated this past Thursday—a young nurse gone missing from the medical building where she worked, her red KIA left untouched in the parking lot. In his four years as detective, he'd worked a total of six murders. Now a possible two in one week? He didn't like the feel of this.

Alexis Greene had been reported missing by her mother, exactly one week after Miskavitch was murdered.

Sheila Greene had called the station late Thursday night when her widowed daughter failed to come home from her nursing job. With a young son at home and no boyfriend, she didn't sound like the party type.

"Come on out, Alexis, show your face," he said into the quiet air, just as Jim Cleary, the dispatch officer, poked his head through the door.

"Jack, we got a DB on the riverbank, over where Shrewsbury Ave. hits the bridge."

"Don't tell me." Jack's stomach dropped.

Jim grimaced. "Yeah. Sounds like Alexis Greene, but maybe not. Doesn't quite fit." He handed him a piece of paper. Jack read it and had to agree. The description fit, but the rest didn't. He grabbed his jacket and headed out the door.

The empty lot where the body had been found was at the edge of the Navesink River. A commercial realtor's sign was posted at the roadside on the open stretch of land. Four cruisers idled in the back corner. Jack parked beside them and approached the patrols, his shoes crunching the frozen ground. They stood in a circle, the vapors of their breath dissipating into the cold air. He noticed Colin Bank, tall and lanky, a head above the others and moved in beside him. The body lay in the center.

Jack's breath hitched when he saw her. His stomach turned in revulsion. His first thought—it's not Alexis Greene. She disappeared in nurse's scrubs.

This poor soul wore an off-the-shoulder red evening gown. She looked like a macabre store mannequin. Her face had gone purple, lipstick had been smeared over her lips, and bright blue eye shadow smudged above the eyes. He took a deep breath, shook his head to rid the image.

"She's done up like she's going to the prom," Colin Bank said.

"Or some very strange affair." Jack's voice cracked. He recalled this past Thursday evening when Sheila Greene had reported her daughter missing. She'd mentioned an identifying mark. He scanned to the left forearm. There, he saw the two-inch pigmentation.

"Dammit." Jack kicked the dirt. "Damn!"

Sheila Greene, such a nice woman, so scared for her daughter. She'd talked of Alexis's five-year-old son—her grandson. It appeared he was an orphan now. It was an ugly, ugly thing.

"Let's get some tape out here!" he shouted.

The M.E.'s van arrived with Kurt Potovich's white Toyota behind it. Jack gave Kurt a few minutes to get settled then took a spot beside him at the body. "How long you think she's dead?"

"Couple days. Looks like cerebral hypoxia."

It certainly did, everything about it, down to the small round bruises on the sides of the trachea. "You thinking what I'm thinking?" Jack asked.

"Strangled just like the girl at the motel?"

"Same marks on the neck." It lay in the cold air between them—the possibility that some kind of sicko was in their town. "Looks like the same M.O., except for the weird dress-up."

Potovich shook his head in dismay. "I can try to squeeze the autopsy in for this afternoon."

"That'd be great." Jack stood and looked out over the field. This one had bad implications. An arch of golden sun was rising on the horizon. It didn't bring any cheer. Two murders in his town. A child, orphaned. He'd tell the woman's mother soon. Hell of a way to start the day.

***

Cally waited anxiously as the gate arm lifted. She pressed the pedal and entered the Two Rivers PD parking lot. Monday morning. First official day on the job about to begin. She ran her hand over her hair, checking to be sure she'd made the bun tight enough. No loose hair, per the manual, low enough so she could wear the cap.

She was to report to Captain Jim McCloskey at eight o'clock. She walked the long hallway, the shiny white linoleum making her feel spiffy in her crisply ironed uniform. She'd been entering this building off and on for more than seven weeks, as she and the other recruits completed the cooperative training program with the Monmouth County Police Academy. But today felt different. Today, she would not head straight down to the lower level where the training rooms were located. Instead, she went straight to the third door on the left where Captain McCloskey sat behind a desk. He stood up and extended his hand.

"Good morning, Captain," she said, shaking his hand firmly.

"Nice to meet you, Cally. Captain Merino had a lot of good things to say about you."

At his invitation, she sat in the chair facing the desk. He passed a nine by twelve envelope her way. "Your schedule's in here. You'll be working days this month, off Sundays and Mondays. You're partnered with Lieutenant Vince Martin. He's been on the force for twelve years. He'll show you the ropes. Listen to him and you'll learn a lot."

"Yes sir."

"Your combination and locker assignment are in the envelope. I'm afraid we don't have a women's changing area. We've never needed one for very long, unfortunately. You'll use the ladies' room for now. We put a locker in there for you, so you'll have a place for your stuff. We're looking into something more permanent." He shrugged his shoulders looking embarrassed. "We have high hopes for you, Cally. Hope you'll be the woman to start a strong tradition of female officers in Two Rivers."

"I hope I can live up to your expectations."

"Best way to get adjusted is to jump in and get your feet wet. I'm hearing talk you may have a very interesting first day." He didn't elaborate, and Cally didn't want to push. "Put your bag and coat in your locker and head down to the break room. Martin will meet you there."

"Sounds great. Thank you."

After she stored her belongings, she headed to the cafeteria. A smell of stale coffee permeated the air. As she got closer, male voices broke into hearty laughter. She entered the room to see four officers sitting at a table. They looked up, and their expressions changed from open smiles to obvious discomfort.

"Hello," she said. "I'm looking for Vince Martin?"

"You the Bank girl?" a guy with curly dark hair and massive arms asked.

"Yes, Cally Bank. Nice to meet you." She extended her hand.

He shook it like she had Ebola virus. Was she imagining it, or had an awkward silence just fallen? Cally looked around the table; all eyes looked at her. She decided to try again. "So, I gather none of you are Vince Martin?"

They all turned to Big Arms who said, "Nope."

"I'm supposed to meet him here."

"Then I guess you better sit down and wait for him." Big Arms pointed to the other table while he shifted inward, putting his forearms on the table and closing her off. He said something to the guy next to him, making it clear his conversation with her had ended.

Well, that's rude, she thought, wondering what the snub was all about. Trying to pay it no mind, she went to the coffee machine and poured herself a cup of muddy coffee. She looked around the room for a discarded newspaper. Not seeing one, she picked up a classified magazine that advertised boats. She didn't know a hoot about boats, but hell, now was as good a time as any to learn. She went to one of the two empty tables and sat.

She sipped her coffee and looked at pictures of boats: sailboats, motorboats, pontoon boats, and cigarette boats. When she couldn't look at one more, she raised her head from the magazine. She'd done a pretty good job of tuning the guys out, and it looked like they were about to leave, gathering garbage and making a mess of their chairs. Just as he was about to cross the threshold, Big Arms turned and gave her a menacing smile. "Good luck."

"Thanks," she replied, squinting like Clint Eastwood. Hell, she could tango with him.

Left alone in the break room she checked her watch. She'd been waiting fifteen minutes. She was debating going back to Captain McCloskey, when a tall thin officer with a slight paunch and grays at the temples entered the room. He walked up and extended his hand. "Cally? I'm Vince Martin. Sorry to keep you waiting."

Cally stood and shook his hand. "No problem."

"It's been a wild morning. A dead body was discovered over in the lot on Mayfair. Our plans for the day have changed." He gestured for her to follow and led her down the corridor. "We're meeting in the chief's office."

Cally's heart pounded. The chief's office!

Cally walked with Martin along the corridor, his efficient strides causing her to nearly jog beside him. When they reached the Chief's office, his tall physique blocked most of the doorway. Soon he moved in, and she was standing at the threshold. Grainer's office was impressive with a wall of windows and an expansive, dark wood desk. The Chief sat in an upholstered chair behind the desk, with Kurt Potovich, the medical examiner, facing him. To Potovich's right, in a worn leather jacket, stood Jack Brant.

A lump formed in her throat. She quickly entered and stood next to Martin. Jack Brant standing in the chief's office talking about a dead body! O...M...G!

He leaned against the window ledge, arms crossed, talking. He glanced at Cally then quickly turned back to Grainer without registering the slightest recognition.

"I don't think so," he said, resuming the discussion. "Looks like she was dead since sometime Friday. More than likely, he killed her at some other location and brought her to the field last night. The guy who found her had his dog out the night before at ten o'clock. The place was empty, definitely no body. He was back with the dog the next morning at five-thirty."

"So now we hope someone saw something." Grainer said.

This was wild! The chief of police was discussing a murder, and she was standing in the room. Cally took a deep breath and tried to look official and quiet the pounding of her heart. She fumbled with her arms and finally crossed them in front like Jack Brant and Martin.

Jack continued. "Patrol did a preliminary canvas of the neighborhood. We're going back out." He turned to Martin. "That's where you come in, Vince. I need you and your new partner," he took her in with the slightest hint of a smile, "to work with me for the next couple days."

"No problem. We're all yours."

Cally's heart was still racing. She wanted to go grab her phone out of the locker and text Colin. She was working a murder case! With Jack Brant! She stood up straight and tried to look ready.

"And what about the prostitute?" the chief asked.

"Similar, but different. We'll know more once Potovich does the autopsy. Two victims, strangled, showing up dead within a week, you gotta' think connection."

Grainer nodded agreement. He looked at his watch then stood. "I have an eight-thirty appointment. Why don't you three spread out in the conference room. Jack, I want you reporting in twice a day. Keep me informed of any developments." He came out from behind his desk and gave Jack a pat on the arm then he came over to Cally. "Officer Bank, pleasure to have you aboard." He extended his hand, and she shook it gratefully.

It was more than she could have dreamed. As she walked out of the chief's office behind Jack Brant and Vince Martin, she felt a velvet fit, more perfect than any glove, any shoe, any slipper she'd ever worn.

***

Luther stared out over the water. The window rattled with the morning wind, and he leaned his cheek against it, let the cold glass cool his racing heart. He twirled Alexis Greene's ponytail band in his fingers, round and round like a New Year's noise maker. He thought back to the crowd he'd watched from across the river, surrounding his model in her beautiful red organza gown, loving the feel of his heart pounding in his chest, feeling alive, feeling more invigorated than he'd ever been in his life.

The house was a raised ranch with a garage and a workroom on the ground level. The sewing machine sat in the far corner. God, he loved that sewing machine since he was a kid. Since he was ten years old and his father brought it home in the trunk of the car—so proud of his five-dollar garage sale purchase. From that day on, Luther waited for those precious times when his father would be at work and his mother would go food shopping, or clothes shopping, or to the doctor—anywhere. Just out of the house, so he could sew. He was an expert at raiding the Good Will bin down the block. The one with the rickety metal door that never closed properly. Tucked away in the far corner of the shopping center lot, it housed worn sheets, bedspreads, men's pants, big lady dresses—all kinds of things. He never took enough that the skinny man who emptied the bins would notice. Anything would work as long as it fit under the presser foot of the old Singer. He'd pull the rags apart, redesign, then throw them back in the bin. Too bad a bunch of poor people were the only ones who ever saw his creations...until now.

Now. He couldn't wait to show everyone what he could do.

He pressed his cheek against the glass, cooled his flushed cheeks, willed his heart to stop pounding inside. To think—people everywhere would know him. People everywhere would respect him. They may not know what he looked like; they may not know his name, but they would admire his work...and they would fear him.

Chapter 5

On the far corner of the table, a carton of Dunkin Donuts coffee had been drained to its last drop. Pink and orange cups littered the table. Cally regretted the two full cups she'd consumed. Her stomach sloshed, and she craved a sandwich to soak up the caffeine that had her jittering. The Hagstrom map had been spread over the conference table. It had been years since she'd seen one of those, but the paper map, spread wide across the table, worked. In Oxford sleeves rolled to the elbows and a yellow highlighter behind his ear, Jack stood at the head of the table updating her and Vince on the latest.

"I've called in two more cops to assist. Anthony Musser and Mike Doolan will be helping out." As he spoke, the rude cop from the cafeteria entered the room.

Cally's first-day nerves spiked. After introductions, Jack told them to take a seat and laid out the plan, which included visiting all of the houses in the neighborhood where Alexis Greene's body had been found.

"One cop to each house," Jack directed. "Get the info and move on. Question every member of the household. Nobody home, mark it. Anything unusual, call me." He pulled the marker from behind his ear and pointed. "Musser and Doolan, you take First and Second Avenues. Martin and Bank, you take Third and Fourth."

Vince cleared his throat. "Bank and I will have to stay together, Jack. First week. I can't let her on her own yet."

Cally felt self-conscious as everyone turned to her. How could Martin say that? She could certainly go door to door on her own. She'd done it as a child selling Girl Scout cookies.

Jack eyed her like she was a puzzle to solve. Musser sneered and shook his head as though she was the biggest burden in the world. "Cut it, Musser." Jack tapped his fingers against the table then turned to her. "You can coordinate my paperwork." This made Musser chuckle outright and Jack raised a brow in warning. "Between the three of you, get both sections done. Bank, you come with me."

"You got to clear that with McCloskey," Martin reminded him.

Jack nodded and reviewed the instructions one last time before they cleared the room.

"I'm going to be your secretary?" Cally asked as soon as they left. She knew she sounded piqued, but she couldn't help it.

"Excuse me?"

"Shouldn't I have stayed with Martin? I could have helped him interview the witnesses."

Her question obviously annoyed him. Putting his hand on his hip, he said, "Officer Bank, if I say you're doing paperwork, then that's what you're doing." He gathered the papers and tapped them against the table. "Let's go."

Cally followed behind, double stepping to keep up with his long strides. He stopped in front of the elevators and pressed the down arrow. The Monmouth County Medical Examiner's office leased space downstairs, and she wondered if they were going there now. She had spent a lot of time in the lower level in the training rooms during the last seven weeks, and at one point they'd gone down the hall for a tour. The morgue had fascinated her.

"Where are we going?" she asked.

"M. E.'s Office. The autopsy's scheduled for later this afternoon, but he's prepping her now."

"You're bringing me along?"

"Yes, I'm bringing you along." The elevator door opened and he stepped inside. Cally could see he was mad.

"I thought you were planning on leaving me in the office the whole time."

"I don't know where you got that idea. This is a murder investigation. We move from place to place." The doors shut and left them alone in the very quiet, very small space. "And Officer Bank, please do me a favor and check the over-sensitized feelings at the door. You're less than an hour on the job. You're lucky to be on this case."

Cally let his words sink in as the elevator took forever to drop ten feet. She was lucky to be on the case, and she was lucky to be a cop, too. Wasn't this where she'd always dreamed of being?

"And I already have a secretary." He looked up at the buttons above the door and smiled.

She was reminded of the gym, and the banquet, too. She really had to start watching what she said around this man. There was something about him that made her feel too comfortable.

The doors opened and Jack stepped out. The M.E.'s space was at the end of the hall, and Jack buzzed the intercom when they got there. The man she'd seen in Chief Grainer's office opened the door and they entered the stark, impersonal place. It was cool and brightly lit with florescent bulbs. The linoleum floor was white and shiny. Just ahead, on a table lay a woman in a red gown. Cally's throat clenched and she felt the need to swallow, but she'd suddenly become too parched. As she walked deeper into the room, the air vents in the ceiling seemed to blow cooler. Goose bumps formed on her arms.

The woman's face was contorted and swollen. She wore a red gown. Her dark hair stood out against the white cloth draped over the table. Metal instruments were scattered around her head, and Cally's stomach turned unexpectedly. She looked away.

"You okay?" Jack asked. "You want a cup of water?" He pointed to the water cooler.

Cally shook her head. She forced herself to turn back and look at the woman. The poor, poor woman. Alexis Greene, she thought, forcing herself to put a real person, a mom and a daughter to the dehumanized corpse. The face bothered her most. Cally wanted to grab a cloth and wipe the makeup off. Why should this woman have to stay in this awful condition, makeup smeared over her face like a doll, someone's plaything? Wipe it off! she wanted to shout.

"Kurt, this is Cally Bank. Just graduated from the academy. She's mentoring with Vince Martin and will be helping out the next couple days." Jack was still eyeing her like she might faint at any moment.

She extended her hand. "Nice to meet you." Her voice came out raspy.

"Nice to meet you, Cally." They shook hands and Kurt began. "Jack, I don't know that I can tell you anything new, yet. We'll know more later, once we get the autopsy underway. Like we discussed, she was strangled."

Cally's eyes went to her neck, and she gasped. Jack glanced at her. "Sorry. I'm fine," she assured him.

"Manually," Kurt continued. "So, you have a perpetrator who's probably fairly strong ..."

"Or very angry and disturbed," Jack said.

Potovich nodded.

"What about time of death?"

"She'd been dead a good seventy-two hours. This guy didn't fool around. Probably killed her right after he abducted her, twelve hours, tops. She was dead by Friday morning."

"The bruise at the base of the neck looked pretty serious. Any chance that was the cause of death?"

"You're right, it's quite a contusion. It was quite harmful, clearly. Probably knocked her out at the time. But it's obvious the strangulation killed her."

Jack nodded then flipped the folder shut. "Good enough. Just wanted to drop in. We'll see you later."

It sounded like she would be attending her first autopsy in a matter of hours. Cally shivered. Geez, she hoped she could hold up.

As they rode the elevator, Jack jingled keys in his pocket and asked if she was ready to go for a ride. "I've got several stops. The first involves the Miskavitch case. The prostitute found murdered in the motel. We'll head out to see the manager then swing back to get a bite to eat. Sound good?'

Cally smiled and tried not to look too starstruck. Of course it sounded good! She was riding with the most decorated officer in town working a double murder case. What was not to like? If he wanted to eat, they'd eat.

When they stepped out, the air was crisp and invigorating with a bright sun shining in a deep blue sky. Using his remote, Jack popped the locks of the unmarked Crown Vic. Taking a deep, satisfied breath, Cally buckled her seatbelt and settled in for the ride.

***

Katrina Marley let herself into *Gail & Company*, the swanky fashion boutique on River Road in Rumson, where she'd been working as the manager for the last year. Balancing the cup of mocha latte, she placed her shoulder bag on the shelf and disarmed the alarm. From the backroom, the ringing of a telephone echoed over hardwood floors. Hoping to answer it before it stopped, she rushed through the showroom, past racks of gowns and private dressing rooms, to the cluttered area in the back.

The voice of Gail Stein, the shop's owner, hurriedly wished her good morning then said in a frazzled tone, "Don't forget that the Papell shipment is due this afternoon. You need to eat lunch in. Nanette is not qualified to inspect the garments."

Katrina knew about the shipment and didn't need to be reminded. She also knew that Nanette and the other sales ladies at the shop were not trained to process deliveries. She hung up the phone and glanced at her watch, noting that it was after eleven o'clock. She wondered if Gail was just making excuses to call and check what time she arrived. So, she was a few minutes late, big deal. There were no appointments scheduled. Passers-by who gazed at the windows rarely came in. Prom season was months away, and their wedding business had shrunk considerably since Gail had decided to stop selling bridal gowns. They had taken a big hit in mother-of-the-bride wear, traditionally her biggest niche.

Katrina took a sip of the latte and plunked on the stool. Jack wouldn't have called on the store line, anyway. He would call her cell. Still, she couldn't control the surge of hope that jumped started her heart every time a phone rang. Maybe he would change his mind. But this time, she dreaded it was really over. He had used such strong language driving home after the banquet. He'd seemed so resolute. And she would bet that blonde policewoman was behind it. There was no denying an attraction between the two of them. So how was she going to get rid of her?

As she plotted, the bells that hung on the doorknob jingled. Katrina looked up to see a gentleman enter. Dressed well in a pair of black fitted slacks, a knit shirt, and a leather jacket, he nodded at her. She stood and flattened the wrinkles on her skirt. "May I help you?" she asked.

He told her he was just looking and turned his shoulder. He walked over to the evening gowns and sifted through them. He pulled out the mint silk charmeuse and studied the lines.

"Sure you don't need any help?" She smiled nice and tipped her head endearingly. All she needed was to get him talking.

"No, thank you."

"Browsing for your wife?"

He looked up, annoyed. "Yes. My wife is confined to a wheelchair, so I'm helping out."

Oh. How sad. She thought a minute then said, "Let me help, please. We have a couple of gowns that may be perfectly suited for her, and we can set a private appointment for her to come in." She hoped the guy had money. He looked like he might. "Do you live here in town?"

"Up on Ridge Road."

Eeew, nice address. "Why don't I go get the laptop. I'll see what timeslots we have available." She wanted to nab him now, put his name in the schedule with her name designated as salesperson right next to it. "I'll be right back."

He eyed her strangely, and for the briefest moment she felt a stab of apprehension, but it passed as soon as he spoke.

"I suppose my wife would like to be pampered like that."

Katrina pictured him going home and telling his wife about the fitting he'd arranged. She also pictured the commission check she'd get and the ways she could spend the money.

"Don't move a muscle," she said enthusiastically. "I'll be right back."

She left him alone out front. Scurrying to the back, she thought what a miserable month she'd had—nowhere near her quota, the worst showing since she'd started. And on top of that—the break-up. Oh, she didn't dare think about Jack or she might start crying.

She was so preoccupied and anxious to find the laptop, which had disappeared somewhere in the piles of sample fabrics, that she did not hear her customer. She did not notice that he'd come to the doorway, nor did she see his shadow behind her.

***

The *Cozy Up Motel* was located in the northwest corner of town, a seedier section of high rise, state funded apartment buildings and smaller, shanty-type houses. Bright sunshine poured through the windshield, warming the cold interior of the unmarked police car. Cally rubbed her hands together. They cruised past a group of teenage boys, hoods up, baggy jeans, bling. They huddled together, shoulders hunched against the cold, their breath visible in the clear air. Cally wondered why they weren't in school. Surely, they'd be more comfortable there, than hanging out on the corner.

"Back in high school I was friends with a couple girls who lived over here. It's a whole different set of rules this side. Those girls had to be home, inside, before dark."

Jack shook his head. "Too dangerous?"

"That's right. They could get caught in the middle of something."

"It's true. This is tough duty."

They both sat quietly for a minute. Cally was sure they were thinking the same thing. It was in an alley two blocks away, between the two project buildings, that Clyde was ambushed. Clearing her throat, Cally said, "Thank you so much for what you did for my brother. Our family is forever grateful."

Jack looked across the seat. He appraised her earnestly then said, "Your welcome. I hope the patrols are riding double by the time you catch this assignment."

She'd heard about the departmental discussion which had begun last summer after the shootings. The Township Administrator and Town Board were giving serious consideration to doubling up in this corner of town. "If I'm riding solo then I'm riding solo. I'll handle it like everybody else."

Jack smiled tightly.

Cally decided to change the subject. "So, where's this motel?"

"A little further out, over on Carton, near the train tracks." Cally knew the area. It was an eclectic section of town with residential, commercial, and industrial all thrown together.

Soon they arrived at a run-down motel and got out. In a front window an old painted sign read, *Cozy Up Motel*. Dirty white curtains hung behind it. The office was as uninviting as the exterior—brown indoor-outdoor carpet, a threadbare chair in the corner, an end table stacked with old magazines. Cally clasped her hands in front to avoid touching the counter, which was caked with brown dust. Jack rang the bell. A moment later a middle-aged thin man, wearing baggy blue utility pants and a grimy white tee shirt appeared from behind a curtain.

"Help you?" he asked, wiping the back of his hand across his mouth. He looked up and saw Jack. "Oh. You."

"You get me the books, Lloyd?"

The man shrugged. "It's not gonna do you no good. I told you; the names are bogus. They pay cash, sign a book. It don't mean nothin'."

"I want the books. You don't provide them, I'll get a warrant."

Lloyd sauntered to the back room. He returned a minute later with a spiral notebook and handed it to Jack. Jack took the notebook, flipped to the last page, and asked several more questions about the status of room number nine.

"Hadn't been rented for, like, a week," Lloyd said.

"All the keys accounted for?" Jack asked.

"Probably not. We go through a lot of keys. People always leave with them." He pointed to a board where keys hung from rows of hooks. They were identified by clear plastic tags, the type you could buy in any hardware store, write something and snap it closed. Cally could see that each tag had a number.

The man followed her eyes to the board. "We keep two. One disappears, we make a copy."

"Tell me again where you were that night, between eight and twelve."

"Right here." He pointed to the efficiency area behind the curtain—twin bed, half fridge, microwave and television. "I'm here every night, some days, too."

"Where do you go when you're not working?"

"My sister's got a place."

"No place of your own?"

Lloyd shook his head like it wasn't important.

"So this is your home." Jack looked around. "Not a bad spot, got your own place there. Warm, comfy. You run the office, mind your business, keep everybody's secrets, right? Bet the holding company, Green Grove, doesn't want cops poking around, do they? They tell you to keep quiet?"

He shrugged.

Jack pulled a card from his pocket and handed it to him. "You can do time for withholding information, you know that? I find out you're holding back on me, Lloyd, you'll be sleeping in a cell, no more comfy little apartment. You got that?"

Cally watched and learned. She liked the way he bore down on him, tough but not mean, firm without being too intimidating. They'd been taught the technique in the academy, how to be tough enough to scare, but not scare off. He played it like a pro.

When they were back in the car she asked him about it. "You think he's holding back on you?"

"Maybe. More likely he's lazy. Doesn't want to bother his brain remembering stuff. If he thought good and hard about it, he could probably provide better information than he's giving."

"But you'd think he'd be wracking his brain, trying to help you out."

Jack laughed. "You think? Not everybody thinks like us, Cally. You'll learn that soon enough."

Us. She liked the sound of it. She and Jack Brant, thinking along the same lines, working the same case, riding side by side in the police car.

***

From the corridor, Luther watched the saleswoman. She was leaning over with a shapely derrière perched his way, totally oblivious. She was surrounded by luscious materials of all textures and colors, and Luther wanted to reach out and touch every one. A sunny yellow chiffon flew through the air. A gray crepe—gorgeous! His fingers began to tingle. He watched her rifling through. She would look magnificent in any one of them.

She had a body like a New York model.

He stepped toward her, and his shoe brushed the floor.

The woman whipped around. "Oh! You scared me." Raising a silver laptop in the air, she said, "Found it. Let's go out front."

He stood a moment, debating. She swallowed, and he laughed to himself. The fast-talking salesgirl taken off-guard. No, he would restrain himself. He'd already solved his problem, his reason for coming. By studying a similar garment on the rack, he'd figured out how to get the complex draping he was striving for in his latest work of art.

"I'm going to cancel the private appointment. I'm sure my wife is too bashful for all that attention."

"Don't be silly! We'll make her feel very comfortable, promise. She'll enjoy it. We pamper our guests to death." She marched past him, placed the laptop on the counter, and scrolled along the touch screen. "When is your engagement?"

"March fifteenth," he said, grabbing a date from thin air just to move it along.

"Plenty of time. How about a week and half from now, Thursday, January Twenty-ninth at two o'clock in the afternoon?"

Thursday? he thought. *Sorry, I'll be busy.* He nearly laughed, but instead he said, "That's fine."

"If she needs to reschedule, just call." She handed him a business card.

After giving her a name, address, and phone number, he said good-bye and left. He turned into the alley beside the building and walked to the back lot where he'd parked his car. As he settled into the driver's seat, he looked out over the dashboard, at the small path in front of his parking spot. On each side, a row of arborvitae, thick and green, lined the path, creating a majestic and concealed pathway for guests of Dieci, the restaurant next door. His heart jumped into over-drive. His mind ran three steps ahead. Good Lord, what a gold mine. The spot was perfect.

Chapter 6

Friday evening. Jack walked in the door, dropped onto the couch and turned on ESPN. The Knicks and Bulls were playing, and Jack sat back, ready to zone out. It had been a hell of a week. In addition to the Miskavich and Greene murders, a waitress named Brianna Hemmer had gone missing last night. Her disappearance had been eerily like Alexis Greene's. Apparently abducted, Ms. Hemmer's empty car had been found in the parking lot of Dieci, a fancy Italian restaurant in Rumson, just a few doors down from where Katrina worked. Jack had been holding his breath since last night, hoping like hell to get a call saying she'd returned home. It hadn't come yet.

When his cell phone rang, Jack jumped. He looked at the display and saw it was the station. With trepidation, he flipped the phone open.

"Jack, it's Cleary in dispatch. I hope you're nearby."

"Shit. Don't tell me."

"Yup. We've got another body. Sounds like Brianna Hemmer."

A pit settled in his stomach as he listened to the details. What kind of monster had invaded their town? Was this a serial killer? A spree killer? A cult?

He arrived at Maple Cove Park at ten fifteen p.m. He knew the park well. It was just a few blocks from his apartment. He often launched his kayak from the parking lot then paddled any one of the many options, heading west toward the bridge, or east to the ocean. The trails were beautiful, lush pockets of green reeds that hugged the river's edge to the ocean's door. It was in one of these high grassy areas that the body had been dumped.

Jack pulled into a small parking lot, crammed with five police vehicles. Jack squeezed his car onto the frozen grass. He grabbed his camera and walked toward the crowd. He heard cops mention *waitress, evening gown, sicko.* Jack's heart sank.

He approached three officers, one of them, Clyde Bank. As the highest rank at the site, Bank was issuing orders, covering for him. Bank already had one cop closing the area with tape and a second taking sole samples of all the cops' shoes.

After brief hellos, Jack asked, "Who called it in?"

"Late night jogger ... over there." Clyde pointed back toward the cars. "He's pretty freaked out, trying to keep his teeth from chattering."

"You take his statement?"

"Patrol's doing it now."

Jack sighed. "What've we got?" He hated to look.

Bank turned on his flashlight. The first thing Jack noticed were the colors—the deep green of the dress, the white of her arms and chest, the blue-black tint of her hair. She had been positioned on her back. Her legs were straight, her bare feet together. Two dainty hands were coquettishly placed on her hips. Under the moonlight, the skin of her hands shone like alabaster against the satin finish of the dress, both in vivid contrast to the dark hair. The dress was gathered at the hips and draped down. It had poofy sleeves, and for a moment Jack thought of Katrina and those haute couture fashion shows she watched.

"What's this person up to?" he murmured. What kind of macabre statement was he or she trying to make? These outfits had larger implications than he wanted to consider. He blocked them from his mind, preferring to focus exclusively on this victim and this crime scene. Jack stooped down to get a closer look. Clyde came down beside him. "She's been dead a while."

Jack took photos of the body and the surrounding area. He sketched it out and wrote notes.

"Evening," a female voice said soberly behind him.

"Cally," He moved his body instinctively to shield her from seeing the corpse. "I thought you were taking a few hours off."

"I heard it come over my scanner." Cally stepped in and peered around Jack's shoulder.

"You have a scanner?"

"My sister keeps a scanner in her bedroom." Clyde said. "She's very gung-ho."

"I know that. Why do you think I picked her?" Jack made room for her beside him. This morning he'd given her the news that she and Vince would be helping out indefinitely. Her enthusiastic reaction had quelled any second thoughts he may have had.

Just one week before Alexis Greene's murder, the only other Two Rivers detective had quit to join the Mercer County investigator's office, leaving the department short-handed right at a time when it needed detectives most. That left Jack to work this case alone—an impossible task for one man. The chief assigned Anthony Musser and Roy Doolan to Jack while they stayed on their regular rotation. Grainer told him to choose two other cops to be signed over exclusively to him. They would be taken off the regular rotation and paid overtime if needed. It was decision time for Jack.

Vince Martin was a shoo-in. He was a lieutenant who knew the ropes and worked hard. Cally required a bit more thought. Did he want to keep her around? First of all, she was green. Second, she was a petite woman. What if they ran into a situation where some muscle was needed? But ever since that first day on the job, she'd been working long hours; she never complained. She'd been a big help. She was organized and made insightful observations.

He submitted her name to the chief. Later that evening, while he shaved the stubble from his chin and daydreamed of her sexy body, he wondered if his reasons were purely professional.

"Glad you came down," he said, turning to look up at her. "You saved me a phone call."

"I figured that," Cally squatted down beside him. She took out her pad and pressed the tip of her pen against it. She looked at Jack with those sharp eyes he was growing so fond of.

"Like the last one, she's in a dress."

"A gown," Cally offered.

"Right. He's put makeup on her again."

"But this time he's been more careful," Cally commented. "It's still quite heavy but notice this time it doesn't look clown-like. More like he's trying to actually make her look attractive."

Kurt Potovich arrived, resting a black medical case on the hard ground beside Jack. "My God," he murmured. He turned the body briefly over on its side then let it settle back on the ground. He leaned over Brianna Hemmer and examined her neck. "Marks on the neck. She's been dead a while."

"She disappeared just twenty-four hours ago."

"Then he's moving faster."

Jack leaned back on his heels and sighed. Brianna Hemmer's husband had called last night at eleven thirty from Dieci Restaurant. As soon as the call came in, a morbid pall descended the station. Two disappearances within a week. It didn't bode well for Brianna Hemmer.

Mark Hemmer reported that his wife was always home by eleven o'clock at the latest. He called her cell phone repeatedly, but he got no answer. Hemmer had waited until eleven-thirty, when he'd finally gotten in his car and drove to Dieci's. He found a closed restaurant and her empty car in the quiet parking lot.

Alexis Greene's murder had been front page news for the past few days. Last night, as Jack stood in the lot with Mark Hemmer, he knew exactly what the poor man was thinking.

"Jack?" It was Cally's quiet voice beside him. "Are you okay?"

Her big brown eyes sparkled under the moonlight. She wore her hair pulled back into a ponytail, showing a gentle slope of smooth forehead. Her skin looked creamy and glowed with life. He wanted to reach across and touch her, feel some human connection in the midst of such lechery. She looked different—soft and vulnerable in a light blue ski jacket with a white turtleneck beneath. The collar framed her face, setting her delicate chin and full lips upon a pedestal.

"I'm fine," he responded, but his voice was hoarse. Too much emotion.

He stood and surveyed the scene. Potovich and a crime tech worked the body. Periphery work was under way. Cops used machetes to slice the tall sea grass and placed the dry, wheat-colored stalks in black trash bags. Next to them, smaller bags had been gathered. Trash from the nearby cans, a bit of litter, Jack assumed, but maybe they'd luck out. Maybe the sicko had dropped some piece of incriminating evidence.

***

Static buzzed in Cally's ear. She reached over and hit the snooze button, her body rejecting any thought of getting out from under the cozy, down comforter. She'd set the alarm for six-thirty, but heck, an hour and a half wasn't cutting it. She lingered under the covers as images of the prior night floated into her conscious. Brianna Hemmer, on the cold ground, amidst the reeds.

A stab of adrenaline shot through her, her mind coming fully awake. Now if her body would just cooperate. A hot shower will wake you up, she told herself, throwing the comforter and putting her bare feet on the carpet. Chilly, she quickly threw on her robe.

Forty-five minutes later, wearing the plain clothes that had become her uniform, she entered the conference room. Jack was there alone, seated at the head of the table reading a computer report. "Did you go home?" Cally asked.

"Just to shower."

"You'll never make it through the day."

"I'll make it." Jack stood and stretched his arms toward the ceiling. He grabbed his heavy leather jacket off the back of his chair. "But I need breakfast. Did you eat?" Cally shook her head. She hadn't even stopped for coffee.

"Let's go."

"Where's Vince?"

"Home to sleep. He stayed till six o'clock."

Good man, Cally thought, turning toward the door and hiding a yawn with her cupped hand. Jack was ahead of her, fussing with his jacket. The sleeve had gotten caught inside the body of it. As Cally walked up behind him, he shook the jacket over his head to free the sleeve. The zipper smacked her in the face, causing her to lose her balance. Jack grabbed her arm.

Cally quickened at his touch. He was so close, his face just inches from hers. She found herself looking straight at his lips unable to pull her gaze away. Jack took his hand and touched her chin, raising her face to his.

"Your lip's cut," he said in a low voice. "I didn't see you behind me." Still, he hadn't moved. His hand was like fire under her chin, sending heat all through her. She forced herself to breathe, to respond.

"I'm okay."

He moved in—to get a better look? She stood perfectly still, unable to pull away, mesmerized by his proximity.

"Uh hum." A throat cleared just outside the open door. "Not interrupting anything, are we?" Musser and Doolan stood at the door. Musser's eyes widened. A small smile and a knowing nod made Cally cringe.

Jack dropped his hand. "I smacked Cally with my jacket."

"We bumped into each other," she added.

"Whatever you say." Musser pushed past them and sat at the table. "We're still on eight to fours, aren't we?"

"You're early."

"Is that a problem? You want us to leave so you two can be alone?"

"Very funny, Musser," Jack retorted. "I'm just surprised you're early. Think that's a first."

Cally had noticed that Musser and Doolan were not the most industrious workers. Over the course of the past several days, Jack had to goad them with every job. They didn't want to run computer reports; they didn't want to sift files; they didn't want to do paperwork. All they wanted to do was conduct the interviews—a job which Jack had made clear was best done by a trained detective.

"Cally and I have been working all night. We're getting breakfast then heading out in the field. See that stack of receipts?" He pointed to the table. "Those are credit card receipts of everyone who has dined at Dieci's over the past week. I need you guys to track down the addresses and phone numbers and start calling. Ask the standard questions. Anything sounds the slightest suspicious, call me on my cell. Man the phones. Vince should be back in about two hours."

They left through the front of the station and walked to the diner. Today, the waitress smiled familiarly to her, too. They were becoming round-the-clock regulars. Most of the booths were empty with a stray workman or an early-bird couple seated in a few. They found a table toward the back and sat. A waitress arrived with a coffee carafe in hand and took their orders.

Cally dumped two creamers, a packet of sugar and stirred. The piping hot coffee glided down her throat. She sighed.

Jack drank his black. He took a gulp and said, "I needed that. Your lip's starting to swell."

Cally touched her tongue to her upper lip and felt a bump. "I think the zipper caught it."

Jack pulled several cubes of ice from his glass and folded them into his napkin. He was looking at her lip. He was incredibly handsome. He had a look in his eye that said *I don't care what people think.* It sent the same tingling feeling she'd had at the station.

He pressed the napkin to her lip. She let him hold it there, her own hands heavy as rocks on the table. She gazed into his eyes and her heart thumped in her chest. "Thanks," she mumbled, her throaty response bringing her to her senses. She grabbed the napkin. "I think Musser got the wrong idea back there." She reached for the water and gulped.

"You think? Maybe he had the right idea." He looked at her earnestly. "I'd like to take you to dinner."

"You're coming to our house on Sunday, aren't you?"

"I'm not talking about dinner with the family." His voice was steady, just like his gaze. He was so frank, so unabashed in his pursuit of her. Cally had never met anyone quite like him.

He leaned back in his seat and watched her. "This Musser thing really bothers you, doesn't it?

"Kind of."

"Who cares about Musser? He's a jerk." He shooed his hand.

"Jack, you need to understand something. Nothing is more important to me than my career. I've only been on the job a week. How would it look if I started dating you? You're practically my boss."

"No one will know."

"My brothers would find out. That's like telling half the police department. Besides, I don't want to go out with anyone right now. I want to focus on my career." This insane attraction between them had to stop.

The kitchen door swung open, and the waitress appeared with the plates. The corn beef hash and eggs looked scrumptious. Cally picked up her fork and dug in.

"So, I should forget the date?" Jack said after they'd both eaten a bit.

"We'll still have fun at my parents.'"

"I can't wait." That one, she was sure, was sarcastic.

Chapter 7

Tommy Doone watched the cars pulling into the Bank driveway. He sat on the edge of the bed, peeking through sheer curtains as he'd done for much of his life. The Bank family had always held a certain allure—the perfect family, the best in sports, successful adults. They kind of fascinated him. They kind of made him sick.

Except Cally. Cally wasn't like her brothers. Cally was cool. As a boy, he'd always enjoyed hanging out with her, even though her brothers often wrecked it for them. And as he'd gotten older, well, the attraction to Cally had, shall we say, changed.

Now he sat at the window wondering if she would come tonight. Two of the four brothers had already arrived, and Mrs. Bank was busy setting the table. From the second story window, he could look down and see into their dining room window clearly. The woman always looked so nice. So well-dressed and presentable. So unlike his own mother.

As he watched her place items on the white table cover, he could almost hear the soft clank of ceramic against cloth. It was a sound he'd heard only rarely growing up, at a restaurant here and there, the banquet hall the other night. He watched Judith Bank bending, smiling, and he could not help but compare. How different his life was from theirs ... how different from Cally's. They lived next door to one another, in Colonial homes that looked almost identical, yet the lives within them were completely divergent. His mom was not a stitch like Judith Bank, and his dad? He was unlike Mr. Bank altogether.

He remembered after the banquet, how the Banks had gathered at the bar. As Tommy and his parents passed through, he saw Mr. Bank, standing amidst his children with his glass raised. He announced how proud he was; how he was the luckiest man on earth. Tommy heard the clink of their glasses, the *here here's!*

As soon as they were in the car, his own dad seized the moment to start up again.

"See that? You see how even the girl made it through the academy?"

"Yes, dad, you already mentioned that."

"How come my son has to be the loser, huh? Why me? Why can't I have a normal son like the rest of the men in there, huh?"

His father sped out so fast the tires spit. His mother sat in the passenger seat, bracing herself, trying to clasp the dashboard. He sat in the back, of course. Driving along the four-lane boulevard that ran parallel to the beach, the misty pink streetlamps flashing by, Tommy tried to keep from yelling back, but his throat choked up the words anyway.

"You're the loser and you always will be!" he shouted. "Thirty years on the force and sergeant's the best you could do?"

"Thomas Arthur Doone! Stop that right now! I will not let you disrespect your father like that!"

"Don't bother, Estelle. It's a waste." They drove the rest of the way home in silence. When his father pulled into the driveway, he shut the engine and said, "I want you out of my house."

Estelle gasped, "Frank!"

"It's long overdue, Estelle. He's an ingrate."

"I don't ask you for money."

"Yeah? And what happens when your grandmother's money runs out, huh?" he shook his head. "Don't come running to me. You're a lazy, stinking, ingrate. You got one week to find your own apartment. You got that? If you're not out, your stuff goes on the curb."

"Fine." He got out of the car and slammed the door. He was ready to move out anyway. Why had he waited so long?

Tommy heard the slam of a car door and nearly fell off his bed. He was sweating. He was shaking. Why did he let himself dwell on things? He needed to take positive steps!

And he'd already started, was almost there. Peering out the window, he saw that it was Cally. She had arrived! She looked so pretty in a light blue ski jacket and her hair swirling around her shoulders. He missed seeing her regularly. He missed her. She'd moved out of her parents' home and into the Maple Shade apartment complex last year.

That night after the banquet, after both his parents had gone to bed, he sat alone on his bed until late into the night, until he realized that the expulsion from home had been the blessing he'd awaited. He would get his own apartment ... and he knew where. He'd sunk under the covers and slept.

Tommy watched her walk up the path, pull open the door, and disappear inside. But tonight, it did not make him sad. He knew he would be seeing quite a bit of Cally, very, very soon.

***

Cally hung her jacket on the wooden peg and entered the empty, aromatic kitchen. Whatever her mother was cooking, it sure smelled good. She'd had a decent night's sleep, a productive Sunday at the station, now all she needed was her mom's cooking. She inhaled the delicious scent—rosemary, red wine, beef, mushrooms, and knew immediately her mom was cooking Beef Bourguignon.

Though she'd arrived early to help, it looked like her mother had everything under control. One large pot sat atop the stove. Cally saw what looked like a pie out on the counter. She went over and lifted the white cloth napkin and smelled apples and cinnamon, her father's favorite. Peeking, she saw the lumpy, flaky upper crust. Yum. She couldn't wait. Hearing male voices out in the den, she placed the napkin back and left the room.

The dining room table set with china and crystal. My goodness, she thought, Mom is going all out today. She thought briefly of Jack and clasped her hands. Crossing the hall and living room, she entered the den. Charles stopped talking and put his head down.

"What?"

Charles ignored her question and took a carrot from the *crud été*. Cally walked to the tray and grabbed a celery stick. She dipped it in the ranch dressing.

Charles looked at Chris and raised his brows. Cally hated when her brothers did this—like she could read minds or something just because she belonged to the opposite sex.

"Are you going to tell me or not?" Cally chomped on the moist stick and waited.

"You know how pissed people are that you snagged this murder investigation?"

"What people?"

"Cops who are more senior than you … and that means everybody … are pissed that you got taken off the rotation to work the investigation. It should have gone to somebody more senior."

"He took Vince. The only reason I was brought in was because Vince is mentoring me."

"Bullshit. That makes no difference at all. You could have partnered with anybody after Vince went over. Jack requested you."

Why would Jack request her? It brought an uncomfortable pang. "Who told you that?"

"Doesn't matter. You don't deserve to be working that case. He should have taken a senior officer."

"And I suppose that means you?"

"Me, Chris, anyone in our tier. Not you. You don't know the first thing about protocol or procedure. Why'd he choose you, Cally?"

"Charles, cool it," Chris said.

"No, Chris, let him speak." Cally turned to Charles. "What's that supposed to mean?"

Charles said nothing. After a long silence Chris answered for him. "People are talking." He lifted his hands in defense. "I'm not insinuating anything. I wouldn't have said a word, but since Charles brought it up ... I'm just telling you what people are saying."

"There is nothing between me and Jack Brant!"

"You tell him that?"

"Yes, as a matter of fact, I have! Not that it's any of your business. Unlike you two goons, Jack Brant has been a perfect gentleman."

Charles rolled his eyes. "Not what I heard. You better watch out, pipsqueak. He'll be looking for favors soon."

Favors? Is that what Jack was thinking? But he'd been this way since the first night they met at the gym. Since before he even knew there was a chance of them working together. It was purely innocent—a guy asking a girl out.

"Jack has me on his team because I'm a team player," Cally said indignantly. "I'm efficient, organized, and smart. A lot more so than you two buffoons. Neither of you could find a file or work a laptop if your lives depended on it."

"What's all the arguing about?" Judith Bank entered the room. Cally smelled hairspray and the light scent of Nivea cream.

"Never mind," Cally said, walking over and giving her mom a kiss. Her brothers did the same.

Her mom wore tailored black slacks, a maroon knit turtleneck, and a silk scarf. Her thick hair was twisted in a French bun. She looked elegant as usual.

"You look tired, dear." Judith held Cally's cheeks in her hands. "Big bags under your eyes. Are you getting enough sleep?"

"Not lately, Mom. Have you read the newspaper?"

"Are you kidding? I'm a nervous wreck. Why don't you come home for a couple weeks, just until they get this guy? I hate the thought of you living in that apartment while this lunatic is loose."

"You do know Cally's assigned to the case," Chris said.

"She's the one trying to track the lunatic down." Charles chimed in acerbically.

Judith looked horrified. "What?"

"She's been taken off the regular rotation to work the case."

Cally threw Charles a mean look. "Don't scare her, Charles. It's nothing, Mom. Just ignore him."

Judith raised her hands to her cheeks. "Don't tell me that's true, Cally. I don't want you anywhere near this case."

Charles smiled wryly. "Jack Brant, your knight in shining armor, requested it."

Judith turned to Cally in dismay. "Well then, I'm going to have a talk with Mr. Brant tonight. Your father and I do not want you on that case, *comprend?*"

Cally's heart jumped. "Mother, you will not say one word to Jack! This is my career, and you will leave it alone." She hoped her face showed how serious she was. "Stay out of it!"

Her mom looked like she'd been slapped. Cally immediately regretted her words. She reached out and grabbed her mother's hand. "I'm sorry!" She threw her meanest look at Chris and Charles. "Come on, Mom. Let's go in the kitchen."

When they got to the kitchen, Cally poured two glasses of Merlot. She handed one to her mom and smiled. "The food smells wonderful. Beef Bourguignon?"

"Your favorite." Judith smiled lovingly, making Cally feel more a heel than before.

She sighed. "You understand, don't you, Mom? This is a really great opportunity for me. The other cops are all jealous, even Chris and Charles. I'm going to learn so much. It's more than I could've hoped for, and so soon into my career." But even as she said it, she wondered if what Charles had said was true. It was strange that she was the one chosen. And there was more she did not even want to think about. The truth was, she liked working with Jack. She looked forward to being with him each day. Just one hour ago she'd left him, and she could hardly wait to see him again. This was bad. A mess.

She thought of the look in Musser's eyes when he found them in the conference room. He'd resented Cally from day one. If a rumor had started, he was at the root of it. Still, rumor or not, she would not let the case slip through her fingers. She had every intention of seeing it through. She would just have to be careful around Jack. She couldn't give off any signals that he might misconstrue.

"But it's dangerous." Judith said, removing the lid from the big pot and dipping a finger into it.

"It's not dangerous."

"It is!" The lid clattered loudly as she set it back in place. "Don't you think this guy will know which cops are tracking him? He'll read the papers. He'll follow the case. He'll read everything people write on the internet. Your name will get out, and he could come after you. And you can bet the national news is going to hook into it. They already have."

"I know." Cally rubbed her hands. "It was on the cable shows last night."

"Don't say it like that!"

"You have to admit it's exciting."

"Three women have been murdered! There is nothing exciting about it. What's the matter with you, Callanne?"

"You know what I mean—the national news here in Two Rivers—it's surreal."

"*C'est mal.* This man is evil. I don't want your name or your image entering his mind."

The sound of voices rolled in from the hall. Cally heard her father's laughter and her nephews giggling. Clyde and Jennifer had arrived. Cally looked at her watch. "It's six-thirty. What time did you tell Jack?"

"Between six-thirty and seven. He should be here any time." Her mom grabbed her hand and grinned.

They joined the group in the living room. Her dad distributed beers and poured the wine. Paige arrived and sat down next to Chris on the couch. Cally went over and sat beside her. She liked the fact that her roommate and best friend was now dating her brother except, that recently Paige had been spending a lot of time at Chis's apartment. She missed her. They started chatting as they sat on the couch, Paige asking questions about the job and the case.

Hulky NFL players jumped off the big screen. Ravens versus Steelers in the snow. Cally found herself glancing out the window each time a car drove by. She sipped her wine. She'd been with Jack Brant for nearly forty-eight hours straight, but she sure felt anxious about seeing him now.

Her dad came, sat in the armchair beside her, and patted her knee. His face was big and round and ruddy, just like the rest of his body. He had a thick crop of white hair that stood straight up in a crew cut. He'd had the same head of hair since Cally was a baby, having gone prematurely white at the age of twenty-seven.

"Cally-Bally, how's my girl?"

"Hi, Dad."

"What's the matter? Where's my little firecracker?" The old nickname made her smile.

"I'm a little tired."

"I'll bet. Working triple time?"

"I suppose you think it's dangerous, too?"

"I'm not so sure. My main concern with you being a cop is the logistics. You're a petite woman. Have you been out to the firing range lately?"

"Not since we went together last month."

"You have the best shot of the five of you. Keep it up."

"I'm also the only third Dan black belt in the family, Dad. I think I can handle myself with or without a gun."

Her dad nodded thoughtfully. "Just watch your step. Keep your eyes peeled. This guy is dangerous." He glanced out the window as a car door shut. "Looks like the man of the hour has arrived," he said as his face broke into a broad smile.

***

Jack turned off the Carrera and looked at the stack of cars in front of him. He took a deep breath and sighed. Look at all these cars. He hoped they weren't all there just to honor him. Why had he said yes? But he knew the answer. Mrs. Bank had caught him in a moment of weakness.

Jack opened the car door and reluctantly made his way up to the front steps. Before his finger pressed the bell, the door opened.

"Welcome, Jack." Clyde, Sr. pulled him in and clapped him on the back. Jack shook his hand and looked into blue eyes topped with a fluff of white brows. He felt instantly at home with both the man and his home.

Jack guessed the house was built in the early part of the century. The ceilings were high, the floor, laid in oak, and the center stairway, wide. The runner was worn with what looked like years of traffic. The banister showed nicks and scratches. Warm and comfortable, he thought instantly, but boy what I could do with the place.

"Hey, Jack." Cally appeared behind her father. For a moment they stood awkwardly in the hall. What was the proper etiquette here? Should he give her a peck on the cheek? A handshake? He settled for a nod of the head. She nodded back. He felt Chinese.

"Long time no see," she joked.

Had it really been less than two hours? She'd changed her clothes and let down her hair. Jack realized he'd never seen it down before. It was tucked behind her ears and hung over her shoulders. It swayed when she moved. She wore a cream-colored turtleneck that clung in all the right places. He could watch her all day.

More Banks flowed behind her: Clyde Jr., then Chris, and Charles. Jack wondered what was with all the C's. He said hello to Jennifer and met Cally's roommate, Paige, a curvy brunette. Jack felt like he was on a receiving line and was glad when it came to an end. Clyde, Sr. put his hand on his shoulder and led him into the den. Handing him a beer, Clyde gestured him to the couch. Jack sank into the worn leather. The Ravens were on the ten-yard line in front of him. He could think of worse places to be. Talk wafted around the upcoming playoffs and anticipated trades for next season.

Cally had disappeared. He heard pots and pans clanking in the kitchen and he pictured her there, stirring and mixing and setting silverware on the table. It was a nice image. "Smells great," Jack said to Chris, who sat at the other end of the couch.

"My mom's quite the cook," he replied.

"Is she the one who decided on all the C's?"

Chris chuckled. "That just kind of happened. The way my parents tell it, they named Clyde after my dad, who's named after his dad. My mom named Charles after her dad. Next came me, full name, Christian. I was named after my mom's favorite uncle, who died right before I was born. By the time Colin came along, they didn't want him to feel left out, so my dad picked a nice Irish name."

And what about Cally?"

"Callanne Marie? She's named after my *grand mère*." He said it with a French accent. "She was a real ball of energy."

Then she's aptly named, Jack thought, as Judith Bank entered the room. Jack stood and she kissed him on both cheeks, a bit more reserved than the last time he'd met her. "I hear you've hardly slept this week," she said, clucking her tongue slightly. "We'll take care of you, give you a good meal."

"It smells wonderful."

"I hope you'll like it." She clapped her hands. "Dinner's ready!" She officiated the seating like an orchestra conductor. She tapped Jack's place in the center, far side, Clyde Junior beside him, Jennifer to the other side. Everyone swirled around the room like the snowflakes that had started to fall outside the dining room window. By the time the whirlwind subsided, Jack noticed Judith had arranged the four women intermittently amongst the men, with Cally directly across from him.

After the food was passed and the grace was said, Clyde Senior raised his glass. He looked Jack's way. "Here's to you, Jack. You did a good thing, six months ago." His eyes welled with tears. "We're grateful."

***

Cally gazed across the table at Jack. He looked so handsome. She loved the way he interacted with her father, how her mother gazed into Jack's eyes, how Jack and Clyde and Chris joked around as though they'd known each other forever. She found herself rooting for him, personally pleased that he blended so effortlessly.

"So how are things going with the investigation?" Clyde, Jr. asked.

"Could be better. We've got lots of evidence taking us nowhere. Our leads have all been dead ends." Jack shook his head, his frustration palpable.

"Maybe you need more help."

Cally turned sharply at the bite in Charles voice. Where was he going with this?

"The feds are already helping," Jack said. "We've requested profiling and access to their databases. FBI's giving us two agents full-time." He spoke with command and confidence.

"That's smart," her dad said. "Bring 'em in early. Use their resources. They're good people, despite what you hear."

"Do you really think he'll strike again?" Judith asked.

Jack smiled reassuringly. "I hope not. It's going to be a lot harder for him. We've got extra cops on the street. Citizens are changing their routines. I doubt you'll find many women out alone at night until he's caught." Jack looked around the table. "You guys working overtime?"

"Patrolling the friggin' K Mart parking lot." Charles grumbled.

"Hey, you never know," Jack said good-naturedly. "It could be next."

"Pisses me off. I'm sitting at K-Mart, while my kid sister, who's been a cop for exactly one week, lands the hottest case to ever come to town."

"Charles!" her mother snapped. "That's unnecessary."

But Charles persisted. He turned to Jack. "Why would you pick someone with no experience?"

Jack placed his fork on his plate. He raised his hands to stop the wave of protests that had erupted around the table. "It's okay. I don't mind explaining." He stared down Charles while he spoke. "Your sister and Vince Martin were assigned that first day. Over the course of the next week, Cally was a big help. And she has a great attitude. I picked her to remain on the team for that reason."

"Yeah, right," he mumbled. "Her attitude." He said it loud enough for the entire table to hear. She was mortified. How could he?

"I've got two other cops working for me right now," Jack continued. "They're a lot more senior than Cally, but you know what? I can't stand having them around. They've got bad attitudes." He looked Charles flat in the eye.

Cally felt her stomach lurch. Oh God! Jack was challenging him!

Charles stared back.

"Christian, please pass the egg noodles. Jack how do you like the Beef Bourguignon?" Her mother's voice was smooth as velvet as she held her hand for the noodles. Though she smiled, her eyes glared at Charles.

Jack replied, "It's delicious. I'm going to want to sleep for a week."

Judith laughed. "So where are you from, dear? Did you grow up in this area?" The melodious tone, the erect posture, the slight tilt of her head Charles's way, dared him to say another word. Cally released her breath as the imbroglio melted away.

Jack proceeded to talk about his past. He'd moved to town ten years prior from his childhood home in North Jersey. He saw an ad for cops needed, and said he'd never even heard of Two Rivers before that.

"Does your family still live up north?" Jennifer asked, everyone smiling, happy again, except Charles, who stewed in his seat.

"I brought my mother and my sister down about a year after I moved down. My dad died when I was in grade school."

Judith tsk-tsked and said, "*Ooh la, la.* I'm sorry to hear that. I'd like to meet your mom some time. Does she live locally?"

They talked some more. Cally leaned back and watched. She watched the way his mouth curved in a crooked smile and how his eyes twinkled every time. She watched his muscular forearms as he reached for the breadbasket. She watched his strong hands pull a piece of French bread. She watched him talk with ease to every member of her family, every member except Charles, whose angry glances he managed to ignore as though they were not taunting him at every turn.

Chapter 8

I t appeared they were disbanding. At the moment they were assembled in the center foyer doling out hugs and kisses, and Tommy thought it would never end. The family dinner had lasted hours. He couldn't think of a single time, not even Christmas, when dinner had taken more than a half hour at his house. Course it was just him and his parents. And they never had much to talk about. Still, Cally's life was so much different than his.

Maybe the Maple Shade wasn't such a good idea, after all.

Now Jack Brant, the detective who'd been honored at the banquet, was standing with his coat on, looking ready to go. Tommy leaned closer to the window. His pulse bumped a couple notches. Brant had been sitting across from Cally at the table, but other than that, it didn't look like there was anything between them. Surely, he was a guest of the entire family. He did save the brother's life.

Tommy waited for the endless string of hugs and kisses to come to an end.

Get in the car and leave, would you!

But now Cally came out behind him. Brant turned around when she called him. They stood in the middle of the driveway talking, and Tommy's heart pounded in his chest. She had her jacket on. She was leaving, too.

"Coincidence," he said into the quiet of his bedroom. "She's going home." To her apartment at the Maple Shade.

After what felt like an eternity, Brant got in his car. He put the car in reverse, and when Tommy saw the white taillights illuminate, he exhaled. But then Brant backed up and waited! For Cally to go first! And then he eased the nose of the silver Carrera forward.

Tommy jumped up. He brought his fist to his mouth and bit down on the skin. Why was he following her? Where were they going? God forbid, was she sleeping with him?

He grabbed his keys and ran down the stairs, out to the car, and caught up with them before they turned the last corner in the neighborhood. He followed from a respectable distance. He followed onto Broad Street and watched as both cars drove under the gate and into the police station lot.

He parked at the curb and shut off the car.

They each got out of their cars and walked toward the entrance. At one point Brant put a hand on Cally's back, but it looked innocent enough, more like ushering her through the door.

This was okay. This was fine. They were working.

But he had better hurry it up. Cally Bank would not stay single forever. It was time to take another positive step forward. He reached his hand across and grabbed the hardcover book. His fingers caressed the paper jacket. *Take Charge of your Life*, his bible. He kept it in the car so he could refer to it frequently. He placed it in his lap. Like osmosis, the tomb pumped courage through his veins.

He would ask Cally out. The time was coming. He'd already taken a big step in the right direction, signed the lease and all. And fate had followed him, hovered over his shoulder throughout the entire process. Tomorrow, he was moving into the Maple Shade Apartments. And not into just any unit, either. Tomorrow morning at eight o'clock, he was moving into the apartment right next door to hers.

***

Cally watched Jack. Was it a mistake coming back to the station with him? She'd made the offer without fully thinking it through, without realizing that her feelings for him had changed. Oh, why did he have to come to dinner? Until tonight, she'd convinced herself he was all wrong for her—a fellow cop she could never date, a guy she could never go out with. But she'd seen different tonight. She would never look at him the same way again. She knew now he could have fit perfectly into her life.

Cally turned to the table and saw a file of leads Musser and Doolan had left. She picked it up, thankful to have something to do with her hands. "Shall we sort through this?' she asked. "I'll take half."

He agreed it was a good idea. As he reached for the file, the skin of his hand brushed against hers, and she revved at his touch. She sat down at the table, placed the papers in front of her, and prepared to focus her thoughts on the case, not Jack Brant. The seat he chose was way too close—right next to her. He opened the manila file and took the top paper. He held it out in front and read. After about a minute, he placed it face down on the left side of the open file and took the next paper. He did this three times. How could he be so focused? Her mind was racing in a hundred directions. She was still on her first sheet. Again, she read it top to bottom but couldn't remember a word it said. She sighed.

"It's hard to concentrate." He reached for the papers he'd discarded and read them again. Was he feeling it, too? His arm was so close she could feel the touch of him. "It's an exercise in self-discipline."

"Yes," she replied breathlessly."

"Being so ... tired ... I mean."

"Yes, tired. I'm just so tired I can't concentrate. Maybe some water." Lord knew, she needed it. She stood abruptly and reached for the pitcher in the center of the table.

"Here. Let me get that," Jack offered. He stood and got the pitcher. She reached to take it from him, but he gestured toward the paper cups. She pulled two from the stack and held them in her hands. They faced each other, so close, him with the pitcher, her with the cups.

Energy buzzed between them, prickling every inch of her skin. He poured the water. She held the cups in her hands and looked at him. He placed the pitcher on the table without moving his eyes from hers. He took the cups and put them on the table.

Oh heavens, she was thirsty. But not for water. Not anymore. He moved in close, but she stepped back.

"We can't do this," she said.

"Why not?"

Why not, Cally reasoned. No one is here. No one will know. But she couldn't allow herself to give in. She would regret it later. "We just shouldn't," she said.

He flinched, and she saw the disappointment in his eyes. He asked, "Still leery of me?"

"No. God, no. I'm not leery of you, Jack. I'm leery of everyone else. You know how cops talk."

"Let them talk. Who cares?"

"I care."

"No one's going to make a big deal about you dating me."

"It's not that." She lowered her head.

Jack took her hand. "Then what is it?"

"People are already talking. They're saying that you gave me the spot because you're... interested in me or something to that effect."

Jack nodded his head slowly. "I get it. Musser. The other day. I'm sorry. I didn't realize." He walked over to the window and looked out. "I'll talk to Grainer tomorrow and get him replaced."

"No! Don't do that on my account. I can handle it. Maybe the talk will die down on its own. I'll speak to Charles."

"Why should you have to do that? No, I'll take care of Musser, and I'll speak to Charles. I put you in this position, and I'll get you out." He put a hand on her shoulder and pulled her into him. "But will you do me one thing?"

"What's that?" she asked, feeling her resolve melt.

"Have dinner with me. I have someplace special in mind."

She didn't respond. She couldn't.

"We won't call it a date. Just dinner."

She looked up into his clear green eyes. A sigh escaped her lips. How could she resist this man? "Okay," she said. "I'll go." She just hoped she wouldn't regret it.

Chapter 9

Katrina had just finished lunch and had resumed her job of filling the racks. Gail had asked her to pull some of the older garments, but picking the ones to go seemed an impossible task this afternoon. She separated the hangers and tried to jam the gray crepe between the other size eight dresses. Damn! Too many gowns! She stuck her arm into the crowded materials and shoved the mint charmeuse toward the front. What was she going to do about Jack?

He hadn't been the same since she'd snuck into his apartment. Why, she couldn't figure. Big deal ... she'd snuck in and cooked him a big dinner. You'd think he'd be grateful. She'd made him salmon and asparagus and laid it all out with candles...

Now she hadn't heard from him since Ashley's wedding, and she was starting to think he was serious about breaking up. Adjusting the folds of a gray crepe, she noticed the exceptional draping. She flattened it down then shoved it in. Maybe she should never have copied his key. Maybe he'd figured it out. She should have realized he'd hate the intrusion! But she'd been thinking sex. He certainly valued that commodity as much as his privacy. She'd just hit bad timing. He'd been rushing ... he'd been preoccupied about that prostitute murder ...

She tapped her fingers on the upholstered hanger.

"Don't pack them in like that!" Gail came over and nudged her aside. "What's come over you, Katrina? You know better." Gail's coiffed blonde hair scratched against Katrina's arm. My God, the woman used enough hairspray to stop a train. Gail moved in and started rearranging the gowns.

Katrina didn't care. Let her find the space. She was the one who'd ordered too many to begin with. For probably the first time in twenty years—since she was eight years old and her mother bought her the white patent leather boots which she refused to take off for forty-eight hours—Katrina didn't care about the clothes. She could care less if the whole damn rack toppled over and the gowns were lost in a giant heap of wrinkles.

"Katrina ..." Gail was eyeing the Dominique Sirop. She pulled it out and studied it. "Did you inspect this garment?"

"Yes. I checked the entire shipment."

"And you didn't see this?" Gail raised the hanger in one hand and draped the plum-colored gown over the other forearm. The side seam had split about six inches. Shoot.

Just then, the bells jingled, and the front door opened. Katrina turned and her heart jumped to her throat ... Jack!

"Hello, Jack." Gail laid the gown on the counter and strode purposefully to him. Placing a shimmering diamond hand on his upper arm, she said, "I'm glad you stopped by. We're having a heck of a time with that faucet in the bathroom. That plumber you sent didn't do a thing. I think the whole contraption needs to be replaced."

Jack glanced Katrina's way. Her heart fluttered, and she quickly smiled at him. He smiled back and nodded. Hurray. A good beginning. She moved in toward the two of them.

Jack shifted his feet. After telling Gail he'd send the plumber back tomorrow, he said, "But actually, I'm here on official business."

Gail brought her hand to her chest. "Oh yes, that poor woman. And to think that restaurant is just two doors down! Good Lord, I shudder to think of all the times I've been out back alone." She literally shuddered her upper body to prove the point. "But we were already visited by a couple of policemen. Big, burly guys. I'm afraid we weren't much help."

Jack glanced her way, and Katrina tried to communicate with her eyes how much she'd missed him. He dropped his gaze. She wished she knew what he was thinking.

"I read their notes, but I have a couple of follow up questions."

"Well, certainly come on in. Katrina, be a doll and pour us some coffees, please."

Katrina stiffened. How dare she treat her like a maid! She knew she and Jack were an item. The woman was impossible.

Gail turned her back. She was dressed in a deep purple suit, and as Katrina looked at her derriere, she couldn't help but think of a spring petunia in full bloom. She, on the other hand, felt like the fading pansy in a plain white dress. Gail led Jack to the nook where they served clients coffee and tea. Jack sat in one of the pink upholstered café chairs. He looked oversized and uncomfortable. Katrina poured three coffees and sat down with them, directly beside Jack but on the other side. She made a point of pulling her chair a good six inches closer to him.

As Jack proceeded to ask almost the same questions the two cops had asked, Katrina's spirits began to rise. This was just an excuse! He hadn't come to "follow-up", he'd come to see her. She usually worked alone, and he probably thought they could catch a quiet moment. But Gail was here, and what could he do? Now he was playing this little game.

Katrina answered his questions. She smiled and played along.

When he was done, as he tucked the small flip pad into the breast pocket of his jacket, he asked, "Can you think of anyone or anything that occurred this past week that was out of the ordinary in any way?"

Gail thought about it and shook her head, no.

Katrina was about to do the same when she thought of her most recent client. The way Jack had posed the question, different than the two policemen before him, made her think of the man. She remembered that slight moment of apprehension when he'd looked at her strangely ... then the way he'd come to the back? There had been something unnerving about him. Then she thought about sending Jack on a wild goose chase, with their relationship hanging so precariously. She shook her head, no, just as Gail had.

Plus, she needed that sale. Her numbers were down, and her job performance had not been the best lately. Could you imagine the scandal if she sent cops over to a Ridge Road client's house? Gail would have a fit.

Jack got up to leave, and with Gail sandwiched between them, Katrina walked him to the door. She watched him get into the unmarked car and ease into a line of traffic. If only Gail hadn't been here, Katrina lamented, watching the car make a right and disappear. They could have straightened the whole thing out.

Chapter 10

The light at Broad and Henry turned red just as he reached it. Jack glanced at the dashboard clock and chucked a sigh. He was already late. He tapped his fingers on the wheel, checked both directions. No one in sight. He pressed the pedal and went for it. At the station, he used the side door closest to his office and was glad to find it empty when he arrived. He could use a minute.

He sat at his desk feeling hungry and frustrated. He had skipped lunch yet again, and his pants were starting to feel loose around the waist. Was it the crazy schedule, or was the stress starting to get to him?

The upcoming meeting would surely be tense. How would Bank react? Would he give him a hard time or cooperate? He reached into the bottom drawer and grabbed the bag of sunflower seeds, took one and popped it in his mouth. He leaned back and chewed, separating the seed from the shell and letting his mind wander from the upcoming discussion to the case.

How could it be that nothing was panning out? No witnesses, no bona fide leads? Their killer was crafty, leaving nothing behind except what he chose. Curling his tongue and blowing, he shot the empty shell into the waste bin just as Charles Bank appeared at the door.

Bank put both hands on his hips and asked, "What's this about?"

Jack came out from behind the desk and extended his hand. Bank looked at it then crossed his arms in front.

Fine. If that's how you want to play it. Jack dropped his hand and said, "Have a seat."

Charles remained standing. "Let's get something straight. I don't appreciate being called in early to get a lecture from you. I'm not your report. You're lucky I came in."

"What's your problem, Bank?" He closed the office door.

Bank turned his head and looked at the wall. He rolled a stubborn tongue under his upper lip. Jack could see he was weighing his next move. Leave and piss off the detective and possibly the chief, or put up with him? Jack liked his odds.

"What do you want from me?"

Jack decided to be frank. "I called you in to ask for support. I figured you'd want to help your sister." He went back behind his desk and sat down. Charles widened his stance and crossed his arms.

"Why should she need my help?"

"Because some of the guys are spreading rumors."

Charles raised a brow. "Are they rumors, Brant?"

"Yes, they are."

Bank shrugged. He raised his brows like he didn't buy it then asked, "Say I ... go along with you. What's in it for me?"

"Your sister gets the respect she deserves."

"That's it? Not good enough. I want off the rotation, just like Cally and Martin. And I want a recommendation from you when the case is closed."

"You're bartering your sister?"

"Don't get high and mighty with me. You're the one who put my sister in this position, not me. And on second thought, forget it." He turned and left.

The sunflower seeds had spilled onto the desk. With a full backswing he sent them through the air. Son of a bitch. *Him* hurting Cally? All he'd done was give her the chance to work a once in a lifetime case. Was that such a horrible thing? It was the rank and file who had turned it into something it wasn't.

The seeds pelted the wall as Clyde Jr. came through the door. "Whoa! What's everybody so pissed about?"

"What's with your brother? Why's he mad at the world?"

Clyde took a seat and Jack noticed how big all the Bank men were. Clyde looked to be about six feet, four. He was broad-shouldered and powerful looking.

"Not the world. Just the PD. Charles was recently overlooked for a promotion. It's got him angry at everybody. He can't stand the fact that Cally is working this investigation."

Jack considered the statement.

Clyde continued. "He's been a cop eight years, been itching for detective. Was this close," he held his fingers an inch wide. "Twice."

"You mean Charles was one of the guys that was passed over last spring when they hired Kleman?"

"Him and Musser. Then six months later, after Kleman gets promoted, he leaves and takes the job with Mercer County." Clyde tilted his head, see? "Now this case comes along, and you ask Vince Martin to assist."

Jack leaned back and shook his head. "I've worked cases with Martin. He was the first guy to come to mind."

"I understand. And I told Charles that when he came complaining to me. But try to see it his way: He went through three interviews. He could smell the bacon, was seeing himself in the detective role. So naturally, he thinks he should have been the cop pulled up on this case. Hell, he thinks they should've made him detective as soon as Kleman quit. And to make matters worse, his sister—the rookie—who hadn't worked one single day on the job—gets brought in. You see?"

He did indeed. The paradigm shift—*Seven Habits of Highly Effective People*—one of his favorite books.

"I get it." Now he just had to figure out what he was going to do about it.

***

Luther pulled the paper from the Smith Corona sending a hearty zip through the air. He sat back in the old mission style chair. With his gloved hands, he held the paper and read it through one more time. Then he folded the letter and slipped it into the envelope.

Satisfied, he smiled. This would jettison the story. It was all he'd heard when he was at the department store. Imagine, a huge department store and everyone talking about him. They were all so curious. And so ill-informed. They had the details all wrong, thanks to that lead detective, Brant. If he would only give them the information that they craved! Luther pulled the adhesive strip and pressed the flap, feeling a rush of excitement. If Brant wouldn't provide the details, he would. The people wanted facts; they wanted to know about his art, and he was happy to oblige.

He left the room, walked through the quiet house and went downstairs. He peeked into his sewing room and felt a rush of excitement. In the lurking shadows of darkness, a small red light glowed. The switch to the surge protector. It eyed the old Singer like a loyal watch dog.

"Soon enough," he whispered into the cool air. The patient machine would be spinning its pretty bobbin very soon.

Chapter 11

Cally left through the front door of her parents' house. She'd stopped home briefly—just long enough to borrow her dad's briefcase so that she could bring some extra work home. As she approached her car, a voice called from next door. She turned. A man in aviator shades stood at the edge of the Doone property.

She waved tentatively as he approached.

"It's Tommy, Tommy Doone," he shouted, removing the sunglasses. He smiled broadly and ambled toward her.

"Hello, Tommy. How are you? Sorry. I didn't recognize you. It's been a long time."

"Yes, I guess it's been a while."

"You look great. How's life treating you?" Honestly, Cally could barely believe it was Tommy Doone. He'd always been a tall, gangly kid. Nice as anything, but shy. They'd played together as kids but eventually had drifted apart. This handsome man who stood in front of her barely resembled that person.

"I'm doing great," he replied. "Just moved out of my parents' house." He lowered his head. The modest action was appealing on him, and she remembered how much she'd always enjoyed his company.

"I made the big break last year," Cally cajoled. "Where'd you move?"

"The Maple Shade apartments."

"You're kidding! That's where I live."

"Small world." He smiled warmly. His eyes sparkled. "Did I make a good choice?"

"You did. Once you get settled, my roommate and I will have you over for coffee. When did you move in?"

"This morning. I didn't have much, just some cartons. The new furniture is being delivered tomorrow. I'm in unit twenty-two."

"No way! That's the vacant apartment next to ours. We'll be neighbors again! Not that I've seen much of you. I don't think we've spoken in four or five years." They stood awkwardly for a moment, and she said, "Well, it was great seeing you. I'll be looking for you at the Maple Shade."

"Yeah, that would be great." He nodded and turned back toward his house.

Cally hurried into her car. She felt a ping of nostalgia as she waved good-bye. She hoped she would be seeing more of him in the future.

A half an hour later, Cally reclined on her bed, staring into her open closet. Paige stood before her, dressed in an aqua nursing uniform and rubber clogs. Her thick, dark hair was pulled back in a ponytail, her hands firmly planted on comfortably curvy hips.

"Let me get this straight," Paige said. "You have a date tonight with Jack Brant, the guy who happens to be the most eligible bachelor in Two Rivers."

"It's not a date. He's just taking me out to eat, but if I go, I'm afraid things will get complicated at work. There are already rumors about the two of us."

"I know. I heard. But I thought you said he's a nice guy."

"He is." Cally crossed her arms behind her head. "I don't know what to do!"

Paige sat down beside her. "How many times have guys asked you out and you've said no because you have to go to the gym, or go to some dumb Judo match, or you can't go out with the guy cause he's a cop friend of one of your brothers?"

Cally shrugged.

"A lot! Too often! Read my lips: Go ... out ... with ... Jack ... Brant ... tonight. Stop worrying so much about your career and go have some fun."

Cally sighed. What Paige didn't know was that a swarm of butterflies was having a hoe-down in her stomach. She still believed going out with Jack tonight could send him the wrong message, and she didn't want to mislead him. "I just don't know."

Paige stood up and gestured her hands in the air. "Helloooo?" She grabbed Cally's ankles and started pulling her off the bed. "Jack Brant is handsome. He's rich. He saves people's lives. You need to start getting ready now!"

Cally remembered the night before, how torn she'd felt. It would happen again, she knew it. Half of her wanted to listen to Paige, the other half screamed, "Don't go!"

But she couldn't very well do that. She'd told him that she would go to dinner. At this very moment he was probably driving to the restaurant. She had to get a move on. She couldn't very well stand him up now.

Chapter 12

Cally eased the Pathfinder under the portico of the well-known steakhouse in Long Branch. It was tucked away on an industrial street near the beach, not somewhere you'd expect to find such a fine restaurant. She had never eaten at the popular hot spot, and she was excited to experience the atmosphere and food.

A valet came and opened her car door as she entered the small circular drive. Jack was waiting in the paver area where Cally assumed they would wait for their cars later this evening. A quiet, airy whistle escaped his lips. He brushed a kiss against her cheek. "You look gorgeous. Like those shoes. Don't think I've ever seen you in heels."

She'd decided to dress up a tiny bit, not enough to give him the wrong impression, but enough so that she didn't feel like a bum. She'd chosen to wear a pair of black jeans and a favorite cashmere sweater. Paige lent her the light blue suede heels. They were a definite change from the flats he was used to seeing her in.

"I'm so glad you came." He gave her a peck on the cheek and placed his hand on the small of her back to lead her to the door. His touch sent a warm current up her spine. They ascended a couple of stairs into an amber-lit foyer with exposed brick and weathered woods, where an attractive woman with hair pulled back and a stylish black dress asked for Jack's name. She led them through several rooms, all stylish and trendy in their own way, to an intimate corner table next to a rustic brick fireplace.

The fire crackled invitingly, and Cally thought, oh no, this is not good. This place is way too gorgeous and romantic. All the willpower in the world couldn't help her here. The air smelled of rosemary and raspberries. Other diners talked in low tones at cozy tables. The case and the station seemed far, far away.

"It's beautiful here, Jack. Do you come here often?" It sounded lame to her ears, but Jack didn't seem to notice.

"I do. Actually, I own the building next door, so I come here a lot. I know it's fancy, but you can't beat the steak. You'll feel like a new woman after you eat. Believe me, it's a therapeutic treat." He opened the wine menu and started reading.

"You own the building next door? That's a big warehouse," Cally said. Paige's comment about him being a wealthy bachelor popped to mind. She hadn't given it much thought at the time.

"Yes, that's a big merchandising company. They sell all kinds of household products online and ship them all over. They've been there for many years. They'll probably move once their lease is up. This beach area has gotten too congested, and the rent is prohibitive at this point. They'll do much better moving further west."

"Do you own other buildings?"

"A few. Around town. It's kind of a hobby." Jack put the wine menu down. He looked into her eyes and smiled. "I guess it's more than a hobby. It's a passion. I like buildings and negotiating deals, bringing in investors. I'm accumulating a portfolio."

"How many buildings do you own?"

He pursed his lips, tapped his finger on them. "Let's see … seven … three mixed use residential and retail buildings downtown, two other warehouses out on Industrial Boulevard, an office building on Commerce."

Wow. She was impressed. Here she thought all he did was save lives. The waiter arrived, a younger guy in black jeans, a black t-shirt that carried the restaurant name, and Sketchers type sneakers. All the waiters and waitresses were dressed similarly, and it all contributed to the laid-back but chic atmosphere of the place. He took Jack's wine order with an approving tip of the head. He returned promptly, and Jack tasted the small sample, and they sat quietly while he poured the dark red wine.

Jack ordered a cheese platter for starters and when the waiter left, she asked, "How'd you get started?"

"In the beginning? I flipped buildings. I bought the cheapest things I could find and financed as much as possible. I was always looking for a good deal. Now that I've established a track record, I can be pickier, and I have a number of investors who trust my judgement."

The cheese arrived and he sliced a piece, placed it on a cracker and offered it to her. He told her of the restaurant's reputation as a top-notch steak house. She knew her parents came every year for their anniversary, but she'd never really thought about the place. Now she pictured her mother and smiled. She took a sip of Merlot. The flavors melded into one delicious sensation. How could a hunk of cheese and a sip of wine possibly taste so good?

Tropical EDM played quietly over hidden speakers, stirring her restless senses to the core. Jack reached in and chose a razor thin cracker from among the choices. He spread it with what looked like a Bourgogne cheese and put it on her plate. "Try that," he said, his demeanor quiet, intoxicating in a hushed way.

The evening passed in a sensual blur. The artfully laid entree of filet mignon and asparagus tips melted in her mouth; the triple chocolate dessert nearly did her in. Cally leaned against the upholstered chair.

"You were right. This was incredible, Jack. I feel like I've had a massage."

"I'd like to bring you back sometime," he said earnestly. "I don't want other people to direct our future."

Their future? Cally took a deep breath. She straightened her shoulders and tried to put her thoughts into words. From the first time she'd met him, he'd never played games, never been anything but completely forthright with her. She liked that about him. But did she want the relationship to grow?

Jack reached his hand across the table and took hers. "What I'm saying is that I want to have more than a friendship with you. There's something special between us. Maybe we shouldn't let petty gossip interfere."

Maybe, maybe not. She understood what he was saying, but she needed to consider the trouble it had already caused, the repercussions that would come. She'd worked so hard to be where she was—a police officer, like her brothers. A member of the team. If she started going out with Jack Brant, it would throw a wrench into the entire thing! Before she would even be judged as an officer, she would be known as Jack Brant's girlfriend. So *not* what she'd planned.

She pulled her hand away, feeling a sadness in her chest.

"It's been a wonderful evening, Jack. Thank you so much for bringing me here, but I don't want this to turn into more."

Jack leaned back with a shake of the head. He ran his hand through his thick brown hair and let out a sigh. "Okay. I get it. Just friends."

Chapter 13

The following morning, Holden McKinley, editor in chief of the *Central Jersey Press*, sat facing Grainer. Old school all the way, McKinley wore his usual bowtie-suspender ensemble, today's, a red plaid. Jack couldn't help but like the man. He was a bugger, but he'd always been good to him, never printing anything that might compromise an ongoing investigation. An attractive, exotic woman sat beside McKinley, short skirt, boots, nice legs from what he could see. The chief told Jack to grab a seat, and he pulled a chair beside the window where he could have more space. Jack had been summoned just moments prior. The chief's brief explanation had sent his heart pounding.

"I can't wait on this," McKinley said resolutely, continuing the conversation he'd been having with Grainer.

"You realize you'll be aiding a killer," Grainer replied.

"I don't see it that way. If we don't print the letter, he'll send it to another outlet." McKinley tipped pudgy palms up. "Then it's anybody's game, and the Press loses its shot. I can't let that happen."

Grainer chewed the side of his mouth and turned to Jack. "What do you think?"

Jack glanced at the letter, sent to The Press by the killer. The chief had summarized it over the phone, but now Jack picked up the evidence baggy and read through the plastic. His adrenaline spiked. The words sent chills through him. How could a person think like this?

"I don't see how we have a choice," Jack said. "I agree that he'll go to somebody else. It may buy us a couple of days, but ultimately it will come out. Maybe we can use it to our advantage." Already his mind had begun to calculate what information should be released and what held back. He turned to McKinley. "I'd rather you guys break the story, if you can assure us you'll do it responsibly."

"Of course we will. We live in this community, too. We don't want any more women being murdered. We'll keep it strictly informational so as not to cause panic." McKinley brought his short round body to the end of the seat. "Then it's a go for tomorrow?"

Jack glanced at Grainer who raised his brows. "Tomorrow's Thursday."

Jack knew exactly what Grainer was alluding to. Both Alexis Greene and Brianna Hemmer had been abducted the previous two Thursday evenings. Debra Miskavitch had been killed in the motel room on a Thursday. He wondered if McKinley had put the pattern together.

"They can tie it to another public safety announcement," Jack suggested.

Grainer mulled it over. "Okay. Tomorrow it is." To McKinley he said, "That's providing you play it into a public warning statement. Something about not being out alone and being aware of your surroundings." He turned to Jack. "Switchboard's going to ring off the hook."

McKinley leaned back. He turned to the attractive woman who sat slightly behind him. "Tia will write the article," he said. "Came to us from The Camden Weekly. She's quite a writer. What else have you got for her, Jack?"

"The letter says plenty."

"Ah, come on. People expect to hear from the detective-in-charge. You need to comfort them, tell them you're gonna' catch this guy. Give me a good quote."

"Forget it, McKinley. I'm not commenting."

"How about giving us some details about these murders." Tia Santos spoke in a quiet voice with a soft Latin accent that matched the velvet look of her skin. Pretty lady, but still he wasn't talking.

"Sorry, no additional details. Three women, all strangled, analysis points to one killer."

"How long from the time they were murdered were the bodies later dumped?

"Check your records." He grabbed the letter off the desk. If this sicko wanted to send *The Press* letters, he could, but he wasn't playing the game. "Chief, if you don't mind, I have an investigation to run."

"Go on, head out, Jack," Grainer and pushed his chair back, indicating the meeting was adjourned.

McKinley reluctantly followed his lead, grabbing hold of the armrest and hoisting himself out of the chair. He extended a chubby hand Jack's way, and they shook as Tia Santos settled items in her briefcase.

"Good luck with the article," he said to Tia.

"Thank you." She smiled. "Here's my card if you change your mind."

He had no intention of doing that, but he took the card. He left the room, his thoughts returning to the letter. His fingers tightened around the bag he held in his hand. *Ultimate sacrifice? Art?* He was killing innocent women. Tearing families apart for pleasure. And he called it art? It was lechery, plain and simple. Keep talking, asshole. Keep sending letters. You're finally giving us something.

Jack entered the command center and slammed the door behind him. Cally and Martin were at the table. Both jumped when the door slammed. Cally looked beautiful, seated at the table, interrupted from a moment of concentration. Briefly he recalled her rejection last night, feeling a little sting. No matter. He was a patient man.

"What's wrong?" she asked

"A letter from our killer." He threw the Ziploc bag on the table. Jack waited as they both read it, watching their stunned reactions. When they'd finished, he said, "He sent that letter to the *Press*. It'll be in tomorrow."

"This is awful," Cally said. "But at least they came to you immediately."

"Naturally. They needed to authenticate it," Jack replied. "The details are spot on. It's him, alright. And there's no keeping a lid on this, anyway. It's too sensational. I'd rather let the local paper break the story. The big outlets will call them instead of us."

"Good point." Cally smiled supportively.

God, he wished he could hug her, take her in his arms, feel something good under the palms of his hands. He turned to the stack of papers spread in front of them. "So, what great new leads did you two find?"

"Not much," Vince said, mentioning a couple new bits of information.

Jack took the evidence bag and placed it dead center of the table. "It's not all bad. Truth is, I'm glad our killer sent this note. It's contact. A solid piece of evidence that might actually take us somewhere."

Chapter 14

The dead bolt echoed through the quiet store. Beyond the front windows, a lazy winter evening was underway. Pedestrians hurried along the sidewalk; a lone woman stopped to admire the black velvet display she'd arranged last month. The gowns were so stale. Would Gail ever switch to the spring collection? Katrina adjusted the shutters so that they were set at the three-quarter angle Gail favored for evenings, noticing a couple walking hand in hand.

Her heart clenched. No word from Jack. Oh, it was so frustrating! She didn't know if she could bear a moment more. She missed him so much. She wanted him! Sure, the case was consuming, but couldn't he take one moment away? One second to call her and see how she was doing after he'd treated her so cruelly? Or was he too busy with his new *partner*?

Grabbing her purse, she headed for the back. Since the waitress's murder, she and Gail had decided to keep the back door locked at all times. Now she opened the door six inches and looked out onto the parking lot. It was a big municipal lot, fairly busy most of the time, and she'd never had the slightest apprehension about walking to her car in the past. Tonight, she thought twice. She stood at the door and watched for activity. She looked for men alone, parked in a car or loitering. She saw no one, and she noted that the streetlight by the lot that had been out for weeks had finally been fixed. She remembered the municipal worker a couple evenings back, shining a flashlight up the pole. Initially he had spooked her, with all that was going on, but then she saw that he wore a hard hat, construction goggles, and the heavy brown parka jacket all the public works employees wore. A white town pick-up truck with the town seal had been parked just beside him. Too bad he hadn't been there just a few hours later when Brianna Hemmer was getting off her shift. Things might have turned out differently.

Katrina stepped out and reached into her purse for the key to lock the store door. As she fumbled through her bag, her fingers closed around a key—*the key*. The one she should probably throw away and forget she ever had. She moved passed it, fishing her hand along the bottom of her purse, and grabbed the clunky set of keys with the store key on the ring.

She locked up, walked the twenty yards to her car, passing the streetlight and thinking again of that town employee. Something about him had looked vaguely familiar. It bothered her that she couldn't place him, but as she got in the car, thoughts of Jack invaded her mind once again.

She had to speak to him. If only she could get his undivided attention ... surely, he would be willing to give their relationship one more shot. She glanced at the time on the car's display, still early, just seven p.m. When she brought her eyes back to the road, the light had turned red, and she was just feet from the SUV in front of her. She slammed on the brakes and her purse slid off the passenger seat, its contents spilling all over the floor. Immediately, she saw the lone gold key, lying there on the mat, beckoning her to use it just one more time. Time is running out, she thought. Soon Jack would forget all about her, and it would be over for real. What was the point of copying that key, if not to use it?

Chapter 15

The Maple Shade Apartments comprised eighty single floor apartments in ten buildings. Each unit contained eight apartments, four up and four down. A covered walkway and stairwell provided access to the apartments. Cally hustled toward her door as cold air brushed the back of her neck. Tree limbs rattled with the wind; smoke from a nearby wood stove tickled her nose. It had been a long, but electrifying day.

With the arrival of the letter, she'd sensed a change in Jack. She'd wanted to reach out to him, offer comfort to the angst she knew he was feeling—the angst they were all feeling—but she'd held back. Instead, she tried to make herself useful. She took notes for Jack and handled the coffee runs, recognizing her place as low man on the totem pole. She was happy to do it. Happy to help out in any small way she could.

Tonight, Jack had insisted on following her to the complex gate. Not until she'd passed safely through, did he drive off to take the FBI guys out for a quick bite to eat. As she watched his car leave in the rearview mirror, she questioned, again, her decision to keep their relationship purely professional. There was no denying that they were attracted to each other. What was the point in holding back? Like Jack had said, who cared what people thought?

Maybe she'd call him in a little while—just to check in, say thanks for seeing her home. But for now, she thought, all I want is a hot shower. She reached the apartment door and was opening it as footsteps sounded over her shoulder. Her arm shot up in defense. She spun around.

"Hey neighbor."

"Good God, Tommy! Don't do that!"

"Sorry." He smiled and raised his hands apologetically. "Didn't mean to sneak up on you. Just wanted to say hello, tell you I'm all moved in." He pointed to the door six feet down the walkway. "I was just putting some cartons out by the dumpster." He gestured toward the back lot, the opposite direction from which Cally had come. His arm dropped awkwardly to his side.

She stood a moment without opening the door. She didn't want to invite him in. She was too tired and didn't feel like talking.

"Want to see my place?" he asked. "The furniture came. It's not quite done, but it's coming along."

"Oh, not tonight, Tommy. I'm exhausted."

His eyes registered comprehension. "Rough day?"

"You could say that."

"My dad mentioned you're working the murders. He still keeps in touch with his buddies. Must be wild."

"It is." Cally stifled a yawn and promised she'd stop in soon. She said good-night and opened the door. Inside, she kicked off her shoes and fell onto the couch. She hoped her new neighbor would not take the brush-off personally. She was just too tired to chit-chat. She put her feet up and laid her head back, thought of Jack, decided that yes, she would call him. After a hot shower—just to say thanks for seeing her home.

Chapter 16

Jack left the agents at the front doors of the Molly Pitcher Hotel. The iconic riverfront hotel was close to the center of town, and less than a mile to Broad Street, where he lived in the third-floor apartment of a building he owned. As he drove, he stifled several yawns. The exhaustion left him vulnerable, and he found himself thinking about Cally again. When had he become so smitten? He was pining away like a schoolboy.

He pulled into the lot behind the building and rode the elevator. Ordinarily he would have taken the stairs, but today he was too bushed. The cab rode ridiculously slow up the three floors. He'd spent the better part of six months renovating the large two-bedroom with new oak floors, newly plastered walls, and a brand-new kitchen top to bottom. It was an old, pre-war building with great architecture—high ceilings and tall windows, and you couldn't beat the location right in the center of town.

The ride came to an end and the door glided quietly open. Gratefully, he stepped out, glad to be home and anxious to drop in bed. He opened the door to his apartment and stopped in mid-step. The apartment lights were dimly lit. He was sure he'd turned them off before he'd left early that morning. Stepping cautiously through the door he noted a soft, electric guitar playing over the Bose

speakers. The scent of ... vanilla?

Uh, no. She couldn't have...

"Katrina?"

"Jack," she cooed from the bedroom. "I've missed you."

Jack threw his keys and phone on the coffee table and reached for the lamp. He turned the switch up all three notches. Her dress was slung over the arm of the couch along with her thong lying on top of it. High heels were placed strategically on the floor to look like she'd kicked them off whimsically. Jack knew better. He pictured her arranging everything meticulously and methodically like she did for the fashion shoots.

He grabbed her dress and thong and tossed them in the bedroom. "Please get dressed. How did you get in here?"

"Don't be mad, Jack," she pleaded. "I want to make-up. Come on in here this minute, you silly man, I've been waiting for you!"

"There's nothing to make-up, Katrina. It's over." He wanted her dressed. He wanted her out. He didn't want a naked woman in his apartment—at least not this one. He walked into his kitchen, grabbed a glass, and pressed it under the ice dispenser. The cubes clanked loudly through the quiet apartment. As water filled the glass, he saw her emerge fully dressed from the bedroom and plunk herself down on his couch.

"Jack, we need to talk," she said as his cell phone began to ring on the coffee table in front of her. He watched as she looked at the display, then looked up at him, her eyes narrowing.

He strode to the table and snatched the phone, noting Cally's name on the display.

"Cally?" He winced as he said her name, turning his back from Katrina and saying, "What's up? Everything ok?"

"I just thought I'd call. Thanks for following me home tonight," she said. "How was dinner with the Feds?"

Aach, he wanted to talk so badly—to have an off-duty conversation with her, let the frustrations of the day out to someone he liked and who understood what he was going through, but Katrina was right behind him.

"Dinner was fine," he said. "Can I call you back in two minutes? I'm right in the middle of something."

"Who's that, Jack?" Katrina's voice sounded from behind him, loud and out of place. "Can you help me zip my dress, please?"

Jack felt suspended in time. He didn't know what to say or do. Cally had gone quiet on the other end. He needed time to think, to explain, but he didn't know how to do either. His phone had gone deathly quiet, and he pulled it back to look at the display, saw that the line had gone dead.

"Damn it, Katrina!" He spun around and saw her sitting there, a smug expression on her face. "Leave!" He pointed emphatically to the door. He grabbed her purse and shoved it on her lap.

"You intentionally sabotaged that call. You're a sneaky woman, and I don't like sneaky people."

"And you're a complete jerk! I can't believe I ever considered making up with you."

"I want that key!" He jutted his hand out, palm up. "Give it to me. I know you copied it."

"Fine. I don't want it anyway. I am *not* going to grovel for you." She pulled the key from her purse and chucked it on the coffee table where it slid across and landed on the floor. She jammed her feet into the high heels, and tucking her purse tightly under her arm, she marched to the door. "Good-bye, Jack." With a display of theatrics, she pulled the door open and disappeared into the hall.

Good riddance, Jack thought. He fell into the armchair and let out a long sigh. He stared up at the coffered ceiling, wondering what he was going to do. He took a few deep breaths, letting the anger and bad energy dissipate. He couldn't let this sit. He had to talk to Cally and explain. He picked up the phone and entered her number. She picked up on the sixth ring and sounded quiet.

"I want to explain what just happened," he said.

"You don't owe me any explanations, Jack, really."

"It was this crazy situation. She came over and—"

"Jack ... I'm really tired. I have a department meeting first thing tomorrow and you have the task force meeting." Her tone was strained and reserved.

He hated hearing her that way.

"I'll see you tomorrow. Good-bye, Jack."

Same two words as Katrina only this time the finality scared him. "Cally ... wait ... don't hang up."

Too late. The phone had already gone dead.

Chapter 17

Cally awoke at five a.m., after three hours of restless sleep. Tossing and turning, she'd told herself it didn't matter. She and Jack were not involved. They were not an item. He could do as he pleased. She suspected that last evening her voice had revealed her sense of betrayal. This morning, she was determined to put any hint of hurt feelings behind.

She rose from the bed and headed into the shower. The chief had called a department meeting, eight a.m., attendance mandatory. As she dressed in her uniform, she planned how she would act towards Jack when she saw him. It was important that he understand she was completely disinterested in his personal life. That he was still with Katrina made no difference whatsoever. Their dinner together had been nice—a gracious gesture between staff leader and member—but nothing more. And now she was glad she'd said so that evening.

At five thirty she stepped out the front door and drove to the 7-Eleven. She would get a newspaper there, and a large cup of coffee, which she needed urgently. As she turned through the familiar streets, she wondered if she'd pushed Jack back into Katrina's arms with her rejection at the restaurant. She found herself regretting how definite she'd been and then immediately castigated herself for thinking it. *You did the right thing! You told him no, and you were right to say it! Now he's back with his girlfriend and you are free of any conflicts.* Still a thought niggled the corner of her brain. *Back* with Katrina? Was it possible he'd never left her?

Cally's thoughts shifted when she reached the convenience store and noted the crowd. The 7-Eleven stood across the street from the train station, and today every Manhattan commuter must have decided to stop in the store first. She had to wait to grab a space in the parking lot, which resembled a swarming swath of macadam. Inside, commuters formed a line in front of the piles of papers. As Cally headed to that corner, a sense of dread crept up her legs. She watched as customers stepped up, took a paper off the stack and read before moving to the cash registers.

"I'm not going outside at night ever again," commented a young woman in a long wool coat.

"I just had new locks installed. Don't want my wife home without them," said a gentleman in camelhair.

Cally reached in and grabbed a copy. The headline blazed THE COUTURIER in bold block letters. She cringed. She thought of Jack, feeling her heart go out to him. Suddenly she was anxious to get to the station. She noted how people looked at her in her uniform. How they tipped their heads respectfully. Yes, people were scared. She fixed herself a tall coffee. When she reached the register, she pulled a credit card, but was waved off by a small, older woman with tired eyes who stood behind the counter.

Back in the car, she rested the cup in the holder and patted the paper flat. A photo of the letter was dead center. The article itself wrapped around the photo, and she could see the letter was printed again later in the body of the text. The reporter's name, Tia Santos, was centered over the left column. Pushing her seat all the way back, Cally began to read.

Early yesterday, The Central Jersey Press received what appears to be the first communication from the killer of three women in Two Rivers. The typed letter, sent in a plain envelope, was mailed from the Two Rivers post office. Two Rivers Police Chief, Robert Grainer, has confirmed its probable authenticity.

The women were murdered over the past three weeks with the first murder occurring on Thursday, January eighth. The next two women were abducted on the following two Thursday evenings, leaving local police and FBI agents wondering if the killer might try again tonight.

The following is the transcript of the letter received at the offices of the Central Jersey Press:

To the people of Two Rivers:

Be frightened, people, because your police are keeping secrets. And what you don't know will hurt you. These so-called policemen mock me by assuming these are just murders. They are much more than bodies in the grass. And they know it. These women have sacrificed themselves for the betterment of society by expanding old definitions of free expression in art. They are brave pioneers! These women are human canvases. Each one wears a unique creation worthy of the finest Paris runway. They wear works of art which must be seen and appreciated! Demand photographs from your local authorities! DEMAND that they STOP CENSORING! Soon everything will be censored! Demand the truth! These incompetent authorities are out to take your freedom away! Soon we will be living in a fascistic society! Stand up and take action! These imbeciles must be stopped!

The Couturier

The article proceeded with details—way too many—about the make-up, the strangulations, and projections of where the killer might strike next.

Cally's heart pounded in her chest. Where had the reporter gotten this information? Santos had referenced an "anonymous" source. Who was it? Who would leak information to the press?

The piece concluded with a statement from Chief Grainer. "People should be vigilant. Women should be aware of their surroundings at all times. Do not to linger alone at night. Stay in pairs or groups when possible. The Two Rivers police force has implemented a strategy to maximize security, but we request all citizens cooperate to ensure that no one else is harmed."

Cally dropped the newspaper on the seat, furious. Who was this anonymous source? They'd worked so hard to keep the details from the public, and now in one day, the entire cover was blown. It would make working the case so much more difficult. The national press would be relentless; they'd never leave it alone. Jack would be hounded at every turn. And what would this do to Two Rivers?

Cally started the ignition. She sat for a moment, feeling sad and angry before she backed out. Her car was nose-up to the store and she watched a few customers emerge through the glass doors. They all held papers. The news was spreading. Like an invisible virus that could not be stopped, a deadly disease in the air. Fear was about to grip her beloved city.

Cally headed directly downstairs where Chief Grainer had called the emergency meeting. She knew that Jack would be conducting a task force meeting upstairs, but both she and Vince had been asked to attend the general meeting with Vince acting as liaison to the patrols. She entered the room and looked for familiar faces. The front of the room was set with a podium and a large dry erase board. There were half a dozen rows of folding chairs, four to each side with an aisle running down the center.

"Yo, babe." A voice whispered in her ear.

Cally turned and saw her buddy, Juan, and they gave each other a jovial high five. He'd arrived with two other rookies and the four of them found seats near the front and talked about their first weeks on the job. A current of excitement ran through the room, which was filling quickly. Cops jostled for the remaining seats and began lining the perimeter walls. The chief had made it clear—everyone attends, on or off duty.

The electric atmosphere ran through Cally's bones, and she felt as energized as she'd felt yet. Fellow rookie, Tyler

Hatch, sat on one side with Juan on the other. Tyler talked about how he'd been partnered with her brother, Chris, and what a great cop he was. Cally had gathered that much over the years. At age twenty-eight, Chris was the youngest sergeant on the squad. He'd surpassed many more senior, including Charles. Cally felt a surge of sisterly pride hearing Tyler's praise.

Musser sauntered by. He looked at her but didn't say hello. He went straight to the back and leaned against the wall, crossed his arms and started talking to two of the guys who'd been in the cafeteria that morning three weeks ago. He made a comment, a snide one, by the laughs it got. They all looked at her. She looked right back at them, determined not to let them bother her.

Juan cast his eyes from Cally to Musser. "What's that about?" he asked.

"Never mind," Cally replied.

"Musser's an asshole," Juan said. "Gave me grief in the locker room the other morning."

"What kind of grief?"

"Racial comment under his breath." Juan shrugged it off. "Comes with the territory, babe, you know that. I can accept it."

Cally's heart surged with admiration. At least she had her brothers to lean on. Juan was out there all alone. She thought of her encounters with Musser. With the exception of him and his cronies, everyone else on the force had been great. So why'd there have to be these couple of bad eggs—giving her and Juan a hard time? What was their problem?

Cally heard the rustle of chairs and watched heads turn toward the rear door. Chief Grainer entered the room with Vince in tow. Grainer stepped up to the podium and slapped the newspaper down with a smack. He slowly scanned the cops and drummed angry fingers against the podium. He held up the newspaper and let the bottom half fall open.

"I find out who's talking to this woman, and you're fired! This leak is UNACCEPTABLE!"

Around the room, cops shifted in their seats as Grainer paused. Vince clenched his hands in front and scanned the audience. Cally felt the tension inside her gut, heard it in the silence.

"We are tracking a killer! No one speaks a word! Not to family members, not even amongst yourselves. If you even speak to a reporter, you're terminated. The only words you are permitted to speak are, 'No comment.' That clear?"

Grainer let out a big puff of air. Setting his palms against the podium, he said, "Some ground rules from here on out. First: do not respond to any dispatch calls unless your unit is specifically ordered to do so. The last crime scene was a circus. It was not an *all units* but more than half of you showed up. UNACCEPTABLE!"

Cally thought of how she'd heard the call over her home scanner and had responded—she and just about every other cop on the force. The chief was right. It had been a zoo.

"Now to logistics. You've all seen the paper. We need to be prepared in the event this person tries again tonight."

He introduced Vince's role on the task force and passed the meeting to him.

Using dry erase boards, Vince laid out the plan and schedule. He broke the squad into eight units, assigning geographic areas and manning each of the units with a lieutenant or captain. The units were posted on the boards with Clyde's name along the top of one. Nearly all cops were on tonight, with just enough off duty to cover the following shift.

Cally listened and took notes, ready to relay every bit of information to Jack. If the killer struck again tonight, Jack would need all the help he could get.

***

Jack had heard from everyone on the task force except Joe Clarizio, the FBI profiler. He'd called in to say he was stuck behind an overturned eighteen-wheeler on the Jersey Turnpike, and had entered the conference room a few minutes ago settling himself in the last available seat. Now Jack called for his observations, and Joe sat forward in his chair. He wore thick glasses that rested low on a hook nose. He peered through the bottom of them as he scanned the papers in front of him.

"I've been working the subject for a little over a week now and I have reached some conclusions I can share. First and foremost, let's clarify that we're not dealing with what we would classify as a serial killer. He demonstrates atypical behaviors, contrary to the patterns established by VICAP." Clarizio looked up from his papers to be sure everyone was following him. Receiving nods from around the table, he continued.

"The time interval between murders is extremely short. Serial murders usually wait months, sometimes years, between murders. This perpetrator is waiting only a week between the murders, and he's already reaching out to the media, sending the very clear message that he will strike again, soon. This is a killing spree."

"A killing spree," Jack repeated, the words echoing the very suspicion he'd been denying.

"That's right. Let's take several aspects of these murders. Most serial killers are driven by lust/power motivations. They lust after women, boys, whomever, and often consume excessive amounts of pornography, often sadistic in nature. They carry out their fantasies and frustration on their victims. The fact that our killer hasn't raped his victims is very telling. For him, it's about the message, not the act."

Scanning the table, Jack saw that Clarizio had the rapt attention of every one present. Hearing Joe's analysis was like meeting a person they'd been hearing about for months. They wanted to know everything. "What is the message?" Jack asked.

"Good question. Learn the motivation, you'll learn the message. Spree killers act under different sets of motivations. They are usually people who have deeply seeded anger issues, often abused or traumatized during childhood, and they've reached a breaking point. A particular incident ignites the rage, and when that bubble bursts, all hell breaks loose."

"Like the McDonalds killer back in the 1980s." FBI agent, Mike Tulio stated.

"I would use the example of John Allen Muhammad, the Maryland sniper," Clarizio corrected. "His spree covered a longer time frame, more similar to what is occurring here in Two Rivers."

Jack thought back to the Beltway Sniper. Those killings seemed to have gone on for months. He couldn't let that happen here. "So where is this taking us? What do you think he'll do next and how can we prevent it?"

Clarizio laughed. "I wish I could tell you the magic answer, Jack. All I can do is give you additional observations, and you'll have to take it from there."

Jack heaved a long sigh. "Go on."

"Alright. It appears that the murder in the motel may have been the igniting incident. The crime scene and the perpetrator's ensuing behavior would indicate that that murder was unexpected and unplanned. He left the body exactly as it lay at the moment of death, which would indicate that he was surprised by the outcome and fled immediately. The fact that she was a prostitute in a motel, may be quite telling. Perhaps he couldn't perform, perhaps he's never performed sexually, hence the absence of sex with the other victims." Clarizio sighed deeply and gazed out the window for a moment. "You've run into some luck with this letter. It's all about the message. He's sending information, and you want to keep that line open. We need to extract the essential message or messages in the letter."

"And what do you think they are?"

"Two lines jumped out at me." Clarizio took papers from his bag and removed the clip. He distributed them around the table.

Jack picked up his copy. It was the full text of the letter with two sentences highlighted in green ink. The first line was: *They wear works of art which must be seen and appreciated!* And the second, *These incompetent authorities are out to take your freedom away!*

Clarizio waited until everyone had the sheet then said, "Clearly, the purpose of these killings is to provide a 'coming out' party, if you will, for the killer. From this first line we can glean that he believes he hasn't received the opportunity he deserves to showcase his work. Notice the reference to a Paris runway, as though perhaps he has or had a career that failed in some way. Perhaps he's been rejected by a New York fashion company, or some other established fashion house. Or this rejection could have occurred earlier in his life either by his parents or some authority figure." Clarizio checked around the table for questions.

Seeing there were none, he went on. "The second sentence I've highlighted is the beginning of a series of lines that point to mental illness. We see clear indications of paranoia, possible paranoid schizophrenia. Notice the repetitive exclamation points. The first one occurs after the key line above, but from that point on, every line is punctuated, as though his illness gets the better of him, and he loses restraint. This is typical of the spree killer behavior I was referring to earlier. These are people who are lashing out against the world, and on a more subconscious level, against people in their lives. They always have something to tell the world or to show the world."

"And in this killer's case?" Jack asked.

"His primary message is that the authorities are not to be trusted, that they are out to strip people's liberties and freedom of expression. He sees himself a savior, and he's calling others to action."

"How far do you think he'll take this?" Vince asked.

"Once they begin, spree killers rarely stop. They go and go until they're caught, killed, or very often, kill themselves. Some killers are able to carry on the regular aspects of their lives during the spree; others shut themselves off to the rest of the world until it comes to the inevitable end."

"So, we can expect a grand finale?" Jack asked, his stomach turning over.

Clarizio turned palms up and smiled. "Let's hope this team stops that from happening. One more thing about this creative streak. It's not necessarily typical in spree killings, but it is something we've seen before. The fact that he's dressing the victims in gowns could indicate some kind of creative repression, possibly repressed homosexual tendencies. He is shouting out to the world with these murders. He wants to be noticed. It's hard to be noticed without being revealed."

Jack nodded. He hoped it was true. "What about timing?"

Clarizio raised his index finger in the air. "Aah, yes. Dollars to donuts tonight's the night. He's methodical, obsessive, completely compulsive. He will absolutely feel compelled to kill tonight. He's abducted or killed his subjects the last three Thursday nights. He's created a cycle. He's basically told the community he will do it again. You can bet on it—he'll try tonight."

Jack watched the wave of fidgeting that broke out in the room. It was what every cop, detective, and agent hated to hear. A violent crime and no clear way to stop it. "Any way to predict where he might go next?"

"Beyond the triangulation we've already done?" Clarizio grimaced, and Jack thought of how they'd studied and re-studied the abduction and drop spots. "No more than the theories we've already put forth. Watch the train station, bus stops, parking lots. Watch the bars, the cafés in the center of town."

"We'll be there." Jack assured him, the FBI agent's words like shots of adrenaline. He wanted up and out of the conference room. He wanted out on the street; he wanted to go pump up the rank-and-file downstairs in the meeting room.

"Anyone have questions?" he asked, putting his palms flat on the table. Seeing no takers, he stood. "Then let's get the hell out there."

Chapter 18

Luther lay on the sofa, a wet rag draped over his forehead. The aura stretched around his field of vision—sparking triangles churning in his head, a friggin' conveyor belt of fractured shards of glass. Even when he closed his eyes, he could still see it. He popped three Advil and waited. He knew the kaleidoscope aura would pass in another ten minutes, but it was the migraine pain to follow that could screw up his plan.

His neck muscles clenched, and he told himself to calm down. He'd put more thought into this one than any of the others. He had a cover, and it would work. It was probably even safer doing it this way. He didn't have to worry about someone stumbling upon him during the act ... and every woman in Two Rivers was now on guard. Now that the letter had hit, cops would be everywhere. The parking lots would be swarming with them. That's why he'd go where they least expected him.

No, he wasn't crazy, he was smart. Smarter than them. And this latest plan would run like clockwork.

***

Jack pulled the sedan into the *Central Jersey Press* parking lot and jammed the column shift into park. He turned to Cally who sat in the passenger seat. When he'd seen her in the meeting, four rows back in her blues, his heart had wrenched. He'd reined his emotions immediately, focused on speaking, on the cops who looked at him, their faces intent, looking to him for motivation and instructions. He gave them all he had but, still he was aware of Cally's eyes watching him, couldn't completely escape that frustration from last night. Now he needed it off his shoulders.

"Dammit, Cally. There's nothing between me and Katrina."

"You don't have to explain," she said, turning her head toward the window. She looked crisp and official in her blues.

"I didn't even know she would be there," he said. "I just got home. She was there ... in my apartment. A couple weeks ago I lent Katrina my car. She must have made a copy of the apartment key while she had my keys. Tonight, when I got home, she was there ... waiting for me."

"Waiting for you," Cally said skeptically. She turned and looked at him with eyes that saw right through him. It was like she'd been there in the room with him.

"Aah, hell," he said. "She was ... waiting for me. In my bedroom"

"What!?"

"I told her to get out."

"Oh, please. Don't patronize me."

"It's true. I told her to leave. I even threw her clothes at her."

He had to chuckle. It was so ridiculous, but Cally did not appear to see the humor.

"Jack. You are under no obligation to me. It does not matter whether you threw her clothes at her or you didn't. You and I are just friends."

***

There. She'd said it. That ought to put any romantic notions behind them. Now they could go back to where they'd been a week and a half ago, before her mother ever invited him to that darned dinner. He could do what he pleased with that sharky looking woman.

Jack shut the car off, and she was glad to change the subject. "What are we doing here?"

"We're going to talk to Tia Santos. Find out who her source is."

"What makes you think she'll tell you?"

"She probably won't, but it will give me a chance to let her know how I feel about that article."

Maybe so, but where would that get them? She had a different idea. She'd thought of it as Grainer spoke at the podium. Now she had to convince Jack. "Why don't we follow her?" As she said it a glint of sun bounced off the entrance door. A very pretty woman wearing a skirt, boots and a belted jacket emerged.

"That's her," Jack said.

"Your car's unmarked. Let's see where she goes."

He glanced at the dashboard clock. "I don't have time."

"One stop. Let's just see where she's headed. Come on...it's my first chance to follow a suspect." She tipped her head, raised her eyebrows ... how could he say no?

"If you're going to be a detective, you have to get the lingo down. She's not a suspect." He put his hand on the key. "We'll trail her for a half an hour, that's it."

He pulled out slowly and stayed a good five car-lengths behind as they managed the late-morning traffic. Tia turned onto Main Street then left at Nellie Springs Road. They followed behind as the buildings passed from retail, to commercial, to industrial. They passed a large warehouse. Jack pointed to it, and said, "One of mine."

Wow. It was big—a new steel building with a half a dozen busy truck bays. They talked about his side business as they followed the white RAV4 onto the Garden State Parkway southbound. The car zipped over to the fast lane. Jack remained cautiously behind.

"Wherever she's going, she's in a rush," Cally said, noting that Jack had tensed when Tia turned onto the Parkway. She hoped she had not set them on a wild goose chase.

Jack kept glancing at the clock. As the miles ticked away, she began to regret pushing him to follow the reporter. She knew how focused Jack was on tracking down the killer, and now she'd roped him into what was in truth a self-serving fishing expedition—a plan to bring down Musser.

"Let's forget it," she said. "We should turn around and head back."

Just because Musser had insulted both her and Juan, and just because he clearly resented both her and Jack, didn't mean he would undermine the investigation. Now she had allowed spite to dictate their schedule.

Jack said no, they'd follow her a couple more miles. Cally's eyes stayed glued to the little round taillights. At mile one hundred, nine miles from where they'd started, Tia's directional bleeped to life. She exited onto route sixty-six, a smaller, two-lane highway. They passed a Home Depot and a Walmart then Tia pulled into a cabin style pub aptly named Chandler's Cabin.

Cally had been here before. She'd come with her family for someone's birthday, though she couldn't remember whose. The parking lot was full. An old-fashioned, Western style sign hung from log beams, which flanked the walkway. Cally remembered a cozy, casual feeling inside.

"She's meeting someone," Jack said quietly. "She knows me. You'll have to go in." He looked down at her uniform then reached into the back seat. He handed her a Yankees baseball cap and jacket, and with a sexy smile said, "Here, *Detective Bank*, put these on."

A flurry ran up her spine. He looked awfully handsome. She wondered if he suspected Musser the same way she did...and if more than the article might be spurring him on.

Chapter 19

Cally entered the pub cautiously, not sure who she would see as she opened the door. The foyer was empty, and the hostess station was unattended. To the right, a dining room rustled with voices, plates, and silverware. The bar was to the left, a darker room, with a TV posted high behind an oval bar. Guessing Tia would be on that side, she scanned the bar area. The bar itself occupied a large portion of the room, with dining booths around the perimeter. Cally spotted Tia in a corner booth. Leaning forward, forearms on the table, the reporter was in deep conversation with someone.

Cally's heart raced. She stepped further into the room, peered through the gaggle of heads. She'd had a sneaking suspicion Musser was the informant from the moment she'd read the article. Who else had motive to derail the investigation? Who was pissed at Jack? Who'd been giving her grief since day one? Who had started the rumors?

Now she was about to catch Big Arms red-handed.

Cally took a few steps more to get a clear shot of him. She peered beyond a gray-haired man at the bar.

Tia's lunch partner had broad shoulders...short hair....
She inched further up, pulled the cap low. A couple more
steps and she would have a spot-on view. The hairs on her
arm stood as excitement washed over her. The big gotcha'
moment was coming.

She stood straight on, could see his profile as he looked
into Tia Santos' eyes. It took a second before she gasped,
before reality blasted her like sand. Air stuck in her lungs.
She almost choked out loud. Sitting not twenty feet from
where she stood, breathing down the front of Tia's tight
sweater, sat Charles.

Cally watched her brother take Tia's hand. She watched
them giggle over a private joke. She watched as Tia took
a celery stick, dipped it in dressing and fed it to him.
Charles took his time finishing it, smiling at Tia with each
bite. Cally backed away, her eyes glued on them, on her
brother transfixed in the reporter's gaze. She reached the
vestibule and pushed through the door.

Outside the sun shone brightly. She tugged on the cap,
already low on her forehead. She needed a moment. Jack
waited in the car and now she wished she could escape,
slip around back and pretend they'd never come. What
am I going to say? she worried, reaching the car too
quickly.

"Well?" he asked as she settled into the seat.

She shrugged her shoulders, tried to smile. Decision
time. "Wild goose chase. Sorry for dragging you out here.
Tia Santos is having lunch with a friend and her two
little kids. She's surrounded by booster chairs and dirty
napkins."

"Really." He looked out his window and took a deep breath. "I want you to stick with her for the day. Stake her out. Find out where she's going and who she's seeing next. I'm not so sure following her was a bad idea. Like you said, she's most likely on this story 24/7. Who knows where she'll go next."

Cally couldn't respond, feeling the web of her own lie tighten around her.

"What's the matter?" Jack asked.

"Nothing."

"Good. We'll swing back, grab your car, and you'll be back in half an hour."

Back on the highway, he stared straight ahead. Her mind raced in both directions, one minute wanting to tell him, the next, wanting to talk to Charles first. Surely there was a reasonable explanation. Surely there was an upstanding reason why her brother was having lunch with the very reporter against whom the chief had warned.

As she debated, Jack's cell phone rang. After a short conversation he pumped his fist in the air. "I'll be right there. Give me ten minutes." He shut the phone and looked at her. "Fabric shop in Brooklyn. Owner says she sold a guy red organza and green crepe back satin. Could be our guy."

"Wonderful, Jack. I want to come."

"No," he said firmly. "You're staying on this."

His expression darkened. The change made her stomach flip-flop.

Chapter 20

Cally drummed her fingers against the wheel. The round-trip had taken forty-five minutes and she'd been staring at the pub's front door for another half-hour. She shifted in her seat. She planned to track and pursue all right, but it wouldn't be Tia she'd follow.

Now Cally leaned back and thought for the tenth time, how could you do it, Charles? How could you do it to the force, to our family? She hoped to God she somehow had this wrong, but the facts sure pointed in her brother's direction. During the wait she'd decided that she would give Charles one chance. She owed him the opportunity of an explanation, even if it meant deceiving Jack for a short time. Once she told Jack he would have no choice but to report Charles to the chief, and the chief would refer Charles immediately to internal affairs.

From the corner of her eye, she saw the door open. Tia and Charles emerged. She held her breath and sunk low in the seat, watched from just thirty feet away. They walked to Tia's car where they stopped and stood face to face. Charles bent his head down so that his forehead touched Tia's intimately. Tia reached up and put her hand against his cheek then kissed him. She's using you, Cally wanted to shout. How could he be so naïve?

Tia eventually dipped into her car, then Charles into his white Corvette. Tia turned right out of the parking lot; Charles turned left. Cally fell in behind like a cheesy investigator. The entire day had left her feeling bad. The whole thing—seeing her brother, lying to Jack, now spying like this. She just wanted it to be over.

She followed Charles from a safe distance, weaving through cars to keep up as the Corvette continually raced ahead. At a jug handle, Charles turned north onto highway thirty-five, and Cally breathed a sigh of relief. She could lose him now and she didn't care. She knew where he was headed.

The country road was quiet—no other cars between them, not that it would have mattered. As soon as Charles hit the open road, he floored the pedal and put half a mile of blacktop between them. She saw him turn right, into the small dirt path that was his driveway. A few moments later, she roared in behind him, kicking dry dust though the pines.

Charles was just getting out. "Cally," he said, the Vette door slipping from his hands and clicking shut. His eyed narrowed in suspicion; his head dipped to the side. "What are you doing here?"

"Didn't you notice me behind you?"

"Nice to see you, too, Pipsqueak."

"Or were you too preoccupied from your lunch date?"

Charles turned and walked toward the house. "What lunch date?" he shouted over his shoulder.

Cally scurried behind. "Your date with Tia Santos. Charles, how could you?"

"How could I what? Date a beautiful woman like Tia?"

"Oh, come on, you don't expect me to believe that's all it is, do you?"

Charles unlocked the front door and stepped into his home. Ordinarily she loved the feel of the place. Large wooden beams crossed the high ceiling; slate flooring covered the expansive room. A raised fireplace occupied much of the back wall between two sets of French doors overlooking a veranda and pool. Charles had put his heart and soul into it, and it showed.

He threw his keys in a copper bowl, and they clanked loudly. "What do you think it is?"

"That's obvious, isn't it?"

"You think I'm the snitch?"

"What do you expect me to think?"

Charles frowned. "I guess that's exactly what I'd expect." He turned from her and walked to the closet. "Did your boyfriend put you up to following me?" Taking off his jacket, he pulled the sliding door.

"I don't have a boyfriend. If you're referring to Jack Brant, the answer is no. Why would he do that?" Cally came up behind him determined not to let him off the hook.

Charles snapped around, put his finger to his chin, and said, "Gee, I wonder. Maybe yesterday?" He sneered and turned back to the closet.

"I don't have the foggiest idea what you're talking about."

"Oh no? Ask your boyfriend. And tell you what, Cal, if you're so sure I'm the snitch, why don't you tell the chief? That's what you set out to do, isn't it?"

"How can you even say that?"

"How? You followed me! Your own brother, for God's sake! Congratulations. You'll get a big gold star for this."

"Screw you!"

"You already are. I knew you were ambitious, but I never thought you'd tail your own brother and spy on him in a bar."

"I didn't spy on you," she shouted as a big ball of guilt wrapped around her gut. "You're just jealous that I'm working this case and you're not."

"You're right about that." He brushed past her, then stopped and turned. "You think one of us wouldn't be working that case right now if it wasn't for you? You're a brand new rookie. How'd you get the case, huh, Cal?" His eyes were filled with accusation.

"What are you saying? Jack wanted Vince, not me. I was just part of the package."

Charles sniggered. "Sorry, nobody's buying that."

How could he infer such a rotten thing? How could he? But she'd be darned if she'd stoop to defending herself.

"Are you going to tell me what you were doing with Tia Santos, or not?"

"Not." He smirked.

"Fine." She turned and strode to the door. She yanked the wrought iron knob so hard the door smacked the wall behind. She was through the door and down the steps, getting in the car. He stood on the porch, his hands on his hips, and she glared at him from behind the wheel. Her foot landed heavy on the gas and rocks spit from the tires. She whipped around and floored it. She couldn't wait to be away from him. It would serve him right if she turned him in.

***

Jack stepped into his office and turned on the light. He smacked the briefcase on his desk and dropped into his chair. Outside, the last light of dusk faded into evening. What a huge waste of the afternoon. He had driven all the way to Brooklyn, interviewed an eccentric shop owner, tracked a credit card, and scared an unsuspecting mother of six out of her wits when she saw two NYPD cruisers pull into her driveway. A husband buying supplies for his wife's sewing business—that's all it was.

"How'd it go?" Vince asked, popping his head into Jack's office. "Not well, I assume?"

"Dead end." Jack began sifting through pink message slips. "What happened around here today? Did Musser and Doolan finish the threats to the PD?"

Martin nodded. "They visited a couple people. Former arrests. Guys blowing off steam for the most part. Nothing current."

"What about Cally?"

"I guess she's still out following Santos. Called her a couple times but haven't heard back."

Jack checked his watch. She should definitely have checked in. Under his breastbone a spark of anxiety flickered. He thought of her out there alone; he thought of the public safety warnings. And this guy hated authority. He punched Cally's number on his cell, snapped it shut when she didn't pick up. "I'm going home to grab a shower and dinner. I'll check on Cally." He grabbed his keys and left.

He drove straight to her apartment, vacillating between concern for her safety and what had happened at Chandler's Cabin. Was she hiding from him? Feeling guilty? The more he thought about it, the angrier he became. If the past two weeks had shown her anything, he'd hoped it was that she could trust him. Apparently not.

Hearing her voice over the intercom provided a temporary panacea. He watched the gate rise, glad she was safe, but almost immediately his disappointment returned. She'd let him and the other members of the team worry about her, and that wasn't cool. He parked the car and slammed the door behind him.

Cally answered the door still dressed in her uniform minus the gun.

"Why didn't you call in?"

She dropped her eyes to the floor. "I stopped home for a sandwich. I fell asleep on the couch. The intercom woke me up."

"Can I come in, please?" He said it brusquely, letting her know he was pissed. Falling asleep was a lousy excuse. She stepped back and let him in and he saw a half-eaten sandwich on the coffee table in the living room. The cushions looked rumpled. Maybe she was telling a half-truth, but he doubted it was fatigue that kept her hiding at home.

"What happened today?" he asked, giving her another chance to come clean.

"Not much." She dropped into the couch while displeasure rose in his chest.

So this was how it was going to be. He sat in the armchair across, tapped his palms on the armrest. The light drumming marched across the room. She looked away self-consciously.

"That's not the answer I'm looking for, Cally. How'd it go? What did you find out?"

"Nothing." She avoided his eyes. "After lunch she went back to the office."

"Really."

"I sat out in the parking lot all day." Cally kept her head down, hands fidgeting in her lap. Jack let silence fall. Without moving, he watched her like the countless suspects he'd interviewed at the station. He watched her chest rise up and down with each difficult breath. He watched. And waited.

***

Luther watched the final glow of twilight fade into a dark night sky. It was time. He turned back to the side window of the house and saw the wife, still cutting potatoes. It was a big knife; he'd wait. The husband was somewhere between Hoboken and Jersey City, reading his paper, cramped between hundreds of other rail commuters. The husband was consistent. Hadn't changed his routine all week. Tonight, would be no different. The wife was equally consistent—the perfect Suzie Homemaker. Dinner on the table, waiting. She even set candles every night.

Water splashed over the side of the pot as she cut the last potato and threw the knife in the sink. He could almost hear the clank of metal against metal, breathed a sigh of relief when it slipped from her hand. He reached his hand in his pocket and felt the familiar object. He took a step forward, his boot heavy, his back-up plan secured.

Luther had stumbled upon her by dumb luck. Taking a short cut through the residential neighborhood, that was just two blocks from the train station, he'd seen the husband come home from work one evening, briefcase in hand, and walk right through the unlocked side door.

The fence along the back made it all possible. His only real exposure of being seen was now, while the car was still parked on the side of the house, and he would need to enter through the exposed side door.

He hoped the town seal was enough to quell any neighbor nerves. If anyone later reported the vehicle, he'd send them on a wild goose chase. He stepped out of the car, adjusted the ridiculous orange hard hat and walked up the sidewalk.

The small side stoop was decorated with clay pots of green ivy. He knew from observing the home, that the door lead into a mudroom with the kitchen beyond, affording him a visual and sound buffer. He turned the knob slowly, feeling his heart pound in his chest. The door eased open in silence.

***

"You know, don't you?" Cally asked, finally looking up at him.

Jack didn't reply.

"How'd you find out?"

"White Corvette. Your brother's car. I noticed it while you were inside. I figured you'd come out and tell me—that we'd work it through together."

"I'm sorry." She dropped her head again, but he wasn't feeling merciful.

He'd been prepared to handle the delicate situation with equanimity. Now he wasn't so sure. "You lied to me," he said. "You looked me in the eyes and lied."

"I did. I'm sorry. I thought if I told you, you'd go straight to the chief. I owed Charles the chance to explain."

"And?"

"He didn't even try. He blamed me for everything. He assumed we were following him, not Tia Santos. He thinks you put me up to it, because of something that happened yesterday. What was he talking about, Jack?"

Jack stood up and walked to the sliding doors that led to the small terrace. He looked at the lights of neighboring units, watched a woman in a second-floor window preparing her dinner.

"I called your brother in yesterday. I asked for his help in stopping the rumors that are going around. I figured he'd want to help you."

"You called him in? To talk to him?" Color rose on her cheeks. She looked beautiful.

"It was a confidential discussion."

"I don't care! These rumors are ridiculous. Why should you explain yourself? Why should I?"

Their eyes locked. She was gorgeous when she was mad. A strand of hair fell over her cheek, and she blew it away. "What a mess," she said, smiling, shrugging her shoulders. "I'm sorry I didn't tell you about Charles."

He wanted only to console her, to pull her in and give her a hug, to let her know he cared, but he needed to stop these selfish feelings that threatened to ruin the very thing she cared about most. "Apology accepted," he said. "Next time, if there's an issue, tell me. We'll work through it."

Chapter 21

Jack raised the pasta bowl and drained the last of the juice. He leaned back with a satisfied smile. "That was the most delicious Bouillabaisse I've ever eaten," he said.

"My mom can cook anything. And pack it and deliver it all over town. We're very spoiled."

Cally was glad he'd liked it; glad she'd been able to provide some sustenance. The crazy hours were making them all edgy and cranky, and she blamed some of their recent altercation on that. Still, she knew she'd been wrong to lie to Jack. She wished she'd never done it. Cally took the bowl and rinsed it under the faucet. She placed it in the dishwasher wondering if her mom had dropped the same care package at Charles' house.

Jack must have read her mind because he said, "You know we'll have to talk to Charles."

"I've already tried that. You saw how stubborn he can be."

Jack got up from the table and came to stand next to her. "Then this is his last chance. If he doesn't level with us, we'll have no choice but to go to Grainer."

Oh, she prayed it wouldn't come to that. As angry as she was with Charles, she couldn't conceive ratting him out. She feared she'd be tempted to leave the dirty work to Jack, and she couldn't stand the thought of that, either.

Jack grabbed his keys and tossed them in the air. "We better go. Charles is on duty tonight."

She had changed out of her uniform into jeans and grabbed her apartment keys, locking the door on the way out. As they drove, Jack radioed for Charles' location. Dispatch placed him at the overpass on West Front.

With the city on high alert, some cops were riding solo, some were partnered. As a senior cop, Charles had pulled solo duty. They spotted him sitting in one of the usual speed traps, his car parked in a secluded pull-off behind a train trestle. Jack pulled a U-ey and came up so that his window was next to Charles's.

Charles looked through the wall of glass. He made no attempt to roll down. Jack gave him the roll sign, and after a couple seconds the window came down, his face stone cold. "What do you want?"

Oh man. She hoped the conversation didn't deteriorate into an argument.

"I want you to come clean," Jack said calmly. "What were you doing with Santos?"

"What do you think I was doing?"

"I have no idea."

"Yeah, right."

"Look, Bank, I don't have time for games. Cally's hoping there's an explanation. I'm listening."

"You set me up."

"Bullshit. We staked Santos; she went to you."

Charles studied Jack then turned his eyes to Cally. She returned his gaze.

"All right," Charles challenged. "The happy couple wants to know what I was doing? Come in my car."

Once they were in, Jack in the front seat, Cally in the back, Charles reached for his cell phone. He held it up with an expression that said, "stuff-it." He opened the recording app and hit the play button. His voice came through the speaker in mid-conversation.

"I have to learn you're in town through the newspaper?" Charles's voice was light and flirtatious.

"Sorry, sweetie, did I hurt your feelings?"

"You sure did. I thought I'd be the first person you called." Charles crooned.

Cally listened with fascination. Though she felt like the uninvited guest at the party, she was mesmerized by her brother's intimacy.

"You would have been, except I've been so busy with work. McKinley offered me the job and wanted me here in five days. I had to pack my old place, move, and start writing on top of it."

Another voice entered the tape at this point, a waitress, Cally assumed, and asked if she wanted a drink and did he need a refill.

Once the waitress left, Charles asked, "So how long have you been in town?"

"Couple days. But the minute I reported in, McKinley handed me the Couturier story. I had to research the case, talk to my sources then write the article. I've been busy."

"I'm surprised you didn't call me about it."

She laughed. "Yeah, right. For what? Information? You're not the type, and I know it."

"What makes you think that?"

"You love the job. You talked about that detective spot non-stop last time I was down." She paused. "Sorry you didn't get it,' she said in a soft tone.

"No big deal. Serves 'em right. The guy they picked quit three weeks later for a job in Mercer County. Now they're up shit's creek with only Brant."

"Sounds like a story to me. Bureaucrat police department twiddling thumbs while a killer walks the street. What do you say?" There was a pause in the conversation. "See? I knew you weren't the type. You won't talk bad about the force, even after they screwed you."

"Forget it. I didn't invite you out to talk business." More silence, followed by a sexy coo from Tia. They ordered lunch. They talked about their previous date—comedy night at a club in Asbury Park followed by what Cally surmised was an enjoyable night in Charles's bed. Cally was glad when he changed the subject. "You know they're coming down hard on Musser," he suddenly said. "Had him up in internal affairs all morning. Came out white as a sheet. Definite suspension, probable termination."

"I'm not sure what you're talking about," Tia stumbled.

"You weren't very careful, Tia. Where'd you conduct the interview, in the center of town?"

"I was careful! I'm sure nobody saw us. He's got a big mouth. Maybe he blew it himself."

"Sounds like Musser. He probably bragged to someone about being interviewed by the paper. Like he's the big guy on the case. Still, if we're going to see each other, we need to get something straight. I can't date someone who's jeopardizing such an important case. Seriously Tia, what you wrote in that article could get another woman killed."

Tia lowered her head. "I'm sorry." When she raised her head back up, Jack saw uncertainty in her eyes. "You're right. I hadn't thought about it like that. McKinley got an earful from Grainer already. I think I'm off the story anyway. I feel bad if Musser got caught, but it must have been his own fault. We met in a secure location. No one was following us. No one knew about him but me and McKinley."

Tia quieted. After a minute she said, "Let's not talk business. How 'bout dinner tonight, handsome? Deadline's past, I'm free as a bird."

"I've got a better idea, how about dessert at my house, right now?"

"Sorry, darlin'. Department meeting at three. How about …"

Charles tapped his phone and the recording stopped. "There's your rat. I'll send it to you," he said to Jack. "Now if you don't mind …" He turned on the engine.

"I'll get you that letter of recommendation."

"This is no quid pro quo, asshole. I did it for Cally."

It tore right at her heart. "Charles, I'm sorry."

"Just get out."

She couldn't leave like this. He had to understand. "I'm sorry. But you're wrong, Charles, I didn't think it was you, I knew there was an explanation."

"It didn't sound that way in my driveway."

Cally remembered her words, how strongly she'd come at him. How, in honesty, she'd been blaming him since this afternoon. It was a mess, the whole thing.

She left Charles's car and stood outside in the cold air. Jack started his own car and waited, and she suspected he recognized her need to gather herself. She watched the red taillights of Charles's cruiser disappear down the road.

One thing was for sure: she owed her brother. Even if he'd acted like a jerk; even if he'd insulted her; he'd gone out of his way to help her today. Jack started the engine, and she opened the door. She slid into her seat, and they headed back to the station. As they reached the lot, as the gate arm began to lift, the radio started to crackle.

***

Katrina was alone at the boutique with a half hour until closing. She'd emptied the coffee pots, cleaned the stock room, and had browsed all of the summer catalogues and written her picks for Gail. Let's hope she'd have better luck selling them than she'd had with the current spring line. The season had gotten off to such a slow start. She'd sold just three gowns so far, totaling close to ten thousand in gross sales, but she only had one appointment scheduled for the rest of the month. No way was that cutting it. Earlier today, when Gail had asked her about upcoming appointments, she'd fudged. In a moment of pure foolishness, she'd told her she had three upcoming appointments when she only had the one. Then she'd slid two bogus names into the appointment book. She'd placed them far into the future so Gail wouldn't ask, but still.

Now, she hoped that guy with the invalid wife didn't cancel. She needed at least one of the three to be legit!

Grabbing the laptop, she opened up to the last week in January. She read his name and tapped her fingers on the countertop. Luther Mintman. Good name. Sounded like money. She read the address: 2260 Ridge Road, and the phone number, 555 677-1234.

It probably wouldn't hurt to put in a call. Maybe a thank you call, mention a couple of extraordinary pieces. But Mr. Mintman had said his wife was shy, hadn't he? Too good a chance she might back out if left to her own devices. Maybe, Katrina decided, I'll talk directly to the wife. Butter her up for the appointment. But darn. If only she knew more about the wife's taste. What kind of gown would entice her?

Katrina studied the rack. She remembered Mr. Mintman holding the mint charmeuse. Mr. Mintman likes mint. Hah. Try saying that three times. She pulled it out and studied it. Then she chose two others, the Domique Sirop and the Donatella and picked up the phone. She entered the number and waited. She studied all three pieces, prepared herself to wow Mrs. Mintman with their descriptions.

She grabbed her cell and punched in the numbers. A burst of static was followed by a digital voice telling her that the number was not in service. She hung up and tried again but got the same message. Not good. Either she had somehow gotten the number wrong ... or he gave her a wrong number, which meant he wasn't serious about bringing his wife in.

Shit. Katrina marched her nails across the counter. She needed that sale. She was going to get that sale. Shy or not, that wife was coming in. If she had to drive to the house, pick her up out of her wheelchair, and carry her into the store, the woman was coming.

Katrina grabbed her shoulder bag and locked the front door. Still ten minutes to closing, but too bad. Before she ventured out the back, she checked the parking lot. That light was still burnt out, and it annoyed her. With all that was going on in this town, you would think they'd make sure public spaces were well-lit. How tough could it be to screw in a light bulb? Half of the lot was in darkness! Luckily, she'd parked right next to the building which had its own lighting.

She quickly entered her car feeling a trickle of apprehension, just like last night. She turned up the heat, but only frigid air blew through the vents. What was bothering her? Was it something about that town worker last night?

She drove through the dark lot, thinking about it. She turned onto Broad and noticed that the street was much more quiet than usual. Driving the desolate streets, making good time, she couldn't get the picture of that man—in the hard hat and those thick plastic construction goggles—out of her mind.

Chapter 22

Two patrol cars stood empty, doors ajar, lights flashing. The house was lit up like a Christmas tree, every window ablaze, the front storm door propped open. A lead weight settled in Jack's stomach.

Inside, shiny wood floors and knick-knacks sparkled. Voices came from the rear area. He walked toward them. He reached the kitchen and his first thought—struggle. She'd put up one hell of a struggle.

Two patrols, Mick Halsey and another guy whose name he didn't know were speaking with a distraught man. Short, in a gray suit, the poor guy raked chubby fingers through thinning hair. Around him, evidence of his wife's bravery. A steel pot lay upside down on one of the white floor tiles. The counters were splattered with what looked like potato chunks. He saw a silver frying pan burnt black on the stove, cut asparagus on the counter beside it, and realized the familiar odor he smelled was burnt butter. The faint smell of natural gas permeated the room, and he saw that the burner dial was turned on. He walked over and turned it off.

"Halsey," Jack said. "Close off the street. No one gets in." He told the other cop to stay posted at the front door and to assign someone else to the back. As his gaze followed the trail of water and potatoes, he surmised that the woman had been dragged out the back door.

"You've got to do something!" the husband shouted. His necktie had been pulled open; his glasses sat askew on his nose.

Cally reached out and took hold of his arm. "Sir, sit down, please." Her voice was strong and empathetic. She tugged on his sleeve, toward a chair at the kitchen table, and he sunk into it. She pulled a seat up next to him. Putting a hand on his knee she said, "Sir, we'll get her back. We'll find her." The man looked hopefully to Cally. Jack eyed her on.

"We need to ask you some questions." She took out her pad and Jack noted her hand trembled slightly. "Can I have your full name, please."

He told her his name was Brent Morris then started firing information. He told her he worked in New York and that the moment he walked in the house he knew something was very wrong.

While Cally slowed him down and recorded the information, Jack followed the trail of starchy liquid to the back door. He stepped out onto a patio with interlocking pavers. He noticed a few more chunks of potatoes and spots of moisture leading to the driveway.

Looking up, he saw Charles Bank standing in the middle of the driveway writing notes. He had pulled his cruiser all the way in, through the gated area so that his cruiser was the furthest into the driveway.

"You were first on the scene?" Jack asked.

"Yes."

"You're on the case then."

"That's not necessary."

"It's how I want it. I'm getting rid of Musser and Doolan. You're the obvious replacement."

"Why's that?"

"First on the scene. I should have put you on from the start. I didn't have time to check the files. You're the obvious choice." He didn't want a discussion. "What've you got back here?"

Charles looked away. Furrowing his brow, he stood quiet for a moment. He kicked his shoe on the blacktop then said, "Fresh oil spot on the driveway. Looks like he parked right here." He pointed to the spot.

"I agree." He waited for Charles to go on.

Charles took a deep breath. "Judging from the distance, he pulled a vehicle right here, dragged her out and put her in."

It was a lot of hauling. "Must have taken a couple minutes," Jack said. "Let's hope the guy finally screwed up," He pointed toward the neighboring houses. "One Ring camera. All we need."

But the clock was ticking. He needed eyes. Ears. Lots of them.

"You take charge of the perimeter while I work inside?"

Charles nodded. A smile crept into the corners of his mouth. "Got it."

Twelve hours later, with the morning sun streaking through the blinds, Jack leaned on the windowsill in Grainer's office. Potovich and Tulio had the seats, which was fine with him. If he sat, he might crash. He'd just passed twenty-four hours awake, but the adrenaline was still pumping. He'd make another fifteen if he kept moving.

The chief roamed the room with his arms crossed. He stopped at the window and looked out onto Main Street. Jack tapped his fingers anxiously. He felt trapped. He had so much he should be doing at this instant. Updating the chief was last on the priority list.

"Son of a bitch. How'd he do it, Jack?"

"Looks like he pulled a vehicle in through the gate."

"But the gate crosses the driveway, doesn't it?"

"Yup, at the back corner of the house."

"You mean he pulled in? How the hell did he do that with her cooking in the kitchen?" Grainer asked.

"I don't think he pulled the car in until later."

Grainer paced away from the window. "That would mean he'd have to leave her to get the car." He rubbed his chin. "Means she'd already be dead."

"Not necessarily," Jack replied. "He could have knocked her out. It's consistent with the other victims."

"The other victims, with the exception of the prostitute, suffered strong blows to the back of the skull," Potovich reminded Grainer. "They had scrapes along the backside, consistent with being dragged."

"Do we still have time?"

Jack could see Grainer was grasping for straws. They all were. Anything to give them hope that Hannah Morris was still alive. "We might. But not much." Jack looked at his watch.

"Okay, go." Grainer said, waving them out of the room. "Jack, hang out a minute."

The others left the room. Grainer followed them and closed the door behind them. "Anything new on the leak? I don't want the details of this one getting out there."

"I think it's Musser."

"Musser?" his eyebrows rose.

"I've got a reliable source says so."

"How reliable?" he eyed Jack skeptically.

"Very. But I need more time to pin him."

"Fine. I never liked that cop. He can't bury old history, and this department needs to get beyond it. He's off the case. I'll put him and Doolan where they can't do any harm."

"And I want to replace Musser with Charles Bank." Jack said. "He was next in line last spring, wasn't he?"

"Yeah. Bank's a good cop. Hotheaded—that's why he didn't get it in the first place—but I got no problem giving him a go at it. You want a replacement for Doolan?"

"No. Let's keep it tight—just Martin and the two Banks."

Grainer smiled. "How's the rookie doing? She looks like hell on wheels. Always moving, that one." He looked sideways at Jack. "You know you got to watch it there."

"They're rumors, chief. Strictly rumors."

"Yeah? What about that starry look in your eyes? She gets in a jam, you could do something stupid."

"I just got two medals for doing something stupid."

Grainer smiled. "Just watch your step."

"Ten-four, Chief, can I go?'

"Go on, get outta' here." He slapped him on the shoulder. "You need extra hands, pull them from McCloskey. And keep me posted," he shouted after him. "Twice daily reports."

Jack waved his hand over his head. He didn't turn around. Reports. They were number ten on the priority list with nine other items unchecked. First one—the labs from last night's crime scene.

***

Cally heard Jack's raised voice bouncing off the hall walls as he approached the command center. She sat alone at the table manning the hotline they'd put in place.

"I need it stat!" he shouted. "We gave it to you eight hours ago." He entered the room with the cell phone to his ear. He rounded his eyes in an exasperated expression. "I want it in my hands in one hour." He tapped the phone's display in frustration. "Morons! They're in a staff meeting. A staff meeting! Where's Martin?" he barked.

"He just went down to pick up the latest incomings. He'll be right back."

"Did he order those labs stat?"

"Yes. I was sitting right here when he did it."

"Idiots."

"Jack, calm down."

"Calm down? A woman is about to be killed. How could they hold a staff meeting?" Jack walked to the window.

"I'm sure they're not holding off on the labs for a staff meeting. They're processing, I have no doubt."

Jack released a heavy breath. "I just left Grainer's office. Musser's off the case. Charles is on."

"Charles?" Cally dropped her pencil. "Why'd you put him on?"

"I thought you'd be happy about it."

Was she happy? Did she want him on the team with all that had happened between them? She looked at the table, rubbed the smudge she'd made with the pencil. Some heavy air would need to be cleared before she could work with him.

"I think he'll be an asset," Jack assured her. "He made good observations at the crime scene."

"Great," she mumbled.

"What's the problem, Cally?"

She stiffened. The case and lack of sleep were clearly taking their toll. She needed to back off and keep Jack out of any problems she might have with Charles.

"No problem. It's fine. Charles is a good cop. I'm happy for him."

Jack walked to the door and glanced up and down the hall. Unexpectedly, he closed the door. He looked back at her, and she saw he carried the weight of the past twelve hours on his shoulders. Hannah Morris, Brent Morris. He stepped toward her then stopped. His eyes bore into hers, his gaze, hungry, hunting, a lone wolf in a blizzard. A whirlwind of emotions swirled through her. She felt the full weight of the task at hand, and she wanted to stand up, place her arms around him, support him as more than his assistant.

With his eyes still fixed on her, he said, "I need you with me. Grab your coat."

"Okay." She wanted nothing more, to be with him, all day, alone. If only it was a picnic.

He ran his fingers through his hair. "We need to be back by four o'clock. I need you to assemble the team for a strategy session."

She nodded. He was back. Man on the job.

"Everybody?" she asked, swinging her coat over her shoulders.

"Everybody: FBI, forensics, the whole crew. From here on, we conference every day until we catch him."

They reached Magnolia Avenue within a few minutes. It was a quiet residential street developed more recently than Cally's, probably in the early 1960s. The homes were all similar—square colonials with flat fronts. Some, like the Morris's house, had added front porches.

Jack parked and shut the engine. Cally glanced across the street at the Morris home. A cruiser and two sedans lined the single lane driveway. If not for the patrol cars stationed at each end of the block, the street would be jammed with media vans. As it was, they were camped more than two blocks away on either end.

The Morris home was immaculately maintained. A red heart hung on the front door, reminding Cally that

Valentine's Day was just a few weeks away. The house was a light gray vinyl sided with neat white trim. A garage to the rear was neatly matched. The blacktop was smooth and shiny; the six-foot white vinyl fence tied it all together with trellis work along the top.

"Let's start there." Jack pointed to the house across the street, not updated, but well-maintained, nonetheless. "Your brother's report said she wasn't home yesterday."

The door was answered immediately by a woman who appeared to be in her seventies and wore polyester pants and a red smock-type top. Jack checked his pad. "Lorraine Gorman?"

"Yes, that's me," she replied. She invited them into an orderly home with peach flowered sofas and matching carpet. Jack began questioning her. The woman had not noticed anything out of the ordinary, no unusual cars or pedestrians, no activity at the Morris home in the previous few days. "It's such a horrible thing," she said. "I'm a nervous wreck about it."

Cally smiled and tried to look consoling. Jack folded his pad and handed her a card. "Please call if anything comes to mind," he said as they left. They went to the house next door, where an old man who looked ninety or older, answered.

"Come in, come in. I've been waiting," he said in a shaky voice. He was skinny and stooped with thin brown pants held up by a leather dress belt at the waist. He turned from them immediately and went into the house. He sat on a stiff-backed Queen Anne chair with crochet doilies on the arms. He fingered one lovingly. "My wife made these." Cally knew by his smile that she had passed. "I called this morning because I saw a water worker on the block the past few days. I was going to call you earlier in the week. Lord help us, I wish I had."

A *water worker*? What was he talking about? Cally wondered.

"Did you call today?" Jack asked, flipping through his pad.

"Well, yes, this morning, as soon as I heard what happened."

Cally thought back to the incomings. There were so many. She didn't remember seeing any from neighbors.

"I left my name and number and told them I had information. It was a bad connection. I had terrible time hearing the officer." Cally looked at the hearing aid in his ear. She glanced at Jack.

'Well, I'm glad we made it to you," Jack jumped in. "Tell us what you saw." He spoke loudly.

"I saw him here at least three days. I figured the town was doing some kind of assessment."

"The town?"

"Yes. He drove a municipal car—white with the town seal on the side. He was checking the water meters, but I thought it was odd—him here so much—sitting in his car. Then I heard what happened." He raised a trembling hand, crooked with arthritis, to his forehead. "I saw him walk up the Morris's driveway and read their meter on Tuesday. He did it to the house next door as well. But then I saw him back again Wednesday."

"What time was this around?"

"Probably five or five-thirty, both days." He smiled and looked at crooked hands. "Physically, I'm not so good, but I'm still sharp as a tack." He tapped his forehead.

Jack smiled at him then turned to Cally. "That's late for a municipal worker."

Cally knew the municipal workers started early and ended early. They were usually done by four o'clock.

"Did you get a good look at the man?"

"Not so good. He wore the brown jacket and an orange hard hat."

"The public works uniform?"

"Looked like it." He raised a finger like he'd just remembered something. "And those plastic construction goggles. Now that I think about it, why would he be wearing those to read meters?"

Cally looked at Jack. Finally!

Jack sat forward in his seat. "Was he tall, short?"

"Hard to say. Medium? Maybe on the tall side."

"Heavy-set? Thin?"

The man shook his head, "Couldn't tell."

"Twenties, thirties?"

"Jeez," the old man scratched his head. "I couldn't tell you that, either. He wore that hard hat. The kind you see them wearing when they work in the street—a white hard hat."

Jack looked at Cally. "Check it out," he mouthed and looked out through the door in the direction of the car. She left immediately and dialed her cell phone as soon as she stepped out. She called Martin who patched her through to Public Works. They assured her they'd had no crews stationed on Magnolia. They were two months away from a meter check. Cally flipped the phone shut. It was him. Their first solid lead.

Chapter 23

Jack smelled the pungent odor as soon as he stepped out of the car. Fermenting brush, wet cardboard, the smell of old milk containers hung in the air. The DPW was housed in a one-story concrete building with a large parking lot for the sanitation trucks. Their shoes crunched on the frozen ground as they approached the main door. The town seal was emblazoned on the glass. Any other day, he would not have noticed the typical design of shield and ivy. Today, it made him think.

"You think a public works employee, one of our own, could be killing these women?" he asked Cally as he opened the door for her.

"Out of some sort of jealousy toward the police?" she asked.

"Maybe. The police receive better pay, better work, prestige. Old fashioned class envy." Could it be so simple?

The receptionist pointed them back to the director's office where a white-haired woman talked on the phone. "I have to call you back, Marsha," she quickly said and hung up. "Hello, Mr. Brant. Mr. Jaworski is expecting you. Come this way." She pulled a flowered blouse over a round bottom. As she walked, her pantyhose scratched. She knocked on a closed door and poked her head in before a response. "The police are here, Merle," she announced.

"Thank you, Clara." A tall, older man came from behind a desk. "Merle Jaworski, pleased to meet you." After introductions, Jack and Cally sat. The room was dark and had a slight smell of must. One window faced a line of bare trees against a graying sky. On a credenza beneath the window were piles of Boater's World magazines. At the center of the director's desk was a stack about three inches high of computer print outs.

"This is a list of all current employees." He grabbed the top inch of the stack. He placed it to the side and held up a second. "This is a list of all former employees who worked here in the past eight years. And this," he tapped the last list with his finger, "is retirees. Now would you mind telling me what's going on?"

"A woman was abducted from her home last night. It could be the same person who killed the other women. Neighbors reported seeing a public works employee in the area. But you reported that you didn't have anyone working there."

"Could be a reasonable explanation. It was after hours, wasn't it?"

"Between five and six p.m."

"Could be one of the guys was in the area on a personal matter."

"In a public works car?"

"No sir, not likely. Employees drive personal vehicles to and from work. They take our vehicles out on business only."

"That's what I thought. This person was driving a town vehicle with the seal on the door."

"Should be easy enough to check. All vehicles are logged in and out. Let me see if any cars were checked out overnight." Jaworski reached to a shelf behind his desk and retrieved a wide ledger. "What nights we talking about?" he asked.

"Tuesday and Wednesday, this week," Jack replied. "Anybody have a car out?"

Jaworski opened the book, spreading it wide across the desk. He scanned a page with his finger, then flipped to a second page. "Nobody. No emergencies. No night projects, nothing."

"What was the latest time a car was checked in?" Jack asked.

Jaworski scanned the outer edge of the page. "One of our supervisors, Mel Duncan had a car out till seven. He was working the hydrant bust on Second." He scanned the rest of the page. "Nobody else."

"We'll need to speak to him. Mind if I take a look at that?" Jack stood and went to the book. He quickly deciphered the formula: employee name, car number, time in, time out and signature at the end of each line. It was a lot like the PD. "Anybody witness these signatures?"

"The book's kept out on my desk most evenings. I'm usually here when they come in, but if not, they just sign it."

"Where do you keep the keys?"

"To the cars?" He pointed to a closed cabinet on the far wall. "I lock it every night. If someone comes back late, they leave the keys on my desk."

"Then it is possible that a set could have been copied." He thought of Katrina copying his key.

"I suppose."

It was something. Not much, but something. Jack moved on to the topic of uniforms and how a non-employee might get his hands on a public works jacket. Jaworski informed him that employees purchased their jackets through a series of payroll deductions when they were first hired. Once they finished paying, they owned them outright.

The information brought them full circle, back to the computer lists, sitting not twelve inches from him. He stood up, ready to leave. He wanted the team all over those stacks of paper. He was sure their man had some connection to public works. They just had to uncover it. They each shook Jaworski's hand and thanked him for the help.

"What about neighboring towns?" Cally asked when they were back in the car. "There may be other towns that wear similar jackets. It could be one of their employees. Think about it, Jack. The neighbors think they saw a Two Rivers car, but, honestly, how closely would they have looked? You see a town car, you assume it's legit. I doubt any of them studied the seal up close, or the uniform for that matter."

"You're right." Jack agreed without hesitation. "I'm putting you on that. Check it out." Jack's stomach growled, and he realized he was hungry. A set of golden arches rose on the next corner, and he turned in. At the drive-in, he ordered a Big Mac meal, and Cally ordered the grilled chicken sandwich meal. He pulled into a parking spot and shut the engine.

"So tell me more, m'love," Jack teased, pulling out the fries. "Tell me what your gut tells you. Have you got a theory?" He said it half-heartedly, but he was dead serious. He liked the way her mind worked, liked watching it move behind those pretty blue eyes.

***

Katrina stood in her recently redecorated bathroom. With new gold fixtures, black granite, and a marble floor that was absolutely to die for, it was the masterpiece for which she'd been saving for an entire year. The contractor had finally finished the job last week. Just standing within its hallowed walls should have made her gleeful. Should have. Looking at her reflection in the gold-framed mirror, she saw nothing but ugly and depressed. Her eyes were puffy. Her mouth drooped more than usual in the corners. She looked awful.

What did she expect? She'd spent the entire day lying on the couch watching soaps. Now she was due into the store at four to work the evening shift. Dragging her big slippers across the marble floor, she went to the shower stall and turned on the water. "I don't want to go to work," she moaned.

She didn't want to sit in that stinking boutique for five hours listening to Gail complain about how bad business was. She didn't want to hear her not-so-subtle remarks about her not-so-stellar sales numbers. Katrina stepped into the shower and let the hot water flow over her head and onto her shoulders. Little by little, she started to perk up.

Forty-five minutes later, she grabbed her shoulder bag off the chair, swung a look back at her living room and walked out. She'd purchased the condo two years prior, and the bold colors and sleek furniture she'd been slowly acquiring looked terrific. The place had come together so well, and just knowing that made her feel better ... for a moment, anyway.

Everything cost so much these days! Buying even the most necessary items ran the credit card bills through the roof. She immediately thought of the mortgage payment. The rate had jumped again, and she was two weeks overdue. A moan escaped her throat. How was she going to make it?

In the car, she tried to mentally balance her budget. She seemed to be doing this quite a bit lately. She needed commissions. Either that or she needed to get a second job, which she really, really didn't want to do.

She thought of Mr. Mintman and his invalid wife again. Last night as she lay in bed, alternating between crying over Jack and her finances, she'd gotten the idea to drive by his house today, just to see what kind of money they were talking. If it was one of those gorgeous mansions on a hill, then she would go all out on the appointment.

But as the long night wore on … well, she started entertaining other thoughts about Mr. Mintman. He was handsome. He wore nice clothes … well-tailored slacks, lambskin jackets … He lived at a fancy address … and his wife was incapacitated in a wheelchair …

She remembered how he'd seemed like a considerate guy, coming into a lady's shop and browsing gowns for his wife. How often do you see that?

Now, as she found herself driving on Ridge Road, along deep curves, houses set back, she felt her heartbeat accelerate. Maybe she could do a lot better than Jack Brant.

"Mrs. Luther Mintman." It rolled off her tongue. "Mrs. Katrina Mintman." Even better. She saw herself going to luncheons and charity galas. Oh, the gowns she would wear.

The numbers were climbing fast now. 2120, displayed on a brass plaque discreetly set at the curbside, and beyond—a magnificent Tudor. 2190—carved atop a brick arch. 2220—an elegant Georgian.

She slowed down to a crawl. Here it came. 2260—spray-painted on … plywood? Her jaw dropped. She stopped the car. What the heck was this? Off in the distance was an old, small, rundown ranch. The roof was caving. The white paint had faded to gray and peeled in spots. Heavy construction equipment—a bulldozer and a backhoe were parked off to the side.

A knockdown! What the heck was going on? She let out a long, ailing groan. Maybe he was the new owner? Using the address even though the house hadn't been started? But somehow that didn't fit and she knew it. Why would he give an address at which they obviously wouldn't be living for some time? An unpleasant reality began to soak through. Was it possible Mr. Mintman was a fake? The thought of it threw her back into panic mode. I am really up shit's creek, she thought. She had not one appointment scheduled and knew she'd be lucky if Gail didn't fire her.

Putting her foot to the gas, Katrina whipped the car around. It was two minutes to four. She had better hurry if she didn't want to be late to work. She'd better hurry if she didn't want to get fired.

Chapter 24

It was almost midnight when Luther pulled under the gas lantern. He'd chosen this spot for several reasons. Close enough to the station to tease the police, but out of the view of the video cameras.

Time to get to it, he thought, hating the thought of lifting her. His shoulder muscles already ached, and he could still feel the bump on the back of his head from that friggin' pot. Man, people had no idea how strong these women could get when they were threatened.

He checked the rear-view mirror. Cars passed on Broad, but they were a good block behind. He'd parked the car parallel, nose to tail between two others. He got out and surveyed the space. Plenty of room behind him. His palms began to sweat. Jingling his keys, he stepped back onto the sidewalk and looked up and down the street in both directions.

He slid the key in the trunk and turned. The old Taurus trunk popped loudly and he cringed, checked the street again. Still no one. The lavender chiffon glimmered with fluorescence in the dark space. This latest gown was truly a work of art—the draping, the roping, the absolutely gorgeous soft silk chiffon! It simply had to be seen to be believed. He looped his forearms under her armpits and lifted her up.

***

Tommy paced the apartment. He looked at his watch, walked to the door, poked his head out again. Her Cherokee was still not in its spot. Where was she? It was almost three o'clock in the morning. The day had already turned over to Saturday! Slipping on sneakers, he grabbed the keys and walked out. It was way too cold to be out without a coat, so he hurried his steps to the edge of the building where he could see the full parking lot. Still no car.

She had not come home.

Tommy rushed back inside and rubbed his hands together. Was it possible she was still at the station? Could she truly be working on the spree killer case around the clock? It seemed a bit implausible. People had to sleep, didn't they?

He sure did. But he couldn't.

How could he fall asleep if every time a car passed his eyes popped open? And then he listened for her footsteps. For her key in the lock next door. He wondered if it made more sense to jump in the car, drive to the station and be done with it. At least he'd know where she was. That she wasn't over some guy's house.

Resigned, he walked to the closet to get his coat. He yanked the door but didn't see it. Where had he left it last? As he wondered, the pile of comic books on the top shelf leaned. He watched the stack begin to give way and slowly fall one by one onto the floor. He thought of wet seals.

The Shadow fell last. Tommy looked down at it. It had always been one of his favorites. The first DC issue. On the cover, the Shadow loomed huge over the railroad tracks with the city skyscape behind him. Tommy leaned over and picked it up, mesmerized. He walked slowly toward the couch. Before he knew it, he was sitting. He hadn't read this one in so long. He'd intentionally stayed away from it. Just looking at it brought back memories of that awful day. He was just ten...

He'd been lying on his stomach, on the floor, reading the first DC issue of *The Shadow*. He'd been waiting weeks for it. Downstairs, his mother was clanking pots and pans preparing dinner. It was an Indian summer day. His window was open, and he'd been enjoying the warm breeze, the look of the curtains puffing up each time it blew. He was feeling the complete solace of an unusually warm Saturday in October, nothing to do but read comic books.

"Tommy! Get the hell out here!" He remembered how his father's voice, coming from the detached garage behind the house, had jolted him. His father was mad. Really mad.

What had he done? What had he forgotten to do? With a sudden jolt, he remembered the doll. Cally had been showing him her doll. She'd left it on the workbench when her mother had called her home. Tommy had meant to run it back to her house but had gotten distracted.

With his hands shaking, Tommy folded the comic book closed. On wobbly legs, he raised himself up. He kept seeing that doll, and he knew his father had found it. His father had already forbidden him to play with Cally anymore. Now he would know.

Making his way toward the stairs, he felt his lip trembling. His knees were shaking so bad he had to grab the banister to keep from falling. His mother was standing at the stove, stirring something. She looked at him as he passed, suspicion in the squint of her eyes. "What have you done, now?" she shouted.

The storm door squeaked as he pushed it open. He saw his father—back to him, his short, stout body walking away, toward the garage. Tommy stepped out in his bare feet, but he didn't feel the rough surface of the old bricks that lined the walkway. He was too busy trying to keep his jaw steady, trying to stop the tears from spilling out. He would take it like a man. He wouldn't cry.

The garage door was open, his father, center stage. Around him, tools on hooks: crow bars, wrenches, screw guns, hammers. Paint cans, paint brushes, gasoline cans in neat rows. The lawn mower, the fertilizer, the rakes. Everything. Along the back wall was the workbench, and right on top of it, the stupid, stupid doll. He saw it in his periphery, but his eyes were locked on his father, the way he whipped around, the way he leered at him, the way his neck twitched. He'd seen it all before. The door banged down behind him, shutting off the world, cutting off all hope of escape. Now he felt the cold below his feet. No Indian summer in here. His father walked to the workbench. He scooped up the doll and shook it at him.

"What the hell is this?"

Tommy just stared. His hands were shaking at his sides, and he couldn't speak.

"Huh? I'm talking to you, boy."

"I ... I don't know."

"Like hell you don't. You been playing with dolls again? Huh? You like dolls?" He wound his arm back and threw it at him. The doll hit him in the nose.

A snap cracked the air. Tommy raised his eyes to see his dad unbuckling his belt. He pulled it from his grimy old pants and held it taut in front of himself, then snapped it menacingly at Tommy.

"Do I have to beat it into you? What do I have to do to make you behave like a real boy, huh? You got four boys next door to play with, but instead you play with that little girl. Why, huh?" A fat blue vein bulged from his neck; his knuckles were white where he gripped the belt.

Tommy's nose was running; his teeth were chattering. "Drop those drawers and bend the hell over. I will not have a sissy for a son if I have to whip it out of you."

A sudden bang made him jump. The comic book dropped from his hands.

It took Tommy a moment to realize that Cally's apartment door had just shut. His palms were sweaty, his forehead wet as he wiped his hand across it. Standing, he heard the soft paper beneath his feet and saw that he was wrinkling the precious book. He stooped to pick it up and clasped it lovingly between his fingers. He would take it to bed tonight. He would read until he fell asleep, which he knew would not take long. Knowing that Cally was home, soon to be asleep, alone, in her own bed, he suddenly realized how completely exhausted he was.

Chapter 25

Cally was fast asleep when she heard the knock on her door. She bolted up and looked at the clock beside her bed—two am. Belting her robe around her waist, she hurried to answer it. She had arrived home a few hours ago, a little earlier than the previous night when she hadn't gotten home until just after three. The past three nights, since Hannah Morris had gone missing, had begun to blend into one long, prolonged nightmare. First, her abduction, then the dropping of her body, the endless hours with no new leads, and already, the clock ticking forward to this coming Thursday.

Jack stood at her door, a vagabond in search of shelter.

"Jack, you're exhausted," she said. "When was the last time you slept?"

"Real sleep?" He shrugged. Far away eyes told her he was barely awake right now. "Maybe Wednesday night?" he ventured.

"It's Sunday morning. Do you realize that, Jack? You need to sleep."

"I'll sleep when he's caught." He brushed a kiss on her cheek. "With you."

The softness of his lips sent a warm current under her skin while the unexpected words caught her off-guard. But didn't she wish it, too? Wouldn't she love nothing more than to cuddle up under the sheets with his big, warm body? Her feelings for him had grown deep. She cared for him more than she let on, even to herself.

Now he looked into her eyes, hung his feelings like ornaments on a tree, there for her to see, to celebrate, to take like gifts being offered. She allowed her own eyes to linger; she didn't turn away.

He kissed her again, longer this time, and she responded with the passion she felt. This once. Just this once, she told herself, because we both need it. When they stepped back, their smiles were bittersweet, the evening's circumstances impossible to escape.

"We need to find this guy," Jack said, verbalizing the thoughts that lay heavy in both their minds. "Did you see her? Did you see what he did to her?"

Her heart wrenched for the woman. The image was branded on her brain, Friday evening, one of her worst ever. The call had come in just before one o'clock in the morning. They had been together at the station. Hannah Morris had been placed on the street...just outside from where they were working. She lay exposed in the cold, dark night, her alabaster hand against the black pavement. Her mouth had been contorted into a grotesque smile, the lips closed but crooked as though molded into place by the killer. Like the others, the eyes bulged. Her face and neck were purple, a sickly color chart to the lavender gown.

The last twenty-four hours had been hell. Around midnight, tonight, members of the team had started drifting home to shower and change, catch a few hours of sleep before daylight. Jack had promised he was going home right after her—that was more than two hours ago. She knew that over the past three days Jack had slept only an hour or two, here or there.

"It's two o'clock in the morning. It's your third night without decent sleep. Sleep for a few hours so that tomorrow you'll be refreshed."

"I've got to do more. I've got to get this guy. I will not let him kill another woman. This is it. Last one." He dropped onto the couch.

"You're doing all you can, Jack. The FBI, the entire police department, every expert you could possibly use is involved."

"And those experts were wrong. Clarizio said the killer would use the same M.O. He broke into a house, Cally. Totally different M.O., completely different set of risks. Clarizio got it all wrong. He screwed up. *We* screwed up."

"You can't blame yourself."

"I should never have relied on voodoo science. I told Grainer to send out a broader warning. I should have insisted." He dropped his head back.

"First of all, profiling is not voodoo science. Second, do you honestly think a warning would have done any good? No one listened to the street warning. Hannah Morris knew about the murders. She kept her door unlocked anyway. It wouldn't have mattered."

"We should have put it out."

Cally sat beside him. She took his lifeless hand and cupped it between both of hers. Her touch sparked life into his glazed eyes, but he pulled his hand out and raked it through his hair. He exhaled hard and set his brow in determination. He tried to get up, but Cally held his arm.

"How are you going to function when you can barely speak clearly?"

"I'll manage."

Cally could see she was not going to win the sleep argument. "Fine. You can at least relax for a few minutes. Just put your feet up and recharge." She kept her voice smooth, non-confrontational. "Just rest," she said softly. He put his head back. Sidling out from beside him, she raised his feet off the floor and put them up on the armrest. She removed his shoes. He raised his head to object, but she put a finger to her lips.

"Sssh. Just rest your feet, that's all. Your phone's right here."

"No." he started to get up.

She pushed his shoulders down. "I'm putting on the scanner. We'll hear everything that comes over."

He smiled and put his head back down. His lids slid closed. He opened them a second later, looked around.

"I'll stay awake," she promised. "I'll stay awake the whole time."

"Sure?" he murmured, but she knew she'd won. He was already floating away.

Cally settled into the soft armchair beside him. His hand twitched; his foot twitched. She'd done it. Would his sleep be as fitful as her own had been before his knock brought her fully awake?

She'd been in the midst of a nightmare, she and Jack, running around her old high school track. They were trying to catch up to Hannah Morris while a shadowy predator dragged her off. Cally was trying to reach them, but she couldn't run fast enough. She ran against a wall of wind, while the predator seemed to fly with it. When she was awakened by Jack's knocking, she felt like she'd just screamed.

Ever since she'd entered Hannah Morris's home, since she'd seen the pot on the floor and the potatoes everywhere, it was like a dark wide hole had been carved inside her. A hole that couldn't be filled until they saved Hannah. Until she brought Hannah home and into her husband's arms. She'd genuinely believed they would do that. That they would find the killer before he did it this time.

When dispatch called the command center late Friday night—a DB in the center of town, right outside the station, she felt like she'd been punched. She and Jack looked at each other, and she knew he was feeling the same thing—they'd failed her. They'd done absolutely nothing to save Hannah Morris from the hands of a murderer. There would be no swat team assembled, no doors kicked in, no rescue. Nothing at all done for Hannah Morris, and it left a horrible, gaping hole in the pit of Cally's stomach.

Sitting in the armchair, she thought of Alexis Greene, of the tag on her foot as she lay on the cold metal table in the morgue. She thought of Brianna Hemmer, hidden between the reeds on the cold ground by the river. And now Hannah.

She didn't want to see her! She'd looked so pretty in the framed pictures all over the house, so full of life, all smiles, big brown eyes, beautiful clear skin. Cally's eyes filled, and tears slid down her face. She wiped them away, took a deep breath and stared up at the ceiling. They had to do more.

Cally got up and walked to the front door where she'd dropped her briefcase. She took out her notes and laid them out on the table. The public works employees were all being investigated. Nothing had materialized yet. They'd scrutinized the families of each victim, friends, lovers, but they'd cleared them all.

They'd been researching the theory that one of the victims was the true target and the rest were decoys. They were checking into Hannah Morris's routine, her habits. As Jack had said, the killer had stepped out on a limb with her, taken more risks. Could she be the true target, the others set up merely to throw them off track? Could the profiler be wrong?

But their investigation had revealed no hidden activity or enemies. Hannah's life was as normal as white milk, her marriage, strong. A big fat goose egg. No, Hannah Morris was just the next in his twisted series, his line of haute couture.

At four-thirty Cally took a shower. At five o'clock she went to the kitchen and began cooking pancakes, eggs, sausage. She brewed a full pot of coffee. At five-forty-five she nudged his shoulder. She'd pushed the limit. Any longer and he'd be mad.

Jack woke immediately, shaking his head violently. Confusion turned to recognition, and he pulled her hand to sit beside him. "How long did I sleep?" He closed his eyes again.

"Just a couple hours."

"We have to go," he mumbled.

"In ten minutes. I made breakfast."

"What time is it?" He stood up and stretched his arms above his head. His flat, contoured tummy peeked out from below his shirt. He looked darn sexy.

"There are clean towels in the bathroom. Clean boxers and a shirt, too. They're Chris's, but they should fit. You realize I took the scanner into the bathroom while I showered?" she asked lightly, trying to put new life into the day, to compartmentalize the killer's latest lechery.

"You're so dedicated," he responded with a hint of smile.

While he was showering, Cally went back to the kitchen and finished cooking. She removed a tray of lasagna from the freezer. She'd cooked it a couple weeks before in preparation for her new schedule, never imagining how busy her life would actually become. Now she placed it in the oven and set the timer for six o'clock, the cook-time for forty minutes. If need be, she'd stop home and bring the whole tray to the station. She could not handle another cold take-out dinner.

Jack walked out as she was finishing up. "Where's Paige been?" he asked settling down on a counter stool. She set a plate of eggs, pancakes, and bacon in front of him, then grabbed one for herself and came around.

"Over Chris's. She practically lives there now. Just comes home to grab clothes. It's like I don't have a roommate anymore."

"That's convenient." His eyes sparked.

She smiled. Remembering last night's kiss sent a warm current under her skin. She had no regrets, looked forward to repeating the experience, but today had its own priorities.

Chapter 26

They arrived at headquarters at six-thirty. Jack stopped into his office; Cally went straight to the conference room. Charles was already seated at the table looking at the Morris crime scene photos. Cally stopped dead when she saw him.

"Morning," Cally said hesitantly.

"Morning." He stood and put his hands in his pockets. "Uh, Cal, listen, I'm sorry. I said some mean stuff. Forget it?"

He was so hard to read. She wanted to forget everything he'd said about her and Jack and their family. But his words still irked her. "Do Chris and Colin really think I'm tromping all over the family?"

"Nah, not at all. If anything, I egged them on. I was jealous." He looked embarrassed. "They're happy for you. So am I."

They were happy for her. Now *she* felt selfish. In a way, she'd wanted this case to be hers alone. Hadn't Charles waited a lot longer for an opportunity like this?

"You deserve to be here more than I do," she said. "I'm glad you're here." She looked at him and smiled. He felt like her big brother again. "And I'm sorry for thinking the worst when I saw you with Tia."

"Hey. We're human, right? When Musser started blabbing about walking in on you and Brant, I believed it."

"I got hit in the face with Jack's jacket!"

He raised his hands. "Let's forget it, okay? We're done with it."

Cally let out a long sigh. She was more than happy to let it go. She looked down at the array of pictures spread in front of Charles. The 5 X 7 photos were arranged like tiles. The driveway, the gate, the kitchen. How could they quibble about petty issues while looking at this?

"It's getting hard, Charles. This last one was really awful. It's starting to really affect me."

"I know." His voice was heavy.

"I wanted to say thank you."

"For what?"

"For sticking up for me. I can't figure out why Musser's being such an asshole. Why would he be so nasty? I never did anything to him."

"There's history there, Cal. Don't worry about it. Looks like his days are coming to an end, anyway. I did what I did for Dad as much as for you. Anthony Musser's father had it in for Dad. Hank Musser despised and badgered Dad until the day he died."

"Why did he have it in for Dad?" Cally asked, shocked to hear this new information. "And how did he die?"

"He dropped dead of a heart attack on the job last year. I think Anthony somehow blames Dad." Cally gestured for him to keep going, and he continued. "About eight years back, there was a spot open on the force. Grainer and Dad hired a female officer name Jen Woods, over Anthony Musser. Anthony's credentials weren't as good, but Hank didn't care. When Anthony had to wait till the next academy session to be hired, Hank flew off the handle. Started talking all this crap, none of it true, and bringing other cops along. Jen eventually quit and filed a lawsuit, and Dad caught a lot of grief that he didn't deserve. He never did anything except hire her, but he was the guy in charge."

"I never knew any of that."

"Course not. It stayed behind these walls. But I suspect both of the Mussers gave Jen a hard time, and she quit. Now somebody's talking to the press. I thought immediately of Musser. Then, when I heard Tia was on the story, well, I had an in." He shrugged, and disappointment creased his brow. "I used it."

"Do you feel bad about it?"

"Not for Anthony. Doubt I'll be seeing Tia Santos again, though."

He clearly seemed to care. Cally couldn't say the same. At the moment, she was pretty pissed at the pretty reporter. Sighing, she looked across the large expanse of table. The public works printouts sat calling them at the other end. They seemed a good place to start the morning.

Chapter 27

Tommy paced the apartment. It was a little after six p.m., and Cally had just arrived home. This was his chance. He'd been here two weeks, and he still hadn't asked her out. They hadn't even had that cup of coffee yet. Tonight was the night.

He rubbed his hands. Could he just go over and say hello? Or should he use some pretext? Cup of sugar? Flour? He drummed his fingers against his jeans. He heard her moving through the thin walls. A loud thump sounded, and he wondered what she was doing. It was followed by an even louder bang against the wall, and he suddenly knew exactly what he would say.

He went to the bathroom and checked his appearance in the mirror. He ran his hands over his new George Clooney haircut. He was looking good, if he did say so himself. "Wish me luck," he whispered.

He went to her door and rang the bell.

"Who is it?" her voice called out.

"It's me, Tommy."

A moment later the chain unlocked followed by the bolt. She opened the door. She looked great in jeans and a sweatshirt. His heart started to race. His palms heated up.

"Hi Tommy." She said it kind of brusquely.

He hesitated, but no, he would not back out. He plowed ahead. "Everything okay? I heard a loud bang. I just wanted to check."

Her mouth turned up in a smile; her shoulders relaxed. "Thanks. That's very nice of you."

"With what's been happening around town, and you being alone." He peeked in through the entryway. "Where's Paige been lately?"

"Boyfriend's. My brother's."

"Oh." he glanced past her into the apartment. "You're ok then?"

"I was trying to get something out of my coat closet. The upper shelf fell, along with all the coats and two hundred pounds of junk."

"It fell? You're lucky you weren't hurt." He stood awkwardly trying to muster his courage. "Need help putting it back up?" he blurted, rubbing his sweaty palms on his pants.

She stepped back and smiled. "You wouldn't mind?"

"Not at all."

Like a ballerina, she extended her arm, inviting him in. The closet door was open beside them. Just like his, it was a wide closet with two sliding doors. The upper shelf and the attached hang bar had collapsed, bringing with it all the coats and a huge pile of stuff: a brown carton filled with flags, a zippered gym bag, a white bag of rock salt, wool hats, gloves, sneakers, a bag of colorful toys. "Let me get a screwdriver," she said and disappeared in the direction of the kitchen.

"How did it drop?" he called after her.

"What's that?" she shouted back. She was fumbling in drawers. He heard the sound of paper crunching, chains against wood.

"How'd it fall?" he asked again. But he was getting nervous. Why did he have to get this way around women? They were just humans! He clenched his hands; his fingernails dug into his palm.

"Got it!" she shouted.

He jolted. Good God, Tommy, keep it together. She was coming back.

She walked into the foyer and Tommy managed to smile and say, "Excellent."

When she turned toward the closet to survey the damage, he wiped his palm on his pant leg. She turned back to him all smiles and determination.

"Okay. If you hold this end up right where you see those screw holes, I'll set the first screw on this end."

"You don't want to take the clothes off the bar?"

She laughed. "What's the matter? Think we can't lift it?"

Shoot. Of course they could. "I just think it might be less cumbersome," he stumbled through. Oh, this was torture.

She pondered it for a quick second. "You're right. Let's take them off."

She asked him to hold the bar while she took handfuls of coats off the bar and walked them into the living room. He felt useless and self-conscious, holding the bar while she did all the lugging back and forth to the living room. Shouldn't he be doing more? What would her brothers do? And damn. His arms were starting to shake. The bar was sagging. She came and took another handful. She turned to the living room. He couldn't hold it another thirty seconds, so he followed, holding the bar like a dumb weightlifter while the coats swayed back and forth making each step nearly impossible. His arms were screaming now. Would she think he was a weakling? Dammit. He was right behind her now.

She turned around and almost plowed right into him.

"Oh! I didn't hear you. What are you doing?"

"I'm putting them here." His voice heaved as he dropped the bar onto the couch. He plastered a smile on his face and tried not to sound too winded. "No use making you run back and forth." He took a handful of hangers, slid them off the bar and handed them to her.

"Good idea," she said all perky. She didn't seem to notice his discomfort at all.

After the last bunch, she stood straight and put her hands on her hips. "Okay," she said, reminding him of a cheerleader. She looked really, really cute. He started to relax. "I need you to hold one end up while I secure the other."

"No problem."

They went to the closet and fitted the pole. She screwed her end in and stepped back. Extending the screwdriver his way she said, "Here you go. Screw in your end."

He took the screwdriver. She stuck her hand in her pants' pocket and pulled out two screws. She held her hand open to him and smiled.

He took the first one from her little cupped palm, found the hole, lined up the bracket. He started turning but pushed too hard. The screwdriver slipped off the head and into the wall, making a distinct thwack. The screw fell to the ground.

"Shit," he said, looking at the hole in the wall then down at the screw by his feet.

"Here. Take this one. I'll get that." She held her hand open again. The second screw lay in her small palm.

They were in the closet together. In a little tiny space, and his breath ratcheted. He thought he might hyperventilate. He was in a closet with Cally Bank, and he couldn't even get the damned screw in the wall. "Damn it!"

"Don't worry, I see it." She had her head nearly in the carpet. She was so close he could smell her fruity shampoo.

"Got, it," she said, angling her head up triumphantly. She held the screw between her thumb and forefinger. All he wanted to do was screw the screw in the wall, like all her brothers could do. Surely, he could do that much! Steady, he told himself. Screw the first one in then get the other one. He looked at the X on the screw, slowly fit the Phillips head and turned. He felt it tightening under his hand and felt his shoulders relax. He reached his hand down without looking and let her put the second screw in his hand. The tips of her fingers reminded him of giraffes at the zoo, how their soft muzzles always tickled when he fed them as a boy.

"Oh my gosh, I'm sorry!" Cally cried. "You cut your hand! I should have taken those hangers off the bar, I'm sorry."

"Don't worry about it."

"And you didn't even say anything. You're such a gentleman." She smiled nice. "Thanks, Tommy."

"No problem," he replied and hated himself for saying it again.

"Come in the kitchen, I have a first aid kit." Just then the ding of a timer sounded. "My lasagna." She sniffed. "Smell that?"

Tommy did notice a pleasant tomato aroma now that she mentioned it.

"I heated a big tray. Would you like to stay for a quick bite?" She grinned invitingly.

"Sure." His heart revved and his smile was almost painful. Maybe, just maybe, things would work out.

"I have to eat quickly because I'm bringing most of it to the station, but we may as well eat while it's hot." She sent a big, wide, cover girl smile right at him. Oh, man.

His nerves released like pollen in spring, up and away, and he felt himself take a free, clear breath of air. It was going to happen! She liked him!

***

Cally removed a stack of Styrofoam plates from the cabinet and set them on the counter. She cut two pieces from the tray and looked down at the mush of sauce and cheese. "I don't get it," she said to Tommy. "It's always too juicy no matter how much paste I use." She shook her head in dismay then placed tin foil over the casserole dish. Mushy or not, she would bring it to the station.

Carrying both plates to the table she sat across from Tommy. He took a forkful and smiled, and she tried hers, too. It tasted good—the tomatoes were fresh; the garlic, just right, not too overpowering; the noodles, a perfect consistency. She just needed to learn how to get it to hold its shape.

"I think it's delicious," Tommy said. "You're quite a cook."

Cally laughed. "Not really. To be honest, lasagna is one of about four meals I know how to make. I should take lessons from my mom."

Tommy seemed to be enjoying it. He took another forkful and waved his hand in front of his face as the heat overwhelmed him. "Hot!" he puffed. He looked cute. She smiled at him, and he smiled back. She liked the way his eyes crinkled.

"I'm glad you moved next door, Tommy. I haven't seen much of you since we were kids. You kept to yourself after a while."

"I was a shy kid." He dropped his eyes. "But we all grow up at some point, don't we?"

Cally thought of the case. She had grown up a lot in just two weeks. "Yes, we do," she said. Tommy's smile was tentative, and she thought he looked a bit stressed, too. "Would you like a glass of wine?" she asked.

He said that he would, and she was glad. She could use a glass herself. After she had poured, she raised her glass to his. "Here's to being friends, to getting to know each other after all these years." She had known him, after all, since she could remember. "It makes sense that you would keep to yourself. I guess my brothers can seem pretty intimidating. Very competitive."

"And I was never much of an athlete," Tommy added. "It was never much fun. Eventually, I just stayed away."

Cally felt a gush of sympathy. He was incredibly honest. "I don't blame you. I would have done the same. It was kind of like that for me, too. The only difference was that I couldn't stay away. They were my family. So instead, I worked really hard. By the time I was seventeen, I was beating them."

"Really? How?" He leaned back.

"I practice Judo, for one thing. That gives me a lot of confidence in many situations." Cally thought of all the hours she'd put in at the studio and in competition. Hours and hours, perfecting throwing, grappling, and striking techniques.

"No kidding. Good for you." Tommy took a sip of wine and studied her for a moment. He raised his glass. "To sticking up for yourself!"

"Here! Here!" He wore a cute smile on his face. He reminded her a little of Colin—modest, funny, kind of quirky. A bit on the outside of things. She said, "Don't get me wrong. I love my brothers. They'd do anything for me. It was just a little tough sometimes, know what I mean?"

He looked at her with understanding in his eyes. "I do, Cally. I know what you mean."

He said it just the right way—not making a big deal of it, and she was suddenly reminded of playing with him long ago. "Remember when we used to play together?"

He dropped his head and smiled.

"We had fun." She remembered how much she liked him, the old connection they'd shared. After all these years, she decided she liked him still. Not a physical attraction, and she hoped he realized that, but it would be nice if they became friends. She took a comfortable sip of wine as the phone rang.

Her heart skipped a beat. She had to get used to that—the way she instinctively brightened every time it rang. She hoped it was Jack. She couldn't wait to talk to him.

She excused herself from the table and answered the phone. Jack's voice sent a wave of warmth through her. "Hi!" she said. She turned her back from Tommy and cradled the phone against her shoulder. She'd left Jack less than two hours ago, but she missed him already.

"Just checking in," he said. "It's quiet here. Why don't you stay home and get some rest?"

"But I made the lasagna."

"We ordered Chinese. Save it for tomorrow night."

Just then Tommy shifted behind her. She heard his chair push back and she turned around. He'd stood up. "I'll be right back," he said. "Boys room."

He passed behind her toward the bathroom. She wondered if he was being chivalrous, giving her privacy.

"Who was that?" Jack asked.

"My neighbor. We're having dinner."

"Oh." Dead silence.

She laughed. "We're just friends, Jack." A moment later she heard the door snap closed. Something about the way it clicked, quiet and careful, made her wonder if Tommy had been listening.

"Did I say anything?" Jack replied playfully, but she heard a touch of defensiveness in his voice. "Get some sleep and I'll see you bright and early."

She put the phone back and released a big, contented sigh. Tommy returned at that moment. He suddenly looked ill at ease, and she knew he'd heard the conversation.

"Let's finish eating," he said, his voice with an edge. They sat back down but Cally felt weird. She suddenly wondered if he'd had other intentions.

"I'm gay, you know," he said, catching her completely off guard. "I'm not out of the closet, so I hope you can keep it quiet."

She felt honored. A wave of respect washed over her. She thought of him growing up next door to her rough and tumble brothers. It must have been hard. He looked insecure, cute, and cuddly. "Of course I will! I'm so glad you told me, Tommy. Really. I'm honored you feel you can trust me."

"It's been hard. You know, my dad, he's a real hard ass."

Cally tried to picture Frank Doone. "Actually, I hardly know your father. I don't think I've spoken to him in twenty years."

"You're lucky."

"Aah, he can't be that bad."

"Trust me." He rolled his eyes. "Anyway, I just want to be friends." He raised his glass. In the ambient light of the dining area, his eyes shone.

"That works for me." She raised her glass to his. "To being friends!"

Chapter 28

Tuesday morning and the mall was quiet. Katrina idled along, wishing she had money to spend. The Nordstrom windows were already displaying cruise wear; so were Macy's. The Victoria's Secret windows were dressed with giant, close-up posters. Ann Taylor showed slacks and colorful spring blouses. She wished Gail would hurry and decide which spring gowns she wanted in the window display. Prom season would soon be here, and they were losing precious sales days. As she meandered the main concourse, a newspaper displayed in a booth carrying magazines and trinkets caught her eye. In bold letters, the paper's headline read, **Couturier Strikes Again.**

She thought immediately of Jack and her heart raced. She missed him so much. She yanked two singles from her Coach wristlet and paid the man behind the counter. With a pounding in her chest, she chose an empty bench and plopped down with the newspaper.

Another body had been found last night and left outside the police station under a streetlight. She laid the paper on her lap, brought her head up slowly. The streetlight. That town worker in the parking lot behind the shop. She suddenly pictured Mr. Mintman and the paper slipped off her knees to the floor. Holy Shit. Mr. Mintman. That municipal worker under the streetlight had looked just like him.

She contemplated telling Jack, but he would just think she was making things up to bother him. He would throw her out of the station like he'd thrown her out of his apartment. No, she was done being humiliated by Jack. She stood, marched to the mall exit, threw open the doors, and chucked the newspaper in a nearby bin. She would not tell him about Mr. Mintman. She was done with Jack Brant for good.

***

Luther stepped into the room and looked around. His workshop. So quiet, so peaceful. Lord, he loved it in here. But it was looking a bit messy. His materials were scattered around the room: little pieces of red, lavender, and blue fabric. He grabbed a large plastic crate and started stuffing everything inside. He tucked the crate on the bottom shelf of the utility room. He took a deep breath. Better. Much better. He saw today's newspaper on the workbench and grimaced. He was getting coverage, but not the kind he wanted.

The damn reporters had him all wrong. Even the cable channel talking heads. They said he hated women. He didn't hate them! He loved them. Especially these women. He loved talking to them, placing his creations over their accommodating bodies. They were his muses. They gave him inspiration, ideas. They never talked back, never complained, never told him he was pathetic. How could he possibly hate them?

He went upstairs. The rooms were cold and damp, but he didn't care. He went to his grandmother's room, to the old desk, and took a piece of her plain paper. The letter would once again be printed from the Smith Corona on untraceable paper and mailed in the most common of envelopes. They'd never catch him. Just like they couldn't trace the letter he'd sent to the newspaper. He was safe, safe, safe.

"Dear Monkeys," he said aloud. He liked the sound of it. He kept talking, typing as the words spewed out, page after page, until he noted the light fading outside. He was getting cold, the dampness settling into his bones. He stood and paced the room.

What color? What Material? Where? How? It was already Tuesday. He had just two days to sew. His thoughts were getting away from him, racing in bursts, and he hated when they did that. But how would he do it? Who could he use as a model?

Each had to be better, more special than the last. A face popped to mind—a bust line and a derriere—the perfect person. And would she ever make a statement! Was she ever relevant! He rubbed his hands, scrunched his shoulders in glee, sat back down. He put his fingers on the keys, added a few choice lines, and signed his pen name.

When he was done, he leaned back in exhaustion, feeling his blood ripple in satisfaction. He would mail the letter today. It would arrive tomorrow. It was perfect.

Chapter 29

*D*ear *Monkeys,* the letter began.

Do you still think you're so smart? Apparently. You're probably patting yourselves on the back right now, just like in those ridiculous press conferences. But you're not kidding anybody. Everyone in the entire nation is watching, thinking what a bunch of incompetents you are. Do you see what they say about you? Small town dummies! Hah!

Me, on the other hand, I am the Couturier. *The elusive artist who is always trending and has you running around in circles. Hah!*

I am almost finished. Soon I will be far away and your chance will be gone. I knew you wouldn't find me. It doesn't surprise me that you never showed my work. That you CENSORED EVERYTHING because you are a bunch of fascists. You keep it hidden away because you are afraid people will use their own minds and like what they see. And what would happen then? How far would it go?

Jack rubbed his cheeks as he read. His face was burning, his head, pounding. How could anyone write this crap? He flicked through the pages. It went on and on for five single-spaced pages. More about the government and authority and new forms of art, a streaming bunch of crap. Jack read on, his stomach tightening, his patience unraveling as he neared the end. When he reached the final lines, his adrenaline spiked. I must be reading it wrong, he thought. He went back and read it again.

My work here is nearly done. I have just one more inspiration to pursue then I will go. A beautiful azure blue charmeuse. I'll need someone with blue eyes. A blonde long-haired model would be best. Thin, of course. Know anyone? What about you, Detective Brant? Good luck! Can you monkeys figure this out? Can you do anything about it? I doubt it. Jack Brant, you should take special interest. Can hero man protect hero woman? LOL! Not a chance. I'll leave her someplace special.

Ciao peasants,

The Couturier

Jack's grasp tightened. He had to keep from tearing the papers in pieces and throwing them in the trash. Son of a bitch! He slammed his fist to the desk. He grabbed the plain white envelope he'd left mindlessly on the desk. It had been postmarked from Two Rivers on January thirtieth. Today was Wednesday, the thirty-first. The letter had just arrived with the morning delivery of mail. He reached for the phone then stopped. He rubbed his forehead, closed his eyes, squeezed his temples.

Cally. His heart galloped in his chest. Where was she? Who was she with?

Alone. She was out alone visiting the utility departments of neighboring towns. Jack looked at his watch. It was just past nine a.m. She had five towns to visit and wouldn't be back for hours. Jack grabbed his phone, prepared to tell her to get right back to the station, then put it back down on the conference table. He knew how she'd react. No, he wouldn't tell her anything yet.

He called the patrol captain. Once he received confirmation that the tail had her in sight, Jack called Joe Clarizio. As much as he hated voodoo science, he needed him. He needed a new profile on this guy—a ledge to grab hold of.

Clarizio was in the building. Jack gave him a copy of the letter and put him in a vacant office to study it. He called the task force to the conference room, including the chief. Ten minutes later, they were assembled.

"In front of each of you is a copy of a letter I received regular mail this morning. The envelope was addressed to me. It was postmarked yesterday from Two Rivers, delivered to the station today."

Charles Bank cursed. When he looked up from reading the letter, his face had gone pale.

"He's showing us his hand," Jack said to him. He looked around the rest of the table. "Obviously, he's targeting Cally Bank."

Clarizio entered the room. He took a seat, and Jack asked him what he'd surmised.

"It fits. He's elevating his message. The first letter alluded to his hatred for the Two Rivers police. This letter acts specifically upon it. It appears he's found a target at which to transfer his rage. We can assume he's a misogynist, and he hates cops, too. Her image has been on news clips. Now he's targeting her. It looks like he may have been following her ... or you."

God, what had he gotten Cally into? Why hadn't he thought it through? He should never have picked her for the task force.

"Her name was in the paper recently," Vince Martin offered. "There was an article about the banquet. The article named the new officers, and I'll have to check, but I believe it mentioned that she was the only women on the force. And don't forget that she's been on TV several times, seen walking beside you, or in the background."

Vince was shaken; Jack could tell. None of them wanted to be having this conversation.

"Let's get back to the letter," he said to Clarizio. "What new information does it give us?"

"I'm sticking with my original assessment—a spree killer with a gripe against the Two Rivers PD, specifically. Have you checked former officers? I'd look into anyone who has been fired over the past five years. The municipal authority uniform makes me certain that he has some connection to the city."

"We've been out all week interviewing ex-municipal workers," he said in frustration. "We're checking some alibis, but to be honest, no one's raised a red flag. Bank, what about the former cops?"

"I'm getting through them one by one. A total of six cops have been terminated over the past four years, not counting about ten new hires that didn't make it through the academy for one reason or another over the past five years."

"I'd start with the six cops terminated," Clarizio suggested, "then to the academy drop-outs."

"Just get to them all. Fast." Jack barked. The nit-picking was killing him. "Pull somebody from patrol." An image of Cally was pressing on him. He didn't want to see it. He wanted her safe. He pounded his fist on the table. Catch him any way you can! he felt like shouting. He pushed his chair back and took a deep breath, looked up to see five pairs of eyes staring at him.

"You want to take a break, Jack? Go splash some water on your face?" the chief asked.

"No."

"We need to re-strategize." Grainer held up the letter. "An officer is now a spree killer's target. How do we play the card?"

Jack stopped dead. "The card?"

"She's tough," the chief said. "I think she could play decoy."

"Play decoy? Are you kidding me? We're talking a rookie cop here—with all due respect, sir, you put her out there and she could get killed."

"We don't put her out there, other women may get killed. She'll be well-protected."

"No way."

"I don't like it either, sir," Charles said.

The Chief waved them off. "Neither of you can be objective. What do you think, Martin?"

"It's up to her. Personally, I think she could handle it. She's a terrific shot, and a Sandan black belt in Judo. I don't see how her being a rookie makes a difference. She'll follow instructions. We'll be right there."

"What do you think, Tulio?" Grainer turned to the FBI agent. "What kind of equipment could you give us?"

"We could run the whole thing for you." He sat forward in his seat. "She'll be fully protected."

Jack threw his pen on the table. "Your troop had the last incident wrong. You said he'd be out in the streets! Now you expect us to trust you with one of our own?"

"I'm responding to your chief's question, Jack. Don't throw shit at me."

"That's right." Grainer glared at Jack. "Get it together, detective, or I'll be forced to remove you from the team." He stood to leave. "I'll take your opinions under consideration and make my decision by the end of the day. I'm inclined to go with Martin and Tulio on this." He looked at Charles. "I can understand your position, she's your sister." He turned to Jack and shook his head. "I think your judgment is clouded due to your personal feelings for Officer Bank."

"That's bullshit," Jack protested.

"What does she have to say about this development, by the way?"

Jack looked at his hands. He hadn't expected the question.

"Detective Brant? What is Officer Bank's opinion?"

"She doesn't know yet."

"She doesn't know she is a target?" Grainer's eyes widened.

Jack shook his head. "We've got her under surveillance. She's safe."

Grainer pointed a finger in his face. "Call her in and tell her what's going on! And that's an order!"

Jack felt his face go hot, and he tugged at his collar. He'd been afraid of this exact thing. He knew that the sting would be suggested, and he knew how she would react. She would insist on participating. The train would run away. He simply could not let her be tied to the tracks.

***

Cally saw Jack as soon as she exited the Tinton Falls Municipal building. He'd been holding his phone to his ear but ended the conversation when he saw her. He looked handsome in the car, his face focused and serious, his gaze following her. But as she approached, she noted discomfort, or maybe distress in his eyes. A wave of dread washed over her. Oh no … not another victim.

"What's up, Jack?" she said cautiously. "Why are you here?" It was just ten thirty in the morning. She was shocked he'd left the task force.

"Hey, Cally." He sounded down.

"What's the matter?"

"I need to talk to you."

Cally's stomach dropped. She didn't like the sound of his voice, and her mind raced. What was going on? Had something horrible happened? She raised her hand to her mouth, flooded with memories of Clyde. "Is everyone alright? Did something happen?"

"No. God, no. It's nothing like that. Something with the case." He reached toward his breast pocket, and she noticed a wad of folded paper. He pulled it out and held it up for her to see. "Come into the car. We got a letter from the killer. He identifies his next target."

"Who is it?"

"It's complicated." He reached over and opened the door from the inside. He eyed her strangely, dead seriously.

"What's going on?" She got into the seat and shut the door behind her.

He looked at her with a mountain of regret in his eyes. In that instant, in that look, she knew.

"You're the target, Cally." He opened the paper and handed it to her.

The paper shook in her hands as she read. She raced through the first bunch of pages, skimming. It was the same gibberish of his first letter but longer. When she got to the last paragraphs, her reading slowed. *Hero man? Hero woman?* Her heart beat against her breastbone. *I'll leave her someplace special.* Her mother's worst fears. Her family's predictions. It was surreal, incomprehensible, too remote.

"Why does he have to target me?" she cried angrily. Everything she'd worked for, everything she'd fought so hard against.

"You're mad?"

"Yes, I'm mad. What did you expect?"

"I was hoping you'd be scared." Jack sighed. "This is real, Cally. Very real. I'm putting you under protection. At least that's what I've recommended."

"Protection? What are you talking about?"

"I'm meeting with Grainer in one hour to review the details. It's just a term, Cally, that's all. We'll keep you under observation. We'll make sure he's not following you, keep a low-key watch over you until he's caught."

"A cop following a cop? What are they going to do, tail me while I'm working the case?" She watched his eyes drop, saw the guilty look on his face. "You've already decided, haven't you?"

"It's for your own safety." He looked away. His jaw was set; his eyes focused out the window.

"For God's sake!" Cally couldn't believe he was being so unreasonable. "We have a perfect opportunity to catch him. Put me out there with a sign on my back! Get this monster off the streets!"

"Cally, you saw those women. You saw what he did to them."

"We have equipment. I'll be safe."

"It's a chance I'm not willing to take."

She couldn't sit a minute longer. She couldn't believe what she was hearing. "I thought you understood me, Jack. I thought you knew who I was. What's important to me." She opened the door and stepped out. She looked back at him, waiting, hoping, but he just looked away, his jaw set tight.

"I'm going to Asbury Park. It's the next town on my list." She slammed the door and did not turn back.

Chapter 30

An hour later, Jack sat in Grainer's anteroom, waiting for the chief to arrive, still smoldering over his argument with Cally. Was he being unreasonable? Was he being motivated by more than sheer tactics? Possibly. But were his feelings for Cally causing him to act irrationally? That was the real question.

He'd always acted on instinct. It was what made him a good cop—why he had three medals on his mantel. So why had Grainer looked at him like this was so much different, like his protective feelings for Cally were so bad?

Did he even care what Grainer thought? Not if it meant the difference between Cally being alive or dead. He would never regret the decision. What he would regret, would be allowing her to get herself killed. No way. He could never live with himself. It wasn't worth the risk. If Cally never spoke to him again, so be it. Maybe someday, she'd come to agree with him. Maybe not. It didn't matter.

Jack heard Grainer's voice approaching from down the hallway. A second voice, low and rumbled responded.

They rounded the corner and Grainer appeared with Clyde Bank, Senior. They exchanged brief hellos.

"Martin and Tulio here yet?" Grainer asked.

"No sir," Jack replied.

"Good. Gives us a chance to talk privately." Grainer led the way into his office with Bank and Jack following. He went behind his desk and sat. Bank and Jack took the seats in front. "See who I've got here?" Grainer nodded toward Bank. "Clyde and I have worked together for over thirty years. I trust his judgment." The chief nodded his head seriously. "Not just that, I wouldn't risk endangering one of his kids without running it by him first."

Jack wasn't sure if he liked the sound of this or not. He shifted in his seat.

Bank turned to Jack. "Jack, I appreciate the fact that you want to protect my daughter. The chief told me your recommendation. He also told me that Tulio can practically guarantee Cally's safety."

"Practically? Is that good enough for you, sir?"

Bank held up his hand to hush him. "Hold on now. Vince Martin says Cally's the best rookie he's ever mentored. He thinks she can handle it."

"I see." Jack rubbed his temples, feeling the pangs of a tension headache.

"I know my daughter." Bank smiled and tipped his head in amusement. "There is nowhere that girl would rather be than dead center of a sting operation."

Jack couldn't believe it. Was everyone so willing to put her in harm's way? Where were his paternal instincts?

"But that's what parents are for—to protect their kids when they might be tempted to take foolish chances, and I have a wife to consider. You've met Mrs. Bank, Jack."

Jack held his breath.

"She never wanted Cally to become a cop. She always hoped she'd change her mind."

"Glad she didn't," Grainer piped in.

"So am I," Bank agreed. "Cally is clearly where she wants to be. But I have to draw the line here. I can't consent to her being used as a decoy for someone as dangerous as this."

Thank God. Jack released his breath. Cally would go into protection.

Bank continued. "It's your show to run, Bob, but that's where I stand. I say keep her safe for a couple days, few weeks, however long it takes to catch this guy. She'll have plenty more opportunities to prove herself."

Grainer nodded. He rubbed his hand to his chin and for a moment Jack wondered if he might move forward anyway.

"All right." His brow furrowed. "I won't say I'm happy with your decision, but I'll respect your wishes, Clyde. I still think she's our best shot at catching him." He turned to Jack. "Where is Officer Bank at the moment?"

"Asbury Park Utility Authority," Jack replied.

"I assume she's got a tail?" Grainer asked.

"Yes. She's not happy about it."

"I wouldn't think so." Bank grimaced. "You better watch out, Jack, she can be hot as chili peppers when she's angry."

"I got a taste a little while ago."

"Have dispatch call her in," Grainer said. "Tell her she's to report to McCloskey for the rest of the afternoon."

"Is that necessary? She can stay on the team. I'll keep her busy inside."

"No," Grainer replied. "I don't want her on if she's the target—too awkward for everybody else. She can work the desk for a spell. She's got to put her two weeks in, anyway. Might as well get it over with now."

Jack remembered his round at desk duty. Rookie cops were required to work several posts in their first year in order to become fully rounded. This included two weeks at the central desk, which entailed fielding calls, filing reports, evidence, and other administrative tasks.

"She'll be disappointed."

"That's the breaks," her father said matter-of-factly. "Better safe than dead."

A tap sounded on the open door. Tulio and Martin entered. For the next thirty minutes they talked strategy. When they finished, Jack returned to his office and put the request to dispatch. He heard the dispatcher's voice calling her car, instructing her to report back, the sound of her disappointed voice responding, "10-4".

Jack heard the frustration. It came through even between the crackles in the radio. He leaned back, clasped his hands at his waist and stared down at them.

He drove the miles with her—ten of them—from Asbury Park to Two Rivers, seeing the route in the palm of his hand, following the lines on the highway. He knew his shot with her had ended before it ever began. He knew it deep in his soul. She would never forgive him for this.

What had this woman done to him that no one else ever had? He'd convinced himself it was the case itself—the senseless, brutal murders that had changed him. The lechery of it had somehow re-opened his eyes, infused him with energy.

But he knew now that it was her—her joy of life. Her energy, her enthusiasm, her pure desire for justice. It was everything he used to love about being a cop—everything that had dulled over the years.

Time was flying. He would be thirty-five next month, never bitten by the marriage bug, never felt the need for a woman in his life. Never wanted one full-time. Suddenly he was entertaining silly visions, like him and Cally sitting in front of a fire ... a yellow lab at their feet, reviewing case files. Bouncing theories off each other as they drank some wine—dumb stuff like that.

And now bringing Cally in from the field was tearing a big hole in his heart. The truth was being a cop was dangerous, and he couldn't stand the thought of her in danger. Look how he'd reacted today. How would he feel when she pulled patrol on the west side? How would he handle that? Best to snuff those silly images right now.

Jack looked down at his clasped hands. A mile left? Maybe less. She'd be almost here.

Chapter 31

Cally eyed Jack, her presence undetected through the window of his office door. He was so handsome, and so grave. He chewed the side of his mouth, his hands clenched. He looked like he carried the weight of the world on his shoulders. She wondered which weight it was.

While she was driving back, she'd called Martin. He'd told her that he and Tulio had supported the sting operation while Jack had argued against it. She'd had to pull over. A knife in the back couldn't hurt so bad. In the parking lot, Jack had admitted he'd recommended desk duty. But he'd done more than that. He'd argued against her when three other cops in the room had supported her. He'd betrayed her.

Cally knocked on the door and stepped in. He looked up and she saw disappointment in the dull of his eyes. Why? He'd won, hadn't he?

"Hi Cally."

"You called for me?" She crossed her arms in front.

"Cally, don't be like this. Come in and sit down."

"Don't feel like it. I talked to Martin. I know you lobbied against me when everyone else in the room supported a sting."

"I told you, it's too risky."

"No, it's not. Even the chief disagreed with you."

"Not after he thought about it."

"He changed his mind because you and my father tag teamed him."

"It wasn't like that." He frowned. By the look of him, you'd think he'd lost the battle. "Why don't you sit down?"

"No thanks."

"Cally, don't be mad. You'll have plenty of opportunities to prove yourself."

"It's not about proving myself! Don't you get that? This is about catching a killer! I am the best shot we've got at catching him and you know it. You're letting some twisted personal feelings get in the way and that is dead wrong."

"Twisted?" Jack stood up and shut the door. "Cally, hear me out. I wouldn't let any female cop do this."

"Bullshit. It's not that out of the ordinary. Female cops offer themselves as bait all the time. How do you think half the Johns out there are caught?"

"That's different. Those men are not killers." He turned from her.

"They could be. How do you know they're not? Departments put women out there all the time with a lot less protection than I would have had. It's routine."

He spun around. "It's not routine to me." His face was set in hard lines. "Starting this afternoon, you report to Lieutenant Nolan. Your tour at desk duty begins today." Then he added, "I'm sorry."

Cally felt her eyes well. She didn't want to cry, but she wasn't sure she could stop it. "I can't believe I ever trusted you."

Jack's shoulders sagged. "Cally, please, don't say that."

"It's true." She hated that tears tumbled onto her cheeks, but she couldn't stop them. She'd come so far; she'd gotten so close to everything. One letter and her life had completely changed. A man she thought she loved and a career she'd always dreamed of—both whisked away in a puff of smoke. This man was a complete stranger. A man who did not stick up for her when others she barely knew did. She took a deep breath and felt her chest buckle. Jack reached out and took her in his arms. He pulled her in and for a brief moment she let him hold her. He put his hand behind her head, and she felt his fingers in her hair, his warm chest against hers.

"Please understand," he whispered. "I can't stand seeing you in danger."

She stepped back and yanked her arm from his. "You don't like that I'm a cop, do you?" The truth of it struck her like a truck. He liked the woman he'd imagined in the gym, but the real her—the woman who wanted to be a cop and be treated like everybody else—well, she was too high of an investment. "Don't dare try to console me. I thought we were a team—that you wanted me by your side, pulling my weight."

"I don't want to lose you to some crazed killer." He reached for her hand, but she pulled it away.

"You don't even understand who I am!"

Suddenly, emotions so hard to battle washed over her—disappointment, frustration, anger—if she stayed a moment more, she might crumble under the weight of them, concede to him, and there would be no turning back. He may have betrayed her, but she would not betray herself. If she backed down, even an inch, she would set a precedent, one she might never break in the future. She would not settle, not for him, or anyone else who claimed to love her. Being here, out there, on the job—was what she was born to do.

And this was about more—more than her personal desires, more than her passion, more than equaling her brothers. This was about justice. She stood straight and looked him hard in the eye. "Jack, you need to understand what's at stake. This is about catching an evil killer. For you to put your personal feelings before that is wrong. Whatever your reasons, they aren't good enough. Whatever your feelings for me, they don't matter. Alexis Greene, Brianna Hemmer, Debra Miskavitch, and Hannah Morris are who matter, and that he doesn't kill again."

"I understand what's at stake." He seemed to have lost his will to argue with her. "And I am not going to let you end up like them." He plunked back in his chair with resignation. "We'll catch him. Without putting your life in danger."

"I sure hope you do." She turned to the door and walked out, feeling the burn on her cheeks. Damn him! Damn him for ruining everything.

Chapter 32

Tommy looked for signs of activity. One of them was on the side lawn, chopping wood—Colin. He bent down, picked up a log, and put it on top of the fat tree stump. Tommy watched as he retrieved the ax, which he'd laid against the stump, and raised it with two hands above his head. The thwack sent a chill up Tommy's spine. Colin had always been a squirty kid, the youngest of the brothers and younger than him by a year. Now he was a tower—the tallest of all of them. A big, tall leaning Tower of Pisa.

"Hey there, Colin, how ya' doing?" Tommy shouted, walking toward the yard. "Long time no see, man."

"Hi." Colin looked back at him like he had snakes in his hair. He squinted his eyes, and Tommy realized he didn't recognize him.

"It's me, Tommy Doone."

"Hey, Tommy. How you doing?" Colin put the ax down and approached with his hand extended. They shook hands like old friends.

"Things must be pretty crazy down there at the station, all that's going on."

"You bet," Colin said.

"My dad's feeling left out of things. How about yours?"

"Probably. He got called in yesterday to consult on something."

"Really? Bet he was a new man when he got home. You know, being called in, feeling needed and all."

Colin looked at him curiously. "I guess. He seems to be enjoying his retirement. Why, is your dad feeling down?"

"Yeah. He talks to me all the time about missing it. I'm taking him out to dinner tonight to take his mind off of it."

"That's nice."

"Anything new with the big case? You guys any closer to getting this guy?"

"If I had a dollar for every time someone asked that question, I'd be a rich man. I'm not even involved. I think they're getting close, but I don't know."

"Good. Hope they get him. My mom's a nervous wreck. You must be nervous, having a sister and all."

"Who, Cally?" Colin laughed. He picked up a round log and placed it end down on the stump.

"Why do you laugh?"

He raised the ax over his head and brought it down. The log split perfectly in half. "She can protect herself."

"I live next door to her now. I try to keep an eye out for her and her roommate."

"Yeah, she told me you moved in." Colin bent down and picked up another log. "Thanks for looking out for her." He placed the log on the stump. He split it in two. He looked back at him. "You look different."

"Do I?" He kicked the toe of his shoe in the grass. He'd come over for a reason, and the question now needed to be asked. He took a deep breath and pasted a grin on his face.

"Hey, let me ask you something. Is your sister ... you know ... involved with anyone?" Maybe he'd jumped to conclusions about that phone conversation. Maybe she'd been talking to one of her brothers.

Colin broke into an enlightened smile. "Aah, so that's the purpose of this visit. You've got the hots for Cally."

"Maybe. Has she got a boyfriend or not?"

"Well, I think she may be seeing someone, Tommy. But you never know, you could ask her out, see what happens. What's the worst she could say?"

See what happens? No thanks. He'd tried that road before. It never worked. He told Colin he'd think about it then said good-bye. The loud thwack of another log jolted him. Nerves prickled yet again as he crossed back into his yard and approached the back door.

Tonight, an important page would turn in the story of his life. He was taking his father out to dinner. Time for Dad to learn that he was his own man—that he lived in his own place, that he was a productive member of the human race. Surely his dad would see that when he took him over to see the apartment after dinner.

He opened the back door. "Dad?" he shouted.

The smell of onions and garlic accosted him. "In here, Tommy," his mother's voice responded. She stood at the stove, wearing the damn apron with the faded pink rose on the front.

"What are you doing, Mom?"

"I'm cooking dinner. Your father said you wanted to come home and have dinner. Just try not to antagonize your father, okay?"

"No, mother, I did not say I was coming home for dinner. I said I wanted to take dad *out* to dinner. Just me and him—out—like adults, you know?"

"Oh." She turned her back and stirred the pot. "I see."

"Are you mad that I want to have dinner with my father for once?"

She spun around. "What do you expect? I cooked a nice dinner—spaghetti with meatballs and sausages. I thought we would have dinner as a family, but I guess you don't want me."

"Aah, Christ, Ma. It's not that I don't want you, it's that I wanted to have dinner alone with Dad, you know, *mano a mano*."

Leave it to his mother to screw things up. He was looking forward to sitting out at a restaurant with his dad, shooting the breeze. He wanted it so bad. He looked around the dreary gray kitchen—the old fashioned white and black stove, the gray Formica countertops cracking everywhere, the dingy blue curtains that hung over the sink. It was depressing. He didn't want to sit in this hellhole for an hour. His mother would dominate the conversation with her mindless blather. No way. He and his father were going out.

"I told Dad I was taking him out to dinner."

"What's that? You want to take me out?" His father entered the room. His broad shoulders eclipsed the doorway that led from the kitchen to the dining room.

"Isn't that what we talked about on the phone?"

"I thought you should eat home. You haven't seen your mother in days. You were going to leave her out?"

"It's one lousy, friggin' dinner. I've been eating dinner with her for twenty-five years. What's one lousy dinner?" Tommy couldn't believe these idiots.

"I'm not going to leave your mother here alone. Look, she cooked."

"Can't you come out without her one lousy night? What's the big deal? Christ, Ma, don't you want a night to sit home and do nothing, no cooking, no cleaning? I thought you'd like that."

"Who's gonna' cook for me, huh?"

She had the lousiest looking scowl you ever saw in your life. He screwed his face back at her. He couldn't help himself.

"Tommy!" his father shouted. "You will not disrespect your mother. I will not have that in this house."

"Are you coming to dinner with me, or not?" His blood was starting to boil. They'd worked it out on the phone. Why'd he have to go and change everything?

"What's so important about going to dinner? Why can't we have dinner here?" his father asked.

"Forget it! You and Mom can eat your lousy dinner here, in this stinking kitchen, but I'm not staying. I hate this place! It's disgusting! How can you live here?" His head was starting to pound.

"Watch your voice, the neighbors will hear," his father shouted.

"I don't care. Let them hear. You and Mom are so concerned about the God damned neighbors. Who the hell cares about them?"

Why couldn't he breathe? Why did he feel like stones were crashing around him?

"They're police officers," his mother replied, but her voice was fading, falling away. "Your father worked with Mr. Bank for thirty years. It's embarrassing."

There was so much noise, roaring in his ears.

Things.

Sounds.

Walls ... closing in.

His father's face was small, tiny in front of him; his voice fading like his mother's.

"You're home five minutes and you're already causing a scene ..."

Tommy stepped back. He had to get away. He clamped his eyes shut. He felt himself lifting ...

***

Cally pulled deep into the driveway and was glad to see Colin out back. Not only would she have someone to hang out with, but he could help buffer the showdown that might come between her and her dad. Colin stood by the garage with an ax in his hand. A freshly chopped pile of wood stood in the iron frame by the back door. The wintry smell of a wood fire caught her nostrils, and she looked up to see smoke coming from the chimney.

"Hey, Colin," she shouted.

"Hey Cally. What brings you home?" he asked, pulling the work-gloves from his hands and dropping them on the top of the wood pile. He held the back door open for her as they went inside. Cally immediately smelled the aroma of rosemary and sage and guessed that a pork roast was most likely in the oven. One of the benefits of having lots of brothers in town—her mom usually cooked enough, knowing chances were good someone would stop by.

"Hello?" Cally shouted as they entered the mud room.

"Cally?" She could hear the smile on her mother's lips and was glad she'd decided to surprise them. Her mother was setting the table, her father, pouring wine. Resting the pile of silverware on top of the tablecloth, she opened her arms wide. "What a nice surprise! We're having pork chops."

"They smell great," Cally exclaimed. "Do you have extra?"

"I certainly do."

Her father blew a kiss. They chit-chatted for a few minutes then settled at the table. An uneasy silence soon descended. Her mother, ordinarily inquisitive, was not asking questions. Her father seemed pensive, his voice strained when he asked, "How was your day, Cally?"

"It was okay. You don't have to pretend you don't know what happened. I know you were involved." Cally had spent the afternoon in the station, arranging her new desk for the next two weeks where she would learn the systems and procedures that made the Two Rivers PD function. She knew it was a duty that all rookies had to endure, but she had not been prepared for the boredom, and she hadn't stopped thinking about the case for a minute.

"Sweetheart, I hope you understand." His father laid his fork on the plate.

"I don't, Dad. I really don't get it at all. We have a chance to catch this guy and instead you're all playing it safe. What if he kills another woman?"

"Would somebody mind filling me in?" Colin asked.

"I was taken off the case today, Colin. Starting today, I am on desk duty, and I have an around the clock guard, too. There's probably somebody parked out front right now."

Her mother gasped. She looked at her husband. "You didn't tell me that, Clyde." She turned to Cally. "Why do you have a guard?" Her voice trembled.

"It's just a precaution, Judith."

"I thought you promised they wouldn't use her in any operations," the panic rising in her mother's voice.

"They're not, mom. I have a guard because the killer sent a letter and now everyone wants to put me in a safe house. Right, Dad?"

"Cally, please don't scare your mother."

"What letter?" Colin and Judith chirped at once.

"Don't panic, Judith. It's just a little more complicated than I explained this afternoon. There was a letter. That's why they wanted to use Cally in the first place."

"What letter? From the killer? What are you talking about?" her mother rat tatted." Why does she need a guard?"

Her dad let out a long sigh and told them what he could about the letter. Judith went pale.

"Grainer called me earlier today," her dad said, turning to Cally. "He told me about the letter and the possibility of using you in the sting. Said he wouldn't go ahead unless I agreed to it. I talked to your mother, not telling her every detail, and we thought it sounded too dangerous."

"Jeez. All this happened today? How'd I miss it?" Colin laughed. Cally flashed him a hard look. How could he joke about it?

"Your father and I would never agree to that!" Her mother shook her head as though the idea was completely preposterous.

Cally shook her head in exasperation. A golden opportunity to catch a horrible killer lost because her parents wouldn't give permission? *That* was preposterous. Would she never escape the coddling? Would she forever be the little daughter who needed watching?

"We love you too much," her mother added, her voice, soft and sweet. The voice Cally could always count on. Honest, sincere—full of all the good things in life. She just didn't want to hear it now. It only made things harder. She took a deep breath, feeling a torrent of emotions suddenly wash over her ... anger, disappointment, guilt ... she feared she might start crying. She placed her hands over her face, lowered her head to hide her feelings. Was she being unfair? Her parents were just trying to keep her safe—what any mom or dad would do.

"Oh Cally, dear," her mom said. After a moment she added, "Maybe we made the wrong decision, Clyde."

"I told you she'd take it hard," he snapped.

"Don't blame me!" she cried. "You agreed with me!"

Her parents were arguing. Impossible. They never argued.

"It's okay," Cally said. She raised her head and smiled at each of them, not wanting to contribute to her mom's distress. "Like Dad said, they'll be more opportunities."

"I don't understand, Cally," her mom said quietly. "Why would you want to do something like that?"

"It's not a matter of wanting, Mom. It's about being involved in something really important. I wanted to stay to the end. To be there when they catch him. To be *a part* of catching him."

Her mother sighed. "And what if you got killed in the process?"

"Then I'd go down doing something I love."

"Go Cal!" Colin raised his glass and laughed.

Cally looked at him and his corny expression made her laugh. Then her mom laughed and her dad too. Hopefully Jack and the team would find this guy in the next day or two. There was nothing more that she could do. She wrapped her hand around the stem of the glass and raised it. "Cheers! To my new desk job!"

Her mom smiled and toasted, "*Salut!* Promise me you won't take crazy chances, and I promise I won't interfere again. *Ca va?*"

Clyde Bank raised his glass to hers. He pursed his lips and blew a kiss toward his wife.

"*Ca va!*" they said in unison.

It goes. It would be okay. Cally had an inkling they were starting to get the message. She wasn't backing down. Come hell or high water, she was in this profession for good.

***

Luther looked around the room, at the dingy blue curtains, the old stove, at the man staring at him, crouched in fighting position. The fist, the scowl, the vein bulging at the neck. Luther smelled the fetid odor, breathed in the stink. He hated this man; he knew that. The man balled his fist and threw a punch, but Luther grabbed his arm and twisted.

"What the hell?" the man shouted and wriggled to free himself. But Luther had him tight.

"Tommy!" the ugly woman screamed.

"Shut up!" Luther shouted back. Why was she calling him Tommy? He was Luther. Luther Minx. He twisted the arm some more, just to watch the man squirm.

"Tommy, let go of your father," she shrieked.

"My name is not Tommy," Luther whispered, but the voice was unfamiliar to his own ears.

"Stop that!" she shouted, the panic rising in her voice. "You're hurting your father."

Your father, your father ... the words echoed in his head, bounced off his temples, pulled at his brain. This man in his tightening grasp, his eyes panicked and hateful. How he despised this man and woman. Their faces forced images he did not want to see, thoughts he could not understand, and an unfathomable reality he could not face.

Chapter 33

It was a little past nine o'clock when Martin told Jack he was going home to say good night to his kids for just the second time in three weeks. "They're starting to think I don't live there anymore. I promised I'd tuck them in." He looked at his watch. "Shoot. I gotta' go." Martin grabbed his coat and cell phone and left the room, leaving Charles and Jack alone at the conference table in the command center.

"You're sure quiet tonight," Bank said after he left. "What's on your mind?"

"Just thinking."

"What about?"

Jack looked up from the call-in stack. They had several good leads, evidence, a profile, but it was all a jumble in front of him. The situation with Cally was making it impossible. He couldn't get her off his mind. Her words kept coming back, *this is about catching a killer....*

Had he put personal feelings in front of common sense? Had he made the wrong decision? He released a loud, long sigh. "I'm starting to think your sister was right. We had a chance to catch him." Jack leaned back in his chair and stared at the drop ceiling above him. The tiled sheets were patterned with thousands of small specks. He looked at them like grains of sand, so many, each like the other. Would it be possible to look away and pick the same one a second time? He thought not. No distinguishing characteristics. They blended in, just like their killer. "He'll kill again, probably tomorrow night. We should have at least considered a sting operation to take him out." Jack shook his head at his own stupidity. "He told us he wanted Cally. It was the perfect opportunity. We could have rigged her to the gills. She would never have been out of sight. She would never have been in danger. It would have been easy."

"Sure," Charles replied. "You say that now."

Bank was right. It was easy to say now, now that the decision was final. He had to remember the pit in his stomach while he'd awaited the chief's decision. "We have to catch him," he mumbled. It was the only answer. The only solution.

Jack stood and went to the dry erase board. He looked at the random words on the board. The handwriting was his, but the words meant nothing now, the link that pulled them together lost for the moment in the shadows of his mind. He grabbed the eraser and wiped them away. "What've we got? What's still hanging?" It was a rhetorical question. Jack was already writing on the board. He wrote the number one and put the word 'Gripe' next to it. "He's got a gripe against the police force. What did Martin come up with today?"

"He checked ex-cops and academy drop-outs. He's still got some guys to visit tomorrow."

Jack nodded and turned back to the board, writing a number two and wrote the word 'Connection' next to it. "There's a connection to the utility authority. Let's cross-reference Jaworski's list to Martin's list. See if there's any familial connection. If any of those ex-cops bumped down to Public Works, we go out right now. What else?"

"DNA."

"We've got DNA, but without a suspect it's not doing us any good. What else do we have to get us there?"

"The profile?"

Jack wrote profile on the board. Beside the word he wrote, twenty to forty, male, Caucasian, educated with a high school degree or higher, local. He stepped back and studied the board. Something's here. It's got to be here. He came back and sat. He tapped his knuckles against the tabletop. "Show me Martin's list."

Bank handed the list. "Ex-cops and ex-recruits."

"I know two of these guys," Jack said. "No way. This third guy, Johnson, I don't know him." He read the next seven names—guys who'd never made it out of the academy. "We got addresses?"

Bank nodded. "And I know this one, Doone."

"What's he like?"

"Little strange. He's our neighbor."

"Can you see him doing something like this?"

"No. But nobody suspected Ted Bundy, either."

"Grab your coat. We get to all of them tonight."

Chapter 34

Dim light shone from the tall window panels on either side of the front door. Bank pressed his face against the glass, his hand cupped over his forehead. "Looks like they're home," he said.

Jack rang the bell a second time and heard the chimes. He opened the storm door and banged on the main door with the heel of his hand. Two cars in the driveway, lights on, it appeared that someone was home. Still, no one came.

He was about to go around back when a tall man stuck his face up against the side panel. He wore jeans and a plain black tee shirt with a white napkin tucked into the neck. When he saw them, he took a step back, hesitated then pulled the napkin from his neck. He disappeared from behind the glass. Jack exchanged a quick glance with Bank, but within a moment, the door opened. "Can I help you?" he asked.

"Detective Jack Brant, Two Rivers police," Jack held up his badge for him to see. "May we come in?"

"What's this about?" He placed one hand on the doorknob and the other on the frame blocking the entry.

"How you doing, Tommy? It's Charles Bank. We just want to ask some questions. Can we come in?"

Tommy Doone's eyes went from Bank to Jack. He seemed confused, disoriented, and Jack wondered why. Had he been sleeping?

Doone stepped back and let them enter. "My parents aren't home. You're looking for my dad I assume?"

"Actually, it's you we want to talk to." Jack watched him carefully, looking for nerves—a tick, a drop of the eyes, something. But Tommy showed nothing. If anything, he looked tired, lethargic, a bit dazed.

He let them into the front foyer and Jack looked around. The house was neat but shabby. "Can we sit?" he asked, looking toward the living room.

"I was just eating. Is this going to take long?"

"Shouldn't." Jack reconsidered Doone's demeanor. Maybe it was annoyance, not fatigue, that he had seen. He smelled the onions and garlic.

Doone scowled. "Alright, we'll sit in here." He went to the living room. He sat in a woolly orange plaid chair with faded arm rests. "What's going on?" His hands fidgeted with the threads.

"We're looking into some old files," Jack said, taking a seat on the couch. Bank sat at the opposite end. "You left the academy three years ago. Why?"

"Why? You kicked me out. I flunked out." His eyes darted to Bank and back again.

"I know that part. What I don't know is why you flunked out. I checked your record. You were a straight A student all the way through high school and your two years at Brookdale, but you scored fifties on the first two Academy written tests. That doesn't make sense to me."

Doone leaned back in the chair and crossed his hands more comfortably at his waist. His knee stopped bouncing. "Want the truth? I didn't want to be there. The old man wanted it, not me. It was easier to go and flunk out than fight him on the idea, you know?"

"You mean you didn't want to disappoint him by saying no?" Bank asked.

"It was easier than arguing about it. Got it out of the way once and for all. Don't tell me you're looking for recruits. I'm not interested." He looked around the room. "And do me a favor, don't mention it to my father. He's finally given up hope that I'm going to become a cop."

"We're not looking for recruits, especially ones that don't want to be there." Jack was feeling the first pangs of disappointment. The department had done exactly what Doone had wanted them to do—expel him. He certainly didn't bear a grudge about it. He asked Doone several more questions. Learned he was unemployed but looking, and he collected contact information from two previous employers. He would check him out thoroughly, but he had a feeling this lead was going nowhere.

Jack looked at his watch. They'd come to Doone's house directly from the station. They still had seven recruits to go, and Jack was hoping to get to all of them tonight.

"Thanks for the information, Tommy." Jack stood. "Mind if we take a look around?"

"Go ahead. You mind telling me why you're really here? I know who you are, Detective. I know you're working the big case."

"If you're reading the news coverage, you know that the killer holds some gripe against the police force. We're not leaving any stones unturned."

"Aah." Doone nodded his head slowly. "Smart. You thought I was pissed off about getting canned." He laughed. Holding his arm out in a gracious gesture he said, "Help yourselves. Look around all you want."

Jack signaled Bank to check upstairs. He went toward the back of the house. In the kitchen he saw Doone's half-eaten dinner, spaghetti and meatballs. He saw nothing out of order and returned to the living room. "You'll be back to your dinner in five minutes. Looks delicious. You cooked it?"

Doone scratched his head. He hesitated, looked around then said, "No. my mom."

"And you said they went where?"

"I don't know where they went. Out shopping, I guess." He shrugged. Confusion creased his brow.

His behavior seemed a little odd, a little out of sorts. Was it possible he was on drugs? Jack made a mental note of the behavior as he poked his head in the laundry room—small basket of whites on top of the dryer. Nothing unusual.

He went through to the dining room. The wallpaper was a faded rose pattern; the large dark table and sidebar reminded him of his grandma's. Jack continued on and found himself back in the center foyer. The central staircase rose above him, a door, which he assumed was the basement, was straight ahead. He turned the knob. "Locked?"

"That's the basement—my dad's work area. He doesn't like anyone going down there, especially my mom. She's got a cleaning fetish."

"Moves his stuff around?"

"Throws it away more like it."

"Do you have the key?"

"Afraid not. He hides it somewhere."

Common enough, Jack thought. Nothing was jumping out at him. Doone was strange but he didn't seem nervous or jumpy. Bank appeared at the upper landing. By the facile manner he bounced down the stairs, Jack could see he'd found nothing either.

"We finished?" Jack asked him.

"Appears so."

Jack turned to Doone, feeling a slight apprehension. "Couple more questions, just for our records ... where were you this past Thursday evening?"

"I was home. I was right here."

"All night? Did you go out anywhere during the course of the evening?"

"No, I was right here all night."

"Was anybody with you?"

"Yeah, my parents were here. They don't go out much."

"Alright." He made a mental note to check it out, return when Frank and Mrs. Doone were home. "Thanks for your time, Tommy. Sorry to disrupt your dinner."

"Tell your mom and dad I said hi," Bank added.

"Sure," Tommy replied. "Will do."

His eyes were getting that faraway look again. He was on something, Jack decided. The guy was strange, no doubt about that. For now, he would stay on the list.

Chapter 35

Is it just me, Cally wondered, or does the air seem charged with energy today? As she walked the hallway, headed to her post in the squad room, uniforms zipped past her, radios crackled, telephones rang. Municipal staff chattered loudly from behind their computers, their high-pitched voices bouncing out to the hallway.

What was all the buzz about? Had word of Musser leaked out? She thought of her conversation with Jack last night. After she'd returned home from the restaurant, she'd called him to tell him about Musser. He was glad to hear she'd roped him and told her he'd take it up with Grainer in the morning. She'd ended the conversation brusquely.

She entered the squad room. At the far end, Juan stuffed colored paper into cubby-holed mailboxes. The back area of the room was partitioned off as an administration area—where she'd settled her desk yesterday. Juan looked up and saw her.

"Yo babe!" He came up and gave her a healthy pat on the back. "Wa' happened, man? I hear you're joining me here."

"I started yesterday. I'm off the case. A target, supposedly."

"I know. I heard. You can keep me company." He smiled supportively.

Cally felt her spirits rise. They'd had so much fun in the academy. At least he'd be here to help pass the boring hours. The room was large with six desks in the center, used for filing reports at shift's end and for inside officers. She and Juan would be seated behind a counter-style desk, behind which were the mailboxes, time clocks, various forms and reports, and dispatch just beyond. They would act as the intermediaries between the cops, dispatch, and private citizens who were admitted back. At the moment, the room was quiet, no private Joes filing complaints. Cally glanced at the clock. Still ten minutes before the shift officially began

"I'm going for a cup of coffee, Juan. Want to join me?"

"No thanks, already had mine."

She headed to the cafeteria, passing the chief's office on the way. Through the open blinds, she saw the chief behind his desk. Musser sat facing him with his commanding officer in the seat beside him. Jack leaned against the window ledge, just like that first morning after Alexis Greene's murder. She saw Musser place his badge on the chief's desk and reach around his belt for his cuffs. His eyes were dark and angry, his expression, grim. A stab of pity found its way under her skin. Why? He'd jeopardized the investigation, spread nasty rumors. Still, she couldn't help but feel a little bad for him.

In the cafeteria, a cop Cally had never met sat at a table reading the newspaper. Cally said hello and he introduced himself, mentioned he was a good friend of Charles. At the coffee carafes, she poured extra dark liquid into a Styrofoam cup. By the bitter smell, she knew it would be too strong. She emptied half in the sink and filled the second half with milk. She dumped two sugar packets and stirred, her mind a jumble of preoccupation. She walked to the window and looked out. Sun glinted off the glass. The pane was cold as she laid her hand against it. The weatherman had called for temperatures reaching no higher than twenty-eight degrees.

The cop at the table folded his newspaper. It crinkled loudly as he put it back in order. He left it on the counter for the next person to read and exited the room. She thought of the meeting taking place in the chief's office not a hundred feet away. She thought of the command center, packed with colleagues she'd come to think of as friends. They both made her feel lonely. She thought of Jack, of their awkward phone conversation last night, how lost they'd both been for words.

"Cally?"

She jumped at the familiar voice. Her heart broke into a gallop at the realization that he was right there, beside her.

"Penny for your thoughts," he said.

She turned to look at him and drank in every detail: his clear jade eyes, his messy boy hair, the broad shoulders she'd wrapped her arms around when they'd kissed.

"How are you?" he asked.

"Fine. You?"

"Fine." He shifted his feet. "How's admin?"

"Fine."

"Boring?"

"Yes. I've got to go." She stepped past him, shut her eyes when she felt his hand close around her arm.

"Can we grab a quick bite after your shift?

"No."

"It's Thursday. I'm worried about you."

Oh, those words. Would she never be free of them? "I'm well protected, remember?"

"I hope so."

He sounded sincere, and she straightened her back, pushing out those feelings that would only interfere with everything she'd worked so hard to achieve. She wanted to be with him, yes. But not as the namby-pamby woman he wanted her to be. She opened her mouth to explain, but why should she? How could she? If it needed explanation, then it was already lost.

"I have to go," she said.

He threw up his hands in frustration. "I couldn't let you do it—to be placed in danger like that. Don't you understand?"

"I do understand. That's the problem." She walked toward the door. When she reached the threshold, she turned. "What happened to Musser?"

"He's suspended. There'll be an investigation."

"And Charles's tape?"

"Didn't need it, thanks to you."

Cally smiled tightly. "Good." At least that much was good.

***

Jack watched her leave, felt her open a big, empty hole between them. What had he done wrong? How had he lost her? He groaned, realizing how much this was affecting him.

Just three weeks ago, he'd been fighting a tie with Katrina and bored with the job. He was a content bachelor and even thought of leaving the PD for real estate full time, and now ... hell, it had all changed. He sure wasn't fighting getting tied down. Work had never been more invigorating, in terms of the routine of it. And it was all because of Cally. She'd managed to change everything.

Now he wondered if he'd done right by her. Should he have said yes, let her participate in the sting?

No way.

Once this was over, once the killer was caught, he'd find a way to make it up to her. He'd find a way to make her understand. But for now, he needed to keep her safe. That had to be his priority. He clapped his hands together. Just keep her safe.

Fifteen people were waiting when he entered the conference room. He laid out the plan. They would operate on two plains: protecting the target and catching the killer.

When he finished, he still stood before them. He had not taken a seat. He crossed his arms in front, knowing that success was the only option.

"This killer is predictable. The killer is methodical. This killer likes Thursdays. It will all come down tonight."

Chapter 36

Four-thirty. Cally straightened the papers at her desk and tapped her fingers on the Formica. She'd finished the work laid out for her and had cleaned out three junk drawers full of old pens, dried out glue sticks, and ancient forms from years back. How would she ever keep busy for the next twenty-nine days?

Everyone in the station had been on pins and needles all day. A dozen cops had stopped in the squad room, all aware that she was the target, all with advice or support. They said things like, "don't worry," "he's dead," "we'll get him." Some made jokes. Colin was one of them, of course. Charles and Chris played it straight and serious, warning her to be careful.

Martin had stopped upstairs, too. Cally wondered if Jack sent him. She didn't ask. He told her that they'd intensified her watch for the upcoming night. Rather than being a respectable distance away in the parking lot, Officer Ron Clayton would follow her body-guard style. When she went in the house, he'd stay by the door. He'd monitor the windows and report in regularly.

At midnight, there would be a shift change. Cally was mortified.

Around two-thirty, Clyde came in and shot the breeze. It was funny that everyone was so concerned. He asked her what she was doing later and tried to convince her to sleep at their parents' house.

"I'll consider it," she told him, knowing she wouldn't.

Paige called around three o'clock. "Hi Cal," she began. She reminded Cally that she was working late. After some stalling, she came out with the real reason for her call: she was "creeped out" and didn't want to stay in the apartment until the killer was caught. She implored Cally to sleep at her parents' house.

"I probably will," Cally lied, wondering if they were tag-teaming her.

"Promise?" Paige pleaded.

"Don't worry about me," Cally said and hung up. Honestly! What did these people think? That the killer was going to sneak through her window with a cop posted outside?

Still, the day made her realize how lucky she was. How lucky she was to have such a great family, how lucky she was to have such a great job, great co-workers, how little she had to complain about.

She thought back to the police banquet—standing on the stage—how happy she'd been just to receive her badge. Where had that simple happiness gone? She wanted it again—that place of contentment before this killer had torn apart their city, and before she'd ever met Jack.

She started to feel sad again and thought, *Forget him! He wants to put you in a box. He'd be terrible for you!* She knew it in her mind, and yet her heart refused to get in line. She thought of him falling asleep on her couch, sitting at the counter in her kitchen, kissing her in the hallway. How long will it take? she wondered. When would she start to feel like her old self again?

"Five o'clock, Babe. You want to go for a drink?" Juan was standing beside her desk. She hadn't even noticed.

It sounded like a good idea until Cally considered the logistics. She pictured Ron Clayton standing in the corner of the bar, watching every sip. "No thanks, I'm going to watch a couple movies and stay in. To tell you the truth, I just want tonight to be over."

"I don't blame you. You want me to come over? Keep you company?"

"No, thanks, Juan. I'm fine. Everybody is being so nice."

When they passed the command center, Cally felt her heart wrench. She thought of stopping in. She wanted to see Jack. She wanted to see everybody for that matter. She could poke her head in, wish them good luck.

An invisible string pulled her away.

In the parking lot, she said good-bye to Juan. She saw Ron sitting behind the wheel of his car, and she knew he'd just come on at four. She waved weakly. Just the two of them until midnight—until the shift change.

***

The paper trail kept disappearing, and yet Jack knew the tracks had been laid. Mindlessly. he drummed his knuckles on the table. Martin, Tulio, and Bank all looked up from their work.

"What's eating you?" Tulio asked.

Jack looked across the table. The command center was a mess of papers, coffee cups, coats, jackets. It seemed the moment Cally left, the place went to pot.

"We've got it right," he said. "I can feel it. Everything's telling us we're on the right track but it's just not taking us there."

"I know." Tulio sighed.

"This asshole has a grudge against the Two Rivers police force. Why? It's somewhere—in the arrest records, or in the personnel files somewhere."

"I agree, but we've been through both with a fine-tooth comb. You visited them all last night, didn't you?"

Jack nodded. Not a single one had given them that ledge to grab hold of. And none had any connection to public works—not on paper, anyway. It gave him a thought, and he picked up the phone and called Jaworski on his personal line. "Jaworski, it's Jack Brant."

"Any luck?" Jaworski asked.

"No. Listen, I've got some names for you, couple ex-cops and some academy dropouts. I'm going to fax the list. Take a look. Let me know if any are familiar. If they have a brother, a cousin, a friend, any connection at all to public works. If they've even stepped through your doors, I want to know."

"You got it."

Jack sent the fax number and five minutes later Jack's phone rang.

"I'm looking over the list," Jaworski said. "I know some of these names from around town. We've got three sons, they all played sports in high school. My middle son was the quarterback, did you know that?"

"I didn't know that." Jack tapped his fingers on the table. "Any connections?" Jack held his breath; he needed a break; one little, stinking break.

"Not a connection exactly." There was hesitation in Jaworski's voice.

"What then?"

"I'm friends with Frank Doone. You know him?"

The hair on the back of his neck pricked and Jack said, "I know him. What about him?"

"Well, like I said, we're friends. We hire per diem workers when we've got jobs that need extra labor. You know, like temporary jobs that we can't staff."

"I'm following you, go on."

"I've used Frank over the years. It's completely legit. If he had a day off, he'd come over and work with us."

Jack's heart raced. "Does he have a uniform?"

"Yeah—I gave him a jacket, too."

The words dropped like rocks.

It was coming fast and it didn't make sense. Frank Doone, Frank Doone. He was way older than the profile, but the voodoo science had let him down before. He thought of his visit last night—the locked basement door—how Tommy Doone had said he and his mother were not allowed down there. How Frank kept the key hidden from them both.

"And Jack?" Jaworski cleared his throat. "One more thing ... about eight, nine years ago, I remember Frank bought one of our auctioned vehicles. A Ford F150, decal still on the door. But when we pass ownership, they sign a form that they'll remove the seal before it's driven. I assume he did."

"And maybe he didn't."

Jack came out of his seat. All three men turned. He thanked Jaworski and hung up. "Bank, you're coming with me. Martin, follow in your car."

"Where're we going?" they asked in unison.

"We're checking out Frank Doone."

"Frank Doone?" Bank's jaw dropped

Chapter 37

Luther collapsed on the couch. His arms pulsed with exhaustion. For chintzy walls they sure came down hard. He looked at the white dust all over the carpet, on the couch, on his arms. He reached his hand to his hair and felt the chalky substance in it.

He put his head back and observed his work. It would suffice. He'd covered his tracks. That closet was so full of crap, she'd never notice. He'd pulled her trash bag of junk up tight against the hole so that it was well concealed. Even if she opened the closet, she wouldn't notice. He was safe.

He thought back to the two times he'd been in her apartment … rather … Tommy had been in the apartment. Tommy, the loser. Tommy, the appeaser. Tommy, the wimp who didn't have the balls to ask Cally Bank on a date, and the guy whose invitation she would never accept, anyway.

"You are a loser. You're never coming back," he whispered in the air. Tommy Doone was finished. Gone. No more. But Tommy could come in handy. He'd certainly gained Cally's trust. Now he would take Tommy's lie and multiply it, gain more trust till he had her wrapped around his little finger.

Luther pinned his thoughts on the brilliant blue charmeuse he'd just completed. He visualized Cally Bank in it. Finally, she could be of use to him. She would wear his gown; she would be immortalized in it forever. His *piece de resistance.*

He closed his eyes and imagined. He imagined tonight. He imagined tomorrow. And he waited. Waited to hear the key in the lock, waited to hear the door shut behind her.

***

It was the tail end of dusk. A sliver of red sun set behind the house as Jack pulled up to the curb. A massive maple loomed over the roof, its shadow casting an ominous pall over the old house. Despite the Chevy in the driveway, the place looked hollow, abandoned. No hunch had ever felt so right.

The click of the car door echoed over the empty street as Jack eased it shut. Charles Bank came up behind him and stood at the ready. They reached the front door, and Jack banged. Crackling maple branches answered him back. Cold air blew over his cheeks. No response. Jack banged again.

"Stay here," he said to Bank. "I'm going around back." He went to the back door and peered through the window. The dinner plate was still on the table, exactly as it had been last night, down to the food. The pot of sauce was still on the stove. Everything was just as they'd left it almost twenty-four hours ago.

A chill ran up his spine. It wasn't right. The scene was definitely not right. He banged on the door. He wasn't surprised when no one answered. The place was an empty shell. He could feel it. His heartbeat accelerated. He wanted to break down the door.

They had him.

He knew it. God damn, he needed to get in there now. He broke into a trot and went back out front. Martin's cruiser pulled up behind his.

"Call the chief," Jack yelled. "We need a warrant now!"

Bank came up behind him. Clyde, Sr. and Judith Bank came out of their house and stood on their front porch. Judith was holding Clyde's arm with a look of sheer panic on her face.

"Go tell your parents everything's cool. Your mom looks ready to faint." Bank hustled off and Jack shouted behind him, "Tell her Cally's fine." His breath hitched as he said it.

Jack went back to his car and shut off the flashers. He motioned to Martin to do the same. In their haste to arrive, they'd kept them on. Now it was time to turn it down, keep things on the QT for as long as possible. The shit would hit the fan soon enough.

***

Cally opened the car door and put her foot on the pavement. She was painfully aware of Ron pulling in right next to her. He reminded her of an old-fashioned beat cop from the 1940s. She stood up and smiled at him. He got out of his car and gave her a quick nod.

"I hear you're my bodyguard," she said lightly.

"That's right." His reply was dry and professional. "I'll be outside until midnight. My replacement will take over from there."

"You really don't have to do this. I'm sure I'll be fine. Why don't you relax in your car?"

"Following orders."

She could see there'd be no convincing him. "I plan on having a nice, quiet evening, watch a couple movies, stay in. It'll be boring for you."

"Go on. Don't worry about me." He shooed her off, and she decided she didn't care. If he wanted to sit outside her door all night, let him.

She entered her apartment and hung her police jacket in the coat closet and went into the bedroom. Releasing the heavy buckle of her uniform belt, she decided she liked the feel of it, the big heavy belt, laden with night stick, flashlight, cuffs, and of course, her gun. Today hadn't been so bad. She'd had fun, plenty of visitors, and if she were to be completely honest with herself, she'd learned a lot. It made her anxious to get out on the street in one month, find out what being a patrolman felt like. She hung her belt in the armoire and changed into her favorite sweats and hoodie.

Next door, she heard Tommy's shower turn on. The walls are so thin, she thought. She debated inviting him over to watch one of the movies with her. Maybe, she decided, but first she'd eat.

She fixed herself a salad with a hard-boiled egg, smoked Gouda cheese, and vinaigrette dressing. Deciding to treat herself, she popped Pillsbury crescent rolls in the toaster oven.

When the timer beeped, she looked through the oven window at the golden biscuits connected together on the cookie tray. She slid them onto a plate and sat down at the table with the salad, the biscuits, and a big wad of butter.

When she finished her third biscuit, she leaned back, full in the belly, heavy in the heart. The couch looked mighty inviting. She wanted to lose herself in it, pick out some good movies on Amazon Prime and just chill out. She was sauntering to the sofa when the doorbell rang.

She groaned, assuming it was her buddy, Ron. What did he want? She peeked out the peep hole, and there he was. When she opened, she was surprised to see Tommy beside him with a bottle of wine in his hand.

"Hey, Cally." Tommy flicked his thumb toward Ron. "Friend of yours?"

Ron darted his eyes from Tommy to Cally. He stood like a barricade between Tommy and the door. "You expecting him?" he asked Cally.

"It's okay. He's my neighbor."

Ron's brows furrowed in concern.

"Don't worry, he's a friend, but thank you." Cally pulled Tommy in and closed the door.

"What's going on?" he asked.

"Don't ask. I have a bodyguard."

"A bodyguard, why?"

"Never mind." She looked at the white wine bottle in his hand. "What've you got there?"

"Pinot Grigio. Thought if you weren't doing anything you might want to have a glass with me." He pouted. "Bad day."

Cally invited him into the kitchen where she took a corkscrew from the drawer. Actually, listening to someone else's problems might just take her mind off her own. Tommy handed her the bottle, and she pulled the cork. "What happened?"

Tommy leaned against the counter with his chin in his palm. "My partner and I had an argument. I'm afraid we may be through." He looked so sad, and Cally felt terrible for him.

"I'm so sorry, Tommy. How long were you a couple?"

He shook his head forlornly. "Two years."

Cally thought of Jack. She'd known him less than one month and the loss still hurt. "Two years," she said. "That's a long time. Poor you. Hang in there." She patted him on the arm. She was about to pour the wine, when she realized she really was not in the mood for alcohol. Her stomach was still full, and she was a little tired, too. What she really wanted was a hot cup of tea.

"I know how it hurts." She said sympathetically. "And I'd like to have a glass of wine with you, but I'm really more in the mood for tea."

"Tea?" He tapped his finger on his chin. "You know, a cup of tea sounds good. Maybe I'll have one instead."

"Are you sure? I've already popped the wine. And you've had a rough day."

"And wine might make me more morose than I already am. No. Tea sounds great. A nice, soothing, cup of tea."

Cally stuck the cork back in the bottle and put a kettle of hot water on the stove. She took two tea bags from the pottery dish on the counter.

"You sound like you were just speaking from experience," he said.

"When?"

"When you said you know how it hurts."

Cally laughed. "Right. Recent experience, my own love life, or lack thereof, I should say."

"Don't tell me you've been dumped."

"Kind of."

"Any guy who would break up with you is crazy." He swatted his hand and smiled warmly.

She liked having him as a friend; she felt better already.

"He's not worthy of you," he added.

"He doesn't understand me," Cally confided.

"Oh no? Why?"

Cally poured the hot water and watched the steam billow. She hooked both cups in her fingers and grabbed the milk with her other hand. "Grab the sugar?" she shouted as she walked into the living room. After placing the cups on the coffee table, she sat on the couch. Tommy sat in the armchair behind the other cup.

Cally sighed. Tommy was the perfect confidant: objective, uninvolved, gay. "I've been working on the investigation," she began.

"The Couturier case?"

"Yeah. But we don't call it that. The newspapers picked up on that Couturier garbage. He shouldn't be glorified."

"What do you guys call him?"

"We don't call him anything. He's a sick, horrible person who doesn't deserve a name at all."

"Oh."

Cally thought he looked disappointed, caught up in the sensationalism, no doubt, just like everybody else. Everyone wanted to hype it to the max.

"Anyway, about the case," he asked. "What does it have to do with your boyfriend understanding you?"

Cally put her feet up on the coffee table. She took a sip of tea. Did she really want to talk with Tommy about Jack?

"Never mind," she said. "It's complicated." And personal. "Let's find a movie and we can both forget our troubles.

She turned on the TV and scrolled thru the Amazon Prime app. They settled on a movie called *Palm Springs*, a rom com from 2020, because it got 5 stars.

Cally went to the slider and closed the vertical blinds. She pulled the shade on the other window. She used the remote to press the play button then went into the kitchen to make a quick bag of popcorn.

While she waited the three and a half minutes, she heard the previews playing in the living room. When the sound of popping subsided, she opened the microwave, split the inflated pouch, and dumped the popcorn into a bowl. She returned to the living room and placed the large glass bowl on the coffee table between her cup and Tommy's. The opening credits were playing. Images of a desert and a pool appeared on the screen. Cally took another sip of tea and settled deep into the couch. "I hope we like this movie. You never know if these reviews are right or wrong."

Tommy put his feet up on the coffee table. "I'm sure it's going to be wonderful," he said, settling comfortably into the chair.

Chapter 38

Jack circled the house again, peering in windows, pacing through the minutes. Neighbors kept a respectable distance. The Banks had gone back inside. It was as though the whole block waited behind closed doors for the warrant to arrive.

He'd made some calls about Frank Doone—a guy who had put in his time, worked his shifts, but never aspired to more. The few times Jack had encountered him in the field he'd seemed cooperative, albeit surly. He thought of Tommy Doone's aversion to becoming a cop. What had caused it? Had something been festering inside his dad for years?

The image of Tommy's half-eaten dinner came to mind. He'd said he was hungry, that he wanted to eat. What had turned his appetite? Who had turned his appetite? Jack looked at his watch. It had been over half an hour since Martin made the call to the chief. Jack wondered which judge was on call. They all lived in town; any one of them would act quickly upon this. It would be any minute.

He reached for his cell and called Grainer.

"I'm getting the warrant," Grainer assured him. "But I'm stumped. I've known Doone thirty years, Jack. I can't picture this."

Jack felt his stomach tighten. Was he chasing the wrong guy? Was he so anxious to catch the killer his mind had run rampant? Yes, the man filled in at public works; yes, he had a locked basement, yes, he bought a truck nine years ago. So what?

He sucked in cold air. He looked up at the old house in the growing darkness. He felt it sure in his bones. This was the place. Frank Doone was their man. And where was he? He was not at home, and it was Thursday night. "Just hurry it up, okay chief? Push it for me."

"What do you think, I'm sitting on my hands?" Grainer hung up.

Jack walked to his car, to the trunk, and got his crowbar. He strode to Bank and Martin. "Vince, I need you to run a DMV search on Doone and his wife. Get the plate numbers on any vehicles he owns. Put an APB out for them," he barked. "Bank, come with me. Let's figure out how we're going in."

Bank looked at the bar in his hand. "You're not going in without the warrant, are you?"

"Hell no. I want this guy behind bars."

They went around to the back door and checked the simple knob lock. The door would be easy to jimmy open. Jack looked through the window again and saw the plate of half-eaten spaghetti. He couldn't wait to get in. It just wasn't right. He walked east and saw a basement window tucked behind some bushes. He squeezed through. The ground below his shoes was hard; prickles scratched his hand. He bent low and peered in. He couldn't make out a thing. The windows were smudged with a thick down dirt. With the heel of his hand, he wiped the dirt, leaving a smudged circle to peer through, but the inside, it appeared, was covered with something—plastic, Jack surmised. He stood up and came out from the bushes. He walked further east, to the far corner of the house, and turned the corner. There had to be another window.

He saw two more on the south side of the house, tucked behind a row of overgrown azalea bushes. He was considering going through when Vince called his name. Jack circled back to the front where Vince raised thumbs up.

Excellent! "We're going in," Jack shouted, knowing a miscommunication at this point could cause a dismissal. Vince nodded confirmation.

At the back door, Jack jimmied the crowbar. The door popped in one crank. After the initial jolt, it glided slowly open, creaking loudly, releasing embers of suspicion into the cold night air. Jack looked at Bank as his hand reached instinctively to his belt. His first step bounced off the vacant walls of the house. Before he took another, he smelled the pungent odor. His heart skipped a beat.

Behind him Bank said, "Uh oh"

"The basement," Jack replied. "Gotta' be the basement."

The crowbar, warm beneath his clenched hand, grew heavy. He raised it as he walked toward the basement door, his anger rising with it. He and Bank had been here last night. They'd sat in seats and talked like gentlemen. What would they find?

The smell intensified when they reached the door. Jack thought of the letter, how the killer had called them monkeys. Had he loathed them all these years? Working beside them, living next door to a house full of cops? Questions swirled like leaves in a storm as he stood at the door, crowbar heavy in his hand.

He jammed the bar in the frame and yanked; the door cracked beneath his hands. He kicked and it flew open, hitting the back wall, banging, but the sound was just background noise. He barely heard it. What he saw took his senses away—no smell, no sound, no touch, just a picture. Frank Doone and his wife, piled on the stairs with marks around their necks. He stared at it until it registered. Until the film started rolling and the sound came back. Until he realized he'd fingered the wrong guy.

***

Luther watched Cally fade away. Just like Tommy's mom every night when she took those pills. Man, they worked great. He leaned forward and inspected her empty teacup. Looking at his, he shuddered. He hated tea. Drinking it had been harder than cutting that hole in the wall.

But it had been worth it. For every sip he took, she took one, too. She drained it all. And now she was sleeping like a baby. A regular Sleeping Beauty. Soon she would be his in the deep dark forest. Or was that Snow White? He could never keep those fairy tale princesses straight. He stood up and went to her. He poked her in the stomach, and she didn't move. He lifted her arm and let it drop. She didn't budge. She was out. Out like a light.

"Not worthy of a name, huh?" We'd see about that. He glanced at the clock on the TV. It was nearly nine o'clock. The movie droned on in the background. He hadn't registered a moment of it. And what had she meant, too "complicated'? Did she think he wouldn't be able to follow her simple boyfriend problem? Did she think he was stupid?

He looked down on her, sleeping, all grogged up, out of it just like Tommy's mother. He hated them all. The father, the mother, the Banks, and yes, even Cally. All those years Tommy had wasted dreaming about her.

Now she would do something for him.

He looked down at her. Her lips, delicate and pink, were parted the tiniest measure. She would look beautiful in indigo blue. Her chest rose up and down. She had the perfect body, would make his art more magnificent than any of the models to this point. He watched her delicate white neck, and his hands started to twitch.

Chapter 39

Jack stood at the bottom of the stairs, the bloating bodies of Frank and Estelle Doone at his feet. They'd been here the whole time. He'd missed them—looked a killer in the eye and missed him completely. God help him if he messed up tonight.

Stepping back, he leaned against Frank Doone's workbench. He took his cell from his pocket and called Sergeant Martin Murphy.

"Murphy, what's the status of our ward?"

"The ward is safe," Murphy replied. "Watching a movie."

"You sure of that?"

"Oh, I'm sure all right. She's more than fine. I spoke to her not long ago."

Jack signed off, wondering briefly what he meant by more than fine. Didn't matter, he supposed, just as long as she was safe.

Jack clenched his hands. He had to move. He climbed the basement steps, making sure not to disturb the bodies on his way. He found Charles Bank at the top of the landing.

"We have to find Tommy Doone." Jack said brusquely. "What do you know about the family? Where would he go?"

"My parents might have some idea."

"Let's go." Outside, neighbors had gathered on the street in front of the house. "Folks," Jack said to the small crowd. "If you could please return to your homes, someone from our investigative team will be coming shortly to question you."

They went next door. Clyde and Judith took seats side by side on the couch in the living room. Charles and Jack sat across, on the edge of the armchairs. "It appears that Tommy Doone murdered his parents," Jack said solemnly.

Judith Bank gasped. Clyde mumbled under his breath, "Dear God. He finally snapped,"

"What's that?" Jack asked.

"Tommy. The kid finally snapped." Clyde clucked his tongue. "Frank abused him something awful when he was a kid. Not physically," Clyde clarified, "not that I know of. But mentally, you know?"

"How so?"

"He bullied him. Nasty to his own kid. I never said anything ..." Clyde dropped his head. "I never liked the guy for that reason." Clyde looked up at his wife then turned back to Jack. "It's no excuse ... I'm not saying they deserved this, just offering perspective."

"What about the mother?" Jack asked Judith.

"We never socialized," she replied in the dainty French accent. "I can count the times on one hand. Hamburgers out back once when the kids were in grammar school.

Christmas Eve when we used to throw our party. She kept to herself. I really didn't know her."

"Where might Tommy go? Do you have any idea?"

Judith shook her head in bewilderment. Clyde came up to the edge of the sofa. "Frank's a fisherman. He's got a boat and a summer house on a lagoon down in Lavallette. Used to belong to his mother, then she passed it on to him. Don't know where. It's possible the son might try to hide out there for a while."

"Do you have an address?"

Clyde told him no, and Jack stood immediately. They needed that address ASAP. He and Charles left the Banks sitting on the sofa, Clyde with faraway eyes that spoke a mountain of regret.

Chapter 40

She couldn't breathe. The giant hand of an ogre covered her mouth. From his belly to his lair, he pulled her ... taking her further and further away ... so dark ... so cold ...

Bile rose in her throat, and with its taste, Cally came fully awake. She couldn't open her mouth. Instinctively, she reached for her mouth, but she could not move her hands. Slowly she realized that her mouth was covered with tape; her hands were taped behind her back. She began to choke. Panic caught in her chest. Sucking air through her nose, she inhaled the strong odors of gasoline and rubber. Where was she? On her side in a small space. Close. Dark.

Her heart pounded. The Couturier. The image of Brianna Hemmer—the makeup, the gown, dead in the reeds beside the river; Hannah Morris, dumped on the road in the dark of night, under the streetlight. Icy fear shot through her veins, surging through her core with an evil so dark, so foreign, she could not comprehend. She lay paralyzed, the frigid air descending over her bones, locking her down.

A screech of metal jarred her. The surface she lay upon rumbled. A garage door, going up along its rollers. I'm in a trunk. Then all was quiet and hard beneath her.

She listened, heard the thumping of boots against concrete. The click of a car door. The distinct thud as it slammed shut, rattling her along with it.

Her mind cried in revolt. No! Move! Get free!

The car started and her body pitched, her shoulder blades banging against cold metal. Then with a jolt, the car moved in the opposite direction, forward, over pavement that rolled like thunder under the wheels. Bolts jutted her ribcage. She winced in pain, tried to reposition, but it was no use. She could barely move. Her hands were bound behind her back, her ankles bound as well. They hit another bump and pain shot through her side.

She flared her nostrils and focused on breathing. She may not be able to move, but she could focus her mind. She counted her breaths, each one, to ten, and then to twenty. Calming, she thought the situation through. What could she do right now to help herself?

She focused. Take note how long you're driving, she thought. Try to determine where you're going. She closed her eyes and felt the road, waited to recognize the familiar turns she'd spent a life upon. But her mind spun round and round, dizziness wrapped her like an unwanted cloak, and she had to open her eyes to keep from being sick. A long, wide turn pulled her off balance, and she winced back the nausea. Then the car came to a stop; a distant sound she knew well: change in the toll booth. He'd just thrown coins in the basket! She knew where they were: southbound, Garden State Parkway. The car straightened. *Follow the miles. Breathe deep, relax. Let the miles quell your nerves.*

Counting, she tried to gauge the minutes, tried to picture the white lines passing one by one under her. How long? How far? How many miles had they traveled?

She was cold, very cold. Her neck ached. She laid her head down against the hard surface, but it banged with each rut. She tried to block out the pain, the discomfort. Envisioning the lines, hearing the roar of tires and blacktop, she closed her eyes and let it take her where it would. She was one with the road; she was helpless, unable to move, unable to free herself from the tape that bound her. She would wait and pray, pray that an opportunity would present itself, pray that she could take advantage of it.

Chapter 41

Luther drove up to the street and was just a block from the summer house when he saw the Lavallette patrol car outside the home. He turned onto the side street, his heartbeat accelerating. He gripped the wheel. How'd they get here so fast? It was not even the midnight shift change yet. That bodyguard must have checked on Cally early, he deduced, with a growing sense of unease.

How would he get Cally in the gown? He drummed his fingers against the cold steering wheel. Turning left, he drove slowly along the lagoon, back onto the main road, then up the next block. He passed the Palella's house, and he paused. They lived directly across the lagoon, a mirror image of his house.

They never came down in winter. They were more predictable than Tommy's father. And their house was a cinch to break into. He'd done it before. Within two minutes, he'd parked in their garage and was sitting in their pitch-black kitchen, watching his own house from the Palella's window. The Lavallette officer got out of the patrol car, quickly checked the perimeter, then went back to his vehicle. He turned on the overhead light and said something into his radio.

A few minutes later, a Two Rivers cop car pulled in next to him. Jack Brant jumped out, carrying a flashlight in his hand, and said a few words to the other cop. He then walked briskly over to the Borough truck, parked in the side spot next to the driveway. He tried the door, found it locked, then peered through the windows. The other cop got out of his vehicle and came to stand beside Brant, who was now shining the flashlight's beam over the house like a big windshield wiper. Luther's hands clenched as he thought of him finding the gown he'd made for Cally. Disappointment flooded his veins. They had ruined his plan. Damn Brant had ruined everything.

***

It smelled of must and mildew. Jack ran the flashlight through the kitchen then moved forward through the living and dining area. Down a hall—two bedrooms. A typical two story raised ranch. He made his way back toward the kitchen and noted a closed door. Opening it, he shined the flashlight down steps to a concrete slab with oil stains in the center.

He took the stairs two at a time. It was a large garage area to one side with a wall that ran the entire depth of the space, splitting the floor plan straight down the center. A closed door led to the other side. He turned the knob, and it squeaked loudly. He was aware of Charles Bank behind him. He scanned the room in clarity and yet it took a moment for the picture to register—the scene he would see for years to come.

Straight ahead, along the length of the room, was a wooden work bench with shelves lined with small plastic bins holding lures, hooks, weights, fishing wire, bobbers. To the right, on a series of hooks, hung hammers, levels, clamps, bungy cords, paint brushes, and electric tools. But it was immediately forward—straight ahead—where Jack's eyes came to rest. Dead center of the room; in front of the workman's stool; upon the otherwise empty wood planks, was a piece of shiny blue material. A gown.

Jack stared at the thin straps, the long train, the draping arranged for the next victim, and fear rose up inside him. The very core of evil had sown that gown and now those hands wanted Cally.

"What is it, Jack?" Bank asked then groaned. "Holy shit."

There was more. Jack saw it all, popping out around him: bits of fabric, red and green and blue. Lavender thread and the shiny roping. Jack turned like a wind-up figurine, his arms frozen at his sides. Behind him, in the back corner was a sewing machine, upon it, scissors and another piece of the azure blue material. It drew him from his shock, and he walked toward it. He felt the smooth material between his fingertips. Thank God Cally was far away from this evil monster. Thank God she was safe, where he couldn't get her, where he couldn't bring her here.

A ball formed in his throat—the enormity, the gravity. If she never spoke to him again, he'd made the right decision. He had to get the maniac behind bars. He had to do it tonight.

His phone twirped and Jack jolted, releasing the fabric from his grasp. He took the phone from his belt and flipped it open. "Brant here."

"Jack? It's Ron McMurphy." The voice cracked, nervous. "I'm here at the apartment with Colin Bank."

"What's wrong?" he asked.

Ron hesitated. The brief catch of his breath sounded an alarm inside Jack. Why was he with Colin Bank?

"It's ... our ward ... she's gone."

"What the hell are you talking about?"

"Give me the phone," a voice shouted behind Ron. "Jack? It's Colin Bank. He dug a fucking hole in the wall. He's got her."

The words refused to register. Jack's heart raced full speed and told him what his mind refused to absorb—Cally—in the hands of a monster.

Charles grabbed the phone. Jack watched him listen to his brother. The world stopped around him as he watched Charles face go pale. Unable to move for that one moment before he was in motion, heading for the stairs. He took them two at a time, nearly kicked the back door open. His hand shaking, he started the car and pulled out. White stones spit from beneath the tires, and he saw Charles Bank running down the steps coming toward the car, but he wasn't waiting; he had no time. What in God's name had he done?

Chapter 42

The slightest ribbon of light wafted through the darkness. Cally kept her breathing steady, tried to focus on the facts she had established. The car had been turned off inside another garage. The driver had gotten out, opened the garage door and driven in; of that much, she was sure. Then he left the vehicle and left her inside the trunk. Now she prayed he would come back before she froze to death. Her teeth chattered under the tape. Her knees knocked together.

What had happened? How had she ended up in the trunk? She remembered Ron at her door, then Tommy … having tea with Tommy … watching the movie … being so sleepy….

Tommy. Had he drugged her? It had to be. But it couldn't.

Maybe he'd been attacked by the Couturier? Ron ambushed and Tommy overtaken? God, let them both be alive. Let them not have been killed because of me!

She thought of Jack. Of his fear, of his worry. Dear God, had he been right? She thought about his concern.

The way he'd been so sure. What had he known that she hadn't?

Lying in the cold trunk, with no means to protect herself, in the hands of a man who surely wanted to kill her, she caught a glimpse of what Jack had seen. Had his decision been based on more than his feelings for her? A more experienced perspective, perhaps? She thought of Jack's medals, all of the commendations he'd received over the years in the Detective Bureau. The murders he'd solved. She thought of how she'd shunned his advice.

And it scared her.

With a sinking heart, she realized he'd been right. She didn't want to be anywhere near this monster. And now? Would he blame himself if she were killed? Would he forever second-guess his decision? She could have been wired, with a van full of agents watching her every move. Would he think that way?

She couldn't let that happen. She had to let him know that she understood, that she knew just where he'd been coming from. She needed that chance.

***

Jack floored the pedal and raced up the Parkway. The speedometer read ninety, one-hundred, one-ten. He let up. Too fast on too crowded a highway. He fought every instinct and slowed the car.

The chief had been right—he was too personally involved. He'd made bad decisions all the way through.

Tommy Doone would be behind bars, Frank and Estelle Doone might still be alive if he had just permitted Cally to move ahead with the sting.

"God, please. Don't let her die because of me."

He thought of Cally, arguing for her chance to handle it like a professional. She would have been wired, with trained professionals monitoring her every move, doing her task like any other cop on the force. And he'd said no! He'd had her removed from the team and sent home—to the waiting hands of a killer! He hadn't trusted her to do her job. That was the crux of it.

He grimaced as he thought of her—the feisty little bodybuilder, the pretty third Dan black belt champion. His eyes watered. She would be okay. She could fend for herself. He just had to get there, fast. Her apartment was the only place to begin.

Patrol cars lined the complex gate and crowded the parking lot. Jack drove up over the curb. Colin was guarding the door like a sentinel. His shoulders sagged when he saw Jack; his face cracked into pain. Jack put his hand upon his shoulder. "We'll get her back."

"I raced over here the minute I heard what happened at the Doone's house. Cally told me the other day that Tommy had moved in right next door. I knew he lived here! I can't believe I didn't mention it to anyone. I just didn't think much about it."

Jack felt his stomach drop at this new information. The killer had been right under their noses this whole time, and they'd missed every opportunity to catch him. Jack patted Colin's shoulder again, unable to reply. "Where's Ron?" he asked instead.

Colin pointed him to where Ron stood, slumped against the exterior wall. "I fucked up. I fucked up," he muttered to Jack. "I let the guy in. She invited him in. She said he was okay."

"Stop. You couldn't have known." Jack took him by the upper arm and pulled him off the wall.

"I didn't tell you he was in there cause I knew you two were …" He stopped himself short. "I thought …"

"Never mind." But it pierced right through Jack. Ron didn't tell him about Tommy because he'd assumed they were romantically involved. Damn Musser! Damn him! Because of a rumor, Ron had kept do-or-die information to himself.

He ushered Ron and Colin into the apartment. As he crossed the threshold he thought of the last time he'd been here. The truth was he loved Cally. Musser had pegged him right from day one. It was Cally who had stopped it from advancing into more. And now she was the one forced to pay the price.

Immediately to the left of the front door was a closet. The coats had been pushed to the far side. Giant black trash bags appeared to have been hauled from the closet into the hall.

"Tell me what you know, Colin."

"Ron said she was inside with the neighbor. When she didn't answer, I busted down the door. We found this." He pointed to the hole. It reminded Jack of Escape from Alcatraz.

"You crawled through?" he asked.

"Yeah. Right away. The place was a mess. Nobody there. There's an attached garage. The door goes from the kitchen straight into the garage. The apartments on that side of the buildings have attached garages. These units you have to walk outside and around."

"A car left through that garage around eleven o'clock," Ron said. "I didn't think anything of it. Just a car leaving an apartment. It never crossed my mind …"

"Why should it?" Jack snapped at him. "It was leaving from a different apartment. It's not your fault."

"Here I thought …"

Jack didn't want to listen. He squatted down and looked through the hole. He could see Doone had used a saw to cut through the sheetrock. The distance between the studs was wide enough for a body—his and Cally's. Sixteen inches, he guessed. Jack climbed through both closets, into Doone's living room where dust, pieces of sheetrock, and fluffy yellow insulation had scattered on the carpet. A standard eighteen-inch saw lay to his right, scissors beside it on the floor. A piece of duct tape was stuck on one of the blades. Jack's stomach turned.

Clarizio was right. It was the end of the line. The grand finale. He'd either disappear or kill himself soon. He'd killed his parents; he'd revealed himself; the game was over. But where would he end it? Where would he take Cally? How could he stop him?

He returned to Cally's apartment, walked to her bedroom, opened the closet door, saw the lavender silk robe she'd been wearing the other night. It hung in delicate folds. He touched it, closed his eyes, ran it over his hands, breathed in the scent of her. *Where are you, Cally? Talk to me, Cally, I love you. Where are you?*

Chapter 43

A voice—mumbling—coming into the garage. The killer, laughing now, high-pitched. Who is it? she wondered, feeling her skin prickle, her body tense in preparation. A key slid in the hole, so close it sent vibration through her knee. Don't panic, she told herself. Work your plan.

The trunk popped and a cheerful voice, almost exuberant said, "Hi Cally! Surprise!" She did not recognize the voice and fear bolted through her. Keeping her eyes shut, she forced her muscles to relax just like she did at the gym. Feigning unconsciousness, she stayed as she was, did not allow her body to tense at his proximity.

"Cally? …. Wake up, Cally." He poked in her stomach.

Her shoulders clenched and she knew she had flinched, but he didn't seem to focus on it.

"God, I hope you're not dead," he said, putting a clammy, cold hand to her neck. She tried to breathe steadily, tried not to pull away from his mucid touch. At least he wanted her alive. She would have time. Be patient, Cally, relax.

His arms reached under her and picked her up. He was strong. His sweat made her nostrils burn. He carried her in his arms and banged her head against a door frame as he struggled to open the doorknob. Three steps, four, five, and she felt herself dropped. She landed on the soft cushions of a sofa.

He didn't speak or move, and she wondered what he was thinking. He put his finger beneath her nostrils and kept it there a minute then stepped back. "Okay, monkeyette. I'm going to watch the show. You stay right there, and I'll be back, 'kay?" His padded footsteps moved away, and she took the chance to open her eyes. A man in a dark ski cap, tall, frame like Tommy exited the room.

Was it Tommy? The hair on her arms stood. A dreadful déjà vu flickered like a strobe light inside her mind. What was it? She closed her eyes, tried to think. What seemed so familiar?

Her mind refused to cooperate. It was useless. Whatever had caused the eerie reaction, she needed to make a plan. She had to get out of this place.

First, she would operate on the assumption that it was Tommy Doone. It had looked like him just now. She was in a basement room—a simple concrete floor with a low-pile area rug. The room was bittter cold, that still, cold air of a room unused and unheated. She'd been deposited on a damp, velour couch. A small T.V. sat on a stand in the corner. Fishing poles leaned in the far corner along with resin deck chairs piled one on top of the other.

Where are you? she asked herself. A beach house? Where?

They'd driven a long time—south. Ocean County. Near the end of the drive, she'd heard sand and gravel under the tires. She smelled the air. Yes, salt, the fresh aroma of the sea. She listened for waves and heard a distant tapping, not waves, too soft, a gentle tapping, the bay, the tide lapping at the bulkhead. She was at the bay, and suddenly she knew: The Doones ... their summer house ... on the lagoon ... all those years ago. She knew where she was.

It sent a pulse of energy, and she pulled her wrists outward, apart. She could break free. She could escape from this place.

***

Jack was back on the Parkway. Driving the dead opposite direction, but he knew it was the right direction this time. Jack thought of Clarizio's predictions, and his foot settled heavier on the pedal. He hoped to God the FBI profiler was wrong again, but he had a feeling that on this, he was right. The big ending? The grand finale? They were living it. Doone would go to the summer house—his studio.

Jack called Charles Bank. "He'll be there. He doesn't know we found his parents. He's not expecting us to enter Cally's apartment for hours. He thinks he's anonymous. He'll go to his studio."

"He should be here by now."

"Maybe he came already. Maybe he saw us and turned around."

"You think he's in the area."

"Damn right, I do."

I'm right, he thought, as he exited the Parkway and headed toward the water. The streets were dark and empty. He flew at highway speeds through pines that cloaked streets, dark summer houses lined one after the other, empty, boarded up, lamps on timers.

And suddenly Jack knew where they were.

***

The tape loosened, not much, but a little. If she kept pulling and pulling her wrists against the tape, maybe, just maybe, she'd get it. She must have done it three hundred times already, but it was finally working. Her shoulders ached, her forearms screamed but she pulled with all her might.

Breathe! Exhale! Pull!

She fell into a trance, her voice repeating over and over in her mind. Her wrists were burned raw, the skin on fire, each pull sending waves of sharp pain up her arms. When she couldn't take the pain, when her muscles cried for her to stop, she heard Jack's voice pushing her on. A small space allowed her to clench her fingers. She pushed them down, into her palm, scratching the soft skin, making room. The tape loosened. Finally, she wiggled her hand out.

She sat straight and grabbed for the tape around her ankles. Frantically she searched for the end of it.

Scratching the tape with her nails, she ran the surface, searching for the edge that would set her legs free. Where is the end? God, where is it? She couldn't find it. She cycled her legs, pulling, stretching, fighting. She forced her hands under the tape and yanked.

A floorboard creaked above her and then another. PULL! The slow, high squeak of a door. Loud, distinct, heavy footsteps, one by one, coming down the stairs, closer and closer. He was coming. This was it. She was out of time.

***

Jack arrived back at the Doone summer house; the street now littered with cop cars. He found Bank on the lower level with the crime scene techs and a couple cops in plain clothes.

"Bank, come with me. Who's in charge, here?" Jack commanded.

A gray-haired man stepped up. "I'm Nate Karner, Chief of Police."

"We need to search the block. Every vacant house. Right now."

The chief stepped back. "I can't do that ... we can't start—"

"Now!" Jack shouted. "A police officer has been kidnapped!"

"You wait a minute."

If the police chief didn't move on it, he would. "I'll break down every door and without a warrant."

The chief looked him in the eye, studying him hard, then without taking his eyes from Jack's, he waved an officer to him. "Go upstairs. Tell them to check the neighboring houses, three on either side and six across the street." He leaned in close to Jack. "If it wasn't for the hostage, I'd throw you out right now. You're in Ocean County, detective. Don't fuck with me." He turned to a colleague beside him. "Get Archer on the phone and get the warrants."

"Screw the warrants."

If Karner thought he was waiting for warrants, he had another thing coming. If he had to go in every house himself, check every corner, every crawl space, anywhere she might be.

She was here. He could feel it. Leaving the room, the hair on his arms stood. He would not let himself think about it. He just had to find her. Bank stayed on his heels as he climbed the stairs and passed through the kitchen. A picture window stretched behind them, the lagoon, in full view beyond.

"Jack?" Bank said.

Jack turned, annoyed at the break in concentration, whipping around, and in the swirl of his vision, he saw something ... a flicker. He stopped. Above the lagoon ... light. Not the beam of moonlight on the water, but above it, coming from across the way, a flashlight, in that house ... that dark house across the lagoon. Jack grabbed Bank's shoulder and whisked him around.

"There!" he shouted when the light beamed again.

"Cops?" Bank asked.

"Can't be. Not yet." His fist tightened. He stared across the water, wishing he could fly, leap across the expanse. They were there—Tommy Doone and Cally; he knew it.

"Get backup!" He shouted as he left. He heard Bank scrambling behind him, but he wasn't waiting. He had to get around. He had to travel all the way back to the main road and then down the next block. It would take minutes. Minutes he didn't have.

***

Cally had taken position. She stood behind the door, waiting as it rolled opened, coming at her in slow motion. She stepped to the side, her back brushing silently along the wall behind her. She let it open, watched his tall dark figure appear behind it, over the threshold. Then he stopped dead.

He stared at the couch. Seeing her gone, he raised a fist and pivoted, turned full around. For a brief second their eyes met—Tommy Doone—but so evil, so different. He'd pulled back to hit her, opened his arms, given her a big juicy target.

She landed her foot, her full weight, upon his chest. He staggered back, twisting, stumbling across the room. She followed in one fluid movement, prepared to kick him again, but he caught her heel, just the edge, enough to push her back, to set her off balance.

She landed on the floor with him coming at her, with her scrambling back to buy time, to get up before he was on top of her. His boot came at her ribs, and she flipped to the side, pushed up on palms, and leapt to her feet. Facing him now, in ready position, hands up, feet apart, knees bent, on her toes, she looked him dead on and said, "Give it up, Tommy. Game's over."

"Tommy?" He laughed. "That idiot? He's gone, sweetheart."

He slapped the air. He was so close. But she needed him close. She knew what she had to do. Instantly, she had her arms around his waist, locking him in. Arching her back, she raised her hips and lifted him off the ground. With all her might she threw him backward, over her shoulder, flipping him so he landed on his back on the floor. Ura nage, the technique she'd practiced hundreds of times, that had won her first and second place wins at tournaments.

***

Jack bolted through the garage and heard grunts and thuds, a loud crash in the next room, followed by a man's groan. He raced toward the open door, desperate to reach her, to get there in time, and then he saw her—standing over Toomy Doone, tense but ready to land her next move.

Doone was down and Cally was safe. Jack felt a wave so strong it nearly bowled him over. He forged ahead to where she stood. When she saw him, her shoulders slumped in exhaustion, her hands dropped at her sides. He wanted to grab her in his arms and pull her in, but Tommy Doone was moving, down on the floor, reaching for his ankle, grabbing something from his work boot.

***

Tommy's head was pounding, roaring, everything crashing. He saw Cally and Jack coming in from the doorway. Why? What had he done?

The images were coming fast now. So fast, flashing. Their faces, their eyes, their bodies, in those dressses, and he couldn't stand the voices, his own voice, spiteful and malevolent. It was him. The Couturier was him, and he felt bile rise in his throat. How could he? How could he do those things?

He saw Dad on the basement steps, Mom, too, and he reached down, felt the gun in his boot. Luther's backup plan, *his* backup plan. *He* was the one who'd put it there. He was the one who'd done everything.

"Shoot them!" Luther's voice shouted in his ears. "Shoot them now!" *His* voice, a distant voice, a mean and hateful voice, but he didn't want to hear it ever again. Never again.

He raised the gun to his temple.

Chapter 44

The shot pierced the air, jolting Cally back to full awareness. Jack pulled his gun and crouched to a firing stance. Her heart hammered in her chest; she watched a small pool of blood seep from Tommy's head. The eyes stared at her as they began to glaze over, fading away with their secrets. Cally couldn't pull her gaze away as a sadness seeped into her core.

But why? Tommy Doone had drugged her, kidnapped her, planned to kill her. He'd killed four other women, used them for his own sick purposes. There was no logical reason to feel bad for this man.

"He's gone," she said quietly, her hands falling lifelessly to her sides. They stood, both of them, staring at Tommy and the red arch growing beneath his head.

"I thought he'd finally come into his own," she said. "He got his own apartment. He seemed happy. He came over tonight with a bottle of wine. I never suspected..."

"I missed it, too." Jack's voice was hoarse, still tense.

He walked up and examined Tommy more closely. "Even last night—I interviewed him. I didn't put it together until Jaworski—even then I thought it was the dad." He shook his head, clearly frustrated at his own mistake. "He killed his parents, Cally. The techs are over at the Doones' house now. This was his big moment, just like Clarizio predicted. I think he planned to do himself in after ... tonight."

Cally shuddered. She knew what Jack had been about to say. She looked down at the man who would have killed her, and dressed her in some horrible gown, and strangely, the anger she'd felt while fending him off had gone. Now only a terrible sense of loss and tragedy remained. So many dead, even him. Why? For what? Why did she feel like she'd missed an important piece of the puzzle?

Footsteps sounded overhead and Charles appeared on the stairs. He ran to her and enveloped her in a tight hug. "My God, Cal, thank God."

Several Lavallette officers followed. The noise rose in her ears until it was a loud jumble of radios, commands, questions. The reality of the scene, of what had nearly happened to her, hit then. The walls pressed in around her.

Jack was behind her, answering questions. She reached out, placed her hand on his shoulder, tapped it to get his attention. He turned, and immediately, his eyes widened. He stepped away from the officers, placed his arm around her waist, holding her steady. "Let's get you outside," he said.

He guided her out a door, and she was disoriented to see that she was on the ground level. She had imagined herself in a basement all along. She inhaled deeply. The cold, salty night air revived her senses, and she felt herself centering. She saw the lagoon behind her. "Where are we? Are we at the Doone's summer house?" she asked.

"No, it's across the lagoon. He planned to bring you there, where he kept a workshop, but the police showed up. So he came here."

"A workshop?"

"A studio—where he kept fabrics, a sewing machine, patterns. They'll be plenty of evidence. The FBI are already there."

She needed to see it. There was something more, she just knew it—something she was missing—as though a giant disconnect hung over her head. If she could see Tommy's workroom, maybe it would come. "I want to see it."

Jack frowned. He raised his hand, then stopped himself. "Okay. If you think you're up to it, I'm not going to stop you." He smiled, and Cally was reminded that she had some apologizing ahead of her.

"You like being in the thick of things, don't you?" he asked.

"I could have done without the ride in the trunk."

He laughed. Her knees wobbled as she walked to the car, and she realized she was still fighting whatever Tommy had used to drug her. Adrenaline had provided a powerful antidote, but now, as her body's natural reflexes waned, her head swam. Jack reached for her hand. He tucked it up against his chest, and she looked at him and smiled.

As they drove down the quiet, waterfront street, darkened homes lining both sides, she recounted as much as she could about the abduction. He told her about the hole Tommy had made in the closet. She remembered back to the night Tommy had helped her hang the clothes bar.

Again, she was aware of a strange sense of dissociation, as though the Tommy of that night was a completely different person than the man who had kidnapped her. It bothered her for the short ride. Soon they rounded the lagoon and were on the Doone's block, where lights, police cars, and activity invaded her thoughts. They found a spot on the white gravel, and the car was immediately surrounded. Chief Grainer was first to her door, opening it and offering his hand to help her out. He gave them both solid pats on the back.

"Good job, Officer Bank. Heard how well you handled yourself, how you brought him down without a weapon." He congratulated Jack next.

"It was all her," Jack replied. "She had the situation under control by the time I got there."

"So I heard. The details are coming over the radios. You'll have a bit of explaining about the gun. He hadn't brandished the weapon up to that point?" he asked Cally.

"I wasn't even aware he had it. It was in his boot the whole time."

"Put it in the report. Chief Extner…" he called, extending his hand toward a man in plain clothes who approached. "Jack, come with me for a minute. Let's fill the Lavallette Chief in."

Cally took the opportunity to slip away. She needed some questions answered.

The house was laid out like the one she had just left. Two large spotlights had been erected in front of an open garage door. A Lavallette officer stood at the entrance. He raised his hand to stop her, but she introduced herself, and he let her pass.

The garage smelled of gasoline and must. Fishing gear, crab traps, and tools lined the walls. To the left, she heard low voices. A glare of light came from beyond an open door about five feet ahead. Her heartbeat quickened. She approached the door and looked through.

An indigo blue gown was laid neatly across the top of a wooden workbench. At the waist a long sash draped over and reached the edge of the floor. She thought of Snow White, laid out on the log, asleep in the forest. She thought of the evil, wicked old woman who had given her the apple.

What had bothered her in the car? What had she remembered? She looked to the corner and saw the sewing machine. Numbly, she walked to it, sat on the simple metal stool behind it. She looked at the thread on the bobbin.

What had he said? She closed her eyes, tried to remember.

"Tommy? ... That idiot? He's gone, sweetheart." His voice had been so strange, so different. That rabid stare, so unlike any expression she'd ever seen from Tommy. In fact, the man who took her from the trunk—the voice, the inflections, his very appearance—they seemed nothing

like Tommy at all. It was as though another person had taken him over completely. She thought of the letter to the police. The wording—not the Tommy she knew. It brought a thought to her mind, and she knew instantly what she had to find, she stood and scanned the room. Where was it? She looked under the workbench, amidst a stack of cartons in one corner. Not here.

She left without looking back, quickly climbed the interior stairs. She noticed Jack, Grainer, and Extner, out on the raised deck, still conversing. She scanned the kitchen, then the living room. It would be easy to spot. She moved on. Beyond the living room, a hallway ran towards what she assumed would be the bedrooms. The first looked like a kid's room with a twin bed and dresser. The second was larger, with an older bedroom set and a full-sized bed centered between two end tables. Along the left wall, on top of a simple desk, was an old-fashioned typewriter.

Cally drew a sudden breath. Though she had been expecting to find it, seeing the machine upon which the Couturier had composed the letters sent a slither of nerves up her spine. Were her suspicions correct? She stepped cautiously forward.

The desk was a dark brown wood, mission design. She sat in the chair and stared down at the old Smith Corona with its orderly metal keys. She imagined the tap, tap, tap as Tommy composed the letters. If Tommy Doone was *gone*, then there would be only one way to learn about the man now known as the Couturier. She hoped her instincts were correct.

Removing a tissue from a box beside the typewriter, she used her thumb and index finger to carefully open the center drawer.

Chapter 45

Cally and Jack spent a couple of hours at the Doone's summer home then stopped at the other two crime scenes. They'd had to report to the hospital as well, where Cally was required to get blood work and a quick physical examination. The doctors had given her the all-clear, and now, as they drove the Two Rivers streets, homes still shrouded in darkness, Cally felt fully awake. The clock on the dash read four a.m., but she could not have slept if she'd tried.

In the desk drawer, she'd uncovered nearly one hundred pages of typewritten ramblings. They shed an eerie glimpse into the seriously disturbed man Tommy Doone had been. The writings would give Joe Clarizio and the FBI invaluable insight into the unraveling mind of a spree killer.

"Do you know much about dissociative identity disorder?" Cally asked, looking out the window, feeling the stillness of the night deep in her bones.

"Not a whole lot. I've read about it, sometimes the egos are aware of each other, and sometimes they're not. From what I understand, it's not uncommon for the alter ego to be aware of the host identity, but if the host becomes aware of the other personality, deep psychosis can set in."

She thought back to her recent visits with Tommy. If he'd known about Luther, he'd done a good job hiding it. She hoped he'd had no idea, but a piece of her guessed he might have realized at the end. "I wonder how many personalities he had," she said. "We may never know."

Tommy, or Luther, had written dozens of pages over the last four weeks, the first detailing what had been the inciting incident at the *Cozy Up Motel.* A prostitute had insulted Luther, called him pathetic, and he wrote of how his own reaction, his strength had surprised him. Clearly, he had enjoyed the fight, but mostly, the victory over her. Cally thought of their childhood, all those years next door, the kids from the neighborhood, playing games in the street. So often, Tommy would lose—*Mother May I, Spud, tag*—he always lagged behind.

Jack pulled into the station lot and shut down the car. "You don't have to do this tonight, Cally. We can write the reports tomorrow." Dark bags circled his eyes and although he looked as bushed as the night before, he still turned and gave her a caring smile. Tired or not, he looked handsome as ever. She felt a tug at her heart as she wondered what would become of them now. When he'd found her—for that brief moment before Tommy shot himself—she'd felt closer to him than she had ever felt to another human being. Had her emotions gotten the better of her? Or had he felt it, too?

His cell phone rang, and he answered it. The Chief was on the other end, and Jack told him they were in the parking lot and would be right in. Cally felt a tinge of disappointment as the opportunity passed. Would she get another chance to talk to him tonight? Would they feel the same way tomorrow?

The night air was cold. Jack held the door and placed his hand at the base of her back as she passed through the entry. When they neared the Chief's office, Cally heard a jumble of voices and nervous laughter. She smelled coffee. They turned the corner, and she was surprised to see a small group beyond Grainer's glass wall. One by one, she saw the members of her family, her brothers, talking, her parents, side by side, all of them turning in unison as she and Jack rounded the corner.

Grainer's desk had been cleared and laid with food, and the Chief stood, plate in hand, all smiles and relief. Beside him, Kurt Potovich, Vince Martin, and Joe Clarizio looked to be eating sandwiches.

Cally looked at Jack whose face suddenly came alive. Her lips stretched into a smile. He grabbed her hand and gave it a squeeze. Her mood lifted like a hot air balloon on a sunny May Day. How lucky was she? To think where she'd been just hours ago.

"Cally, sweetie!" Her mom enveloped her in a hug as soon as she entered the room. She pulled back and looked at her, tears in her eyes. Shaking her head, her mom said, "You must be famished." She handed her a baguette with a generous hunk of sharp Provolone, basil, tomato, and a healthy dose of olive oil and fresh pepper. "I made your favorite sandwiches. And sweetie, I'm so proud of you! I can't believe how you handled that horrible man. Thank goodness you stuck with the Judo classes all those years!"

Her dad rolled his eyes. Into Cally's ear, he whispered, "Now she says it. I always knew that Sandan whatever it's called would come in handy." He smiled down at her and gave her a big hug. "Think I owe you an apology."

"Forget it, Dad."

"You've certainly been baptized by fire. From here on, I promise not to meddle."

Everyone had questions, retold their own experiences, and let both her and Jack know how proud they were of them. One by one, people began filtering out. Her parents left after she assured them that she would come home soon, and sleep in her old bedroom for at least a night or two.

"Leave the reports for tomorrow," Chief Grainer told them as he shut out the lights to his office.

Cally and Jack walked the quiet hallway back to the command center. The room seemed strangely still, as though the energy of the past weeks had leaked away like helium in a mylar balloon.

"I can't believe it's over, Jack. No more worrying about who he'll get next or how we'll ever catch him."

"Thanks to you." He reached over and drew her in. His chest was warm and firm, his eyes looked into hers.

Her heart fluttered. Her knees went weak like jelly. "And everybody else on the team. It takes a village to raise a child, right?"

"Something like that. I'm more a family man, myself."

He smiled, and it was such an open smile, such an inviting smile—just like the one he'd laid on her three weeks ago at the gym. My goodness, what a dumbie she'd been! And wait a minute—what had he just said? Something about being a family man? But he was talking again, and she just listened. Listened and watched the way his lips moved.

"I heard your dad say he owed you an apology. I owe you one, too."

She shook her head. "No you don't. When I was locked in that trunk I kept thinking about you. If anything had happened to me ... I didn't want you to blame yourself. I prayed for the chance to tell you that I understood why you took me off the team, and luckily it all worked out. I think somebody was watching over me."

"You mean like a guardian angel?"

He pressed in tight, and a flush of warmth traveled up her spine. She thought of the banquet three weeks ago, sitting at the family table, waiting for her first glimpse of this man, Jack Brant. She remembered back six months—her beloved brother nearly dead in that hospital bed, and then, the cold, dark trunk of that awful car.

A guardian angel? For sure. But this man who held her so tight carried a pot of lucky gold, himself.

"Yes, you could say that," she replied, allowing herself to sink into the protective arms of the man who loved her.

THE END

Acknowledgements

This book has been a long time in the making. I wrote it a number of years ago, when it won several awards, including as First Runner-Up in Romance Writers of America's Golden Heart Contest. I want to thank the many contest judges who took the time to read the book and excerpts and give me pointers, encouragement, and votes for the book. You gave me the confidence I needed to keep going!

Thank you to my proofreader extraordinaire, Lissy Johnson, who caught typos, spelling errors, and made some very good observations. I have found a valuable reader for my future books!

Very importantly, I'd like to thank *you,* the readers, for taking time to relax and read this story. Your interest means the world to me, and I truly hope you enjoyed Cally's journey. If the book resonated with you, I would be incredibly grateful if you would share your thoughts in a review on Amazon, Google, or on the website of the independent bookseller where you purchased the book. It means more than you know and helps other readers to find the book. And please stay tuned for my next novel, *A Lady Suspected*, to be released May 2026. To receive a Launch Update, please visit my website at www.SusanPaytasBooks.com.

Thank you to my parents, Nancy and Bob, for simply being the best parents a girl could ask for. Married 68 years, and still going strong, they are amazing role models for our family. Thank you for instilling in me a love of the Jersey Shore and buying that first shore house on 93rd Street on LBI! Spending summers at the beach has been one of the greatest gifts you could have given our family. My parents' love of the Jersey Shore was transferred to our entire family and resulted in my husband and me moving here permanently more than 30 years ago.

Most of all, I want to thank my family, my husband, Joe, and our grown children, Harry, and Christine, for putting up with me during all of those hours I spent engrossed at my laptop, and for giving me unending encouragement. I love you all, and our growing family, so much.

www.ingramcontent.com/pod-product-compliance
Lightning Source LLC
Chambersburg PA
CBHW071554150726
48000CB00004B/1460